Clara Mandrake's Monster

Ibrahim S. Amin

Copyright © 2017 Ibrahim S. Amin
All rights reserved.

Book layout by www.ebooklaunch.com

For Kath

Part 1

The Wardrobe

1

Clara Mandrake knew she was doomed. The nightmare tore open, spat her back into the cocoon beneath her blanket. Torments melted at the corners of her mind. But the monster was still there. Its presence, its weight, throbbed in the darkness beyond the quilt.

Dreaming. She was still dreaming. One of those dreams that tries to trick you with its layers. If she just pinched herself… Pain burst between her fingernails and spread across the back of her hand. Breath froze in Clara's throat. Her heartbeat thudded. Its iambs shook her body and spoke the truth.

No *Dream* *No* *Dream* *No* *Dream*

She grabbed fistfuls of fabric and scrunched them to her. Held them so hard it hurt.

Yes *Hide* *Yes* *Hide* *Yes* *Hide*

But Clara couldn't. She had to know. Had to see. She tensed her limbs, inhaled. Her heart thumped faster and louder.

You'll *DIE!* *You'll* *DIE!* *You'll* *DIE!*

She sat up and tugged the blanket down into a coil at her chin. Blackness smothered the room and stole each shape. The moon tried to save her. Silver squeezed through cracks in the shutters, but it drowned and Clara was all alone.

No. Not alone.

She *felt* it first, was already turning towards the far corner even before wood creaked and a hinge groaned. The wardrobe. It was in the wardrobe.

It was in the wardrobe and it was coming to get her.

She screamed. Her jaw shuddered and her whole skull was breaking apart. Opening like a nightmare. Like a wardrobe. Like her ribcage when the monster's claws found her in the dark.

A door flew open and bashed the wall. She shrieked again, clutched the cloth at her throat — half-strangled herself but couldn't stop. The monster loomed over her. A shapeless mass, darker than the darkness. It reached out.

"Clara!"

A hand gripped her shoulder.

"Clara, what's wrong?"

"Mum!"

Shadows shifted. Perception and understanding rattled around her brain. The monster wasn't here yet! There was still time!

"It's in the wardrobe!"

"Wh-"

Clara tossed the blanket away and leapt out of bed. She dragged her mother a couple of paces, before Ella Mandrake cried out and planted her feet.

"Run! There's a... a... monster."

The last word tumbled out, and she realised how stupid it sounded. But... Clara peered into the corner, at the wooden thing that took shape in the gloom, and her heart hammered again.

"A monster?" Ella pulled out of Clara's grasp and sighed. "You just had a bad dream."

"No! It's in there! I heard it move!"

Her mother turned, and Clara waited for her to sense it too. For her to *feel* the malevolence lurking behind that door. Then they'd run, escape. Raise the alarm so their neighbours could come with spears and axes and torches and hounds and-

"A rat."

"Huh?"

Ella stepped towards the wardrobe. Clara grabbed at her.

"No!"

Her mum sighed again.

"I'll light the candle and show you," Ella said.

"But..."

Clara bit her lip. Warmth flooded her face. The sensation from before, that dread, now tottered between certainty and embarrassment. She'd felt something. Hadn't she? Or was she just a stupid little girl who'd let nightmares and shadows frighten her?

Ella went to the bedside table and took out the tinderbox. Clara didn't stop her. She watched the wardrobe, brow knitted. The first click of steel and stone made her gasp and feel twice as foolish. But the flame soothed her. A golden glow drove away the blackness.

Her mother lifted the saucer. A mote of fire flickered and the shadows danced. The light advanced. It washed the wardrobe and worked its way into every curl and crevice. Ella reached for the handle. Clara's breath caught.

The door opened. Darkness parted.

"See? There's nothing in here."

"Oh…"

Ella closed the wardrobe, crossed the room, and set the saucer down on the bedside table.

"Try to get back to sleep."

She smiled and stroked her daughter's arm, but Clara knew what she was thinking. Ten years old and still afraid of the dark… A silly, cowardly girl. Clara Mandrake couldn't look her mother in the eye. Ella's lips hovered over the candle flame, then rose without extinguishing it. Clara's face burned. *The scared little girl needs her light…*

She climbed into bed.

"Goodnight," her mum said.

"Goodnight."

The door closed. Clara stared at the closet and felt nothing. No presence. No horror. Her head slumped onto the pillow.

She shut her eyes.

Floorboards creaked under the bed. Her eyes flicked open, and didn't close for a long, long time.

• • •

Fahmaia Hashad — mawlana of the Kharji people, favourite of Allat the One Goddess, spiritual guide to the great warlord Barzik Khan and all his warriors — scratched her nose. She scratched it again. Then a third time. After that she sighed and decided she couldn't blame an itch.

The mawlana withdrew her hand from her face. She frowned at it. Her markings were as sluggish as her spirit this morning. Calligraphic script oozed across her flesh like half-slumbering serpents. A bad sign, when even miracles succumbed to lethargy.

Fahmaia leaned forward without uncrossing her legs, stretched out, and wafted a tendril of incense smoke towards herself. Cinnamon wrinkled her nostrils. The aroma warmed her sinuses and she envisioned its heat as a golden glow. Aureate light passed into her lungs, diffused throughout her veins.

Her muscles tensed then loosened. She inhaled and exhaled. Her eyes closed. Prayers flitted across her lips, faster and faster till the words blurred in her ears and gained clarity in her thoughts.

But the trance wouldn't come. Darkness occupied the inside of her eyelids, and refused to yield the visions she sought. Allat had nothing for her. The One Goddess was silent, and the mawlana scoured her recent memories for signs of sin. She couldn't think of anything. No folly, no thoughtless impiety which might explain why the prayer trance eluded her. Hubris? Had she become too confident in her abilities?

She found her hand creeping towards her nose again, restrained it, and recited the opening verse of a different prayer.

"Should we announce ourselves?" A man's voice, outside the tent.

"She might be busy." A woman's, with the same whisper that turned her words into blades instead of muffling them.

"We could leave it here."

"Will that offend her?"

"I don't-"

Fahmaia Hashad scowled and wondered how she was supposed to pray with all that babble going on out there. Her lips twitched into a smile. She was looking for excuses again. The man and woman were blameless, whoever they were.

"Come in!" she said.

The whispers stopped. Feet shuffled and cloth rustled around limbs she assumed were performing frantic gesticulations. Then a hand parted the canvass opening. A shape appeared beside it. Leather capped a stump. Fingers and forearm fumbled at the gap, and another hand joined them. Fahmaia half-expected a multi-armed absurdity to flop into the tent.

A man and woman entered instead, after a moment's entanglement in the doorway. She held a baby to her chest. He rubbed the side of his face with the stump. Both of them bowed so strenuously Fahmaia feared they might prostrate themselves as though she were some pagan idol or false living goddess. The movement thrilled the baby, who laughed and clapped.

"Please, sit."

She gestured at some of the cushions and wished she hadn't made such a mess when she'd tried to find a position for her prayers. The man sat. The woman hovered for a moment before she joined him.

"You won't remember me, mawlana," he said.

Recognition startled her when it came.

"Ahmed?" She groped for the family name, worried she'd forgotten it. "Ahmed Al-Shaaf?"

His face lit up. A broad, almost chubby face. She tried to place it alongside the one from her memories, with its dressed wounds, sunken cheeks, and hollow eyes. The man who'd lain in his sickbed and mourned the loss of his sword hand. They might have been cousins instead of the same person.

"This is Nazeen, my wife."

The woman froze, as though they'd caught her in the middle of a misdeed. She didn't meet the mawlana's eyes. But Fahmaia was used to that from people who'd just met her, and couldn't deny that the rest of her visage was far more captivating. Their baby gawped at the markings too. Fahmaia smiled and the child grinned back.

"What's your daughter's name?"

Nazeen's gaze darted to her husband, and the mawlana wondered if she'd said the wrong thing and given the impression she was about to accuse the poor woman of blasphemy or heresy. Ahmed nodded.

"We…" Nazeen looked Fahmaia in the eye for the first time. "We named her after you, mawlana."

"Oh!"

Her mind whirled, and came to rest on those same memories from years ago — of Ahmed, as he lay in the infirmary bed. As he tried to shove something under his blanket before she could glimpse it. The corners of her eyes stung.

"I'm… I'm honoured."

The words sounded hollow in her ears. Inadequate. But Ahmed's smile broadened and Nazeen found the beginnings of her own.

"May I… May I hold her?"

Nazeen hesitated, but only for a second. The elder Fahmaia took her namesake into her arms. The younger Fahmaia grinned, and pawed at the mawlana's face. Her eyes glittered. She slapped and grabbed, marvelled as her hands captured only skin, while ribbons of script flowed beneath them. Her parents gasped. But both Fahmaias laughed and it proved infectious.

"She already loves Allat's scriptures," Fahmaia Hashad said. "Goddess willing, she'll grow up to be a strong, pious woman."

The mawlana cradled the child and let her continue her exploration of the text.

"Where did your path take you, after you left Barzik's warband?"

"I wandered for a while," Ahmed said. "Then I met Nazeen, and we bought a farm with the Khan's gold."

Fahmaia nodded. Barzik Khan was generous, especially to maimed soldiers and orphans.

"Farming's a hard but honest living," she said.

"Nazeen does all the hard work." He waved his stump. "I just keep my bees. Ah…"

Ahmed reached into his knapsack and pulled out a jar.

"Honey."

Fahmaia thanked him, and was still smiling long after the Al-Shaafs had gone on their way. Contentment warmed her and relaxed her body better than the meditation had. She was about to close her eyes, harness this tranquillity. But the pot was right there…

She dipped her finger into viscous gold and sucked it with a pang of guilt and glee. The honey was rich and sweet and sticky and gorgeous. She closed her eyes. Remembered. Ahmed, bandages capping his wounded arm. An infidel's blade had hacked his wrist. Taken his hand and, so he thought, his manhood. He tried to hide the dagger when she came to see him. The dagger which would've ended his suffering. But she saw it, and spoke. Without judgement. Without condemnation. Then prayed with him through the night.

Now this honey existed, something pure and beautiful. And so did that grinning, laughing baby girl. All by the grace and mercy of the One Goddess, who'd helped Fahmaia show him a better path.

Sweetness tingled on her tongue. Her thoughts deepened and the prayer trance began.

• • •

Two scents pulled Clara out of her sleep. The first was the smell of burning. But she wasn't on fire, so that was probably fine. One of her eyes opened partway to make sure. A wisp of smoke rose from the candlewick before the air swallowed it. Her mum must've come in and blown out the flame. That brought back the night and a groan. Clara thought about pulling the blanket over her head and staying cocooned for the rest of her life. But the second scent was a savoury aroma. Egg porridge. Stomach and brain argued. Stomach won.

She swung her legs out of bed. But she pulled them back before her feet touched the floor. It was stupid. So stupid. But... Boards creaked in her brain. Clara leaned over the edge, lowered her head. It was dark under there. One last pool of night.

Clara rose into a crouch and sprang like a cat. She landed in front of the window, undid the latch, pulled the shutters open. Autumn sunlight bathed the room. She got down on her hands and knees, put her chin almost on the floor, and looked under the bed.

Nothing.

Stupid. Stupid. Stupid.

The wardrobe was less ominous now, but she still paused with her hand on its handle. Clara bit the inside of her cheek, told herself to snap out of it. She opened the door. Nothing leapt out, nor dragged her inside to devour her, so she got dressed and continued to hate herself.

Clara went into the kitchen. A bowl of golden porridge steamed on the table. She sat down, picked up her spoon.

"Clara!"

"I…" She braced herself for the lecture. "I'm…"

"Your hair!"

"Huh?"

Ella Mandrake lifted a handful of her daughter's tresses.

"It's all tangled. You didn't brush it."

Clara rose. Her mum pushed her back down.

"I'll do it. Eat your breakfast or you'll be late for school."

She went off to get the brush. Her daughter thanked the universe. Bleary eyes couldn't deal with scorn or sympathy. She ate. Eggs and oats cooked the inside of her mouth.

"How did it get like this?" Ella knelt behind Clara's chair. "It's a mess!"

Clara had no good answer, so she gobbled more porridge. The brush worked at her roots first, pulled her scalp this way and that.

"Argh!"

Her mum attacked a cluster of knots and yanked Clara's head backwards. Agony tore through her skull. Porridge splatted under her spoon.

"Sorry!" Ella said.

Her vision blurred. She touched the bowl. Wanted to grab it. Spin round. Crash it into the side of her mum's head. Blood and shards would rain on the floor, and-

Clara's eyes widened. Her mouth gaped. That image hung in front of her, and she could only stare at it until the bowl scorched her fingers and seared it from her brain.

"Almost done now," Ella said.

Where had that come from? Her cheeks burned. Would her mother see the guilt there? Know what horrible things her vile, ungrateful daughter had been thinking?

"There we go. I told you to brush it before bed."

"Sorry, mum."

Clara picked up her spoon. She managed to get through the rest of her breakfast, but each mouthful was a slap across her face.

When it was time to go, she hugged her mother, kissed her. Ella didn't react for a second or two. Her daughter had grown out of morning affection long ago, and that knowledge was another kick in Clara's gut. But Ella recovered from the surprise and hugged her back.

Clara went out and the air cooled her skin. Orange leaves crunched along the path. She needed to sleep better tonight. Things were bad — her *mind* was bad — when she was this exhausted.

She stopped at the gateposts. Her fingertip found its usual starting point, a groove in the stone. Clara traced a

human figure which a passer-by might've mistaken for a tree. Then her digit jumped to the other image. This one was even less artistic. A series of lines and blobs. But she knew what it was supposed to be, and that made it so. A dragon. A *drake*.

Clara sighed. Touching her father's work, feeling things Saqib Mandrake had carved before she was born, was almost like kissing her mother. On a whim, she kissed the stone too. But it was gritty, rotten. She wiped her mouth, spat, and walked away.

Leaves scattered around her shoes. Each kick arranged them in new patterns, and Clara watched like a woman reading tea leaves. She needed more sleep. She-

"You look like crap."

Clara blinked. The world had moved and her brain hadn't noticed. She was already outside her friend's house. Rayya Shimud's eyes sparkled.

"Feel like it too. Didn't sleep much last night."

"Poor Clara."

"Yeah."

Clara's mouth matched Rayya's smile, and the rest of her face followed before she knew it was happening. Her friend's plait swished back and forth as they walked down the lane, towards the schoolhouse. Rayya ranted about the latest iniquities her parents had inflicted upon her. Clara nodded along and was glad she didn't have to think or say much.

"…and they let my brother do it, when he was my age. But they won't…"

Clara yawned.

• • •

A breeze sliced Silas Renshaw's freshest bruise. The bump throbbed on his cheek and demanded attention, but he didn't rub it. Trainees didn't caress their injuries in public. Not that it mattered this morning. Every eye was on Cryze, who stood midway between the boys' and girls' dormitories like an ebony statue.

"Good luck."

"I'll miss you."

"Congratulations."

"Can I have your stuff? The stuff you're not taking…"

They approached her one by one. Friends first, which didn't take long. Quick embraces. Lucy had to jump to kiss her cheek. Then the rest filed past. Cryze nodded and spoke a few words to each well-wisher. She might've been a mistress inspecting the trainees, not a young woman who'd shared their status just a day earlier.

"Good luck on the road," Silas said. He offered his hand.

"Thank you." She gripped it. "Remember to guard your right."

She released him, clenched and unclenched her fist. The side of his face ached again. Silas stepped away so the last youths could take their turns and pay tribute to the black colossa. He tried not to sigh.

Cryze was better than him. She'd outraced him and outfought him enough times to prove it. Stomped him into the mud both figuratively and literally. She deserved this. And she'd do their school proud, burnish its reputation with her deeds. But Silas felt it all the same. In his stomach and mind and every muscle.

The clip-clop of hooves broke his reverie. Cryze turned on her heel and the others parted to clear her path. A groom led a mare over by the reins. Saddlebags and packs swayed against the animal's flanks. Everything Cryze would take with her, to her new life. She vaulted into the saddle. Silas grimaced. She even mounted a horse better than he could.

A stocky, iron-haired man sat atop the other steed. He looked at Cryze and nodded. She nodded back. And that was it. The two of them rode, and in moments they were gone.

The trainees didn't disperse. Raindrops plinked on their shoulders, but no one wanted to go inside first. Instead they glanced and muttered. Many eyes flicked Silas' way. Jonas' and Lucy's too.

He joined Silas, then she came over and no one bothered to hide their interest any longer. The other trainees kept their distance, but Silas felt their collective gaze — locked on the three of them.

"Black beauty's gone," Jonas said. "It'll be one of us next."

"Maybe," Lucy said.

But they all knew it was true.

They eyed one another, while the rain fell. Lucy, short but broader across the shoulders than either of them. Jonas, lanky and sinewy. Almost as tall as Cryze though half as heavy. And Silas, who still wore the last traces of his old life's fat but knew he could contend with either of them.

Lucy put her hand out. The boys followed suit. They shook, and none of them blinked.

• • •

Darkness soothed Clara's bedroom. It pressed against the shutters, sealed the window. Muffled the moonlight. The wind was gone. Swaying branches, cats' wails, owls' hoots. It silenced them all. Shut them out so she could sleep in peace.

Across the room, something bumped.

Only the wind, Clara told herself. The wind. Nothing else. Just the wind. But there was no wind, was there? It was gone and she was here. A rat! That was it. Must be it. Yes, a rat looking for food or a place to sleep. Disgusting but harmless.

Hinges rasped like dying men.

And Clara knew the darkness wasn't her friend, wasn't there to keep out the world while she slept. A floorboard groaned. The darkness trapped her. It would feed her to the monster.

Another groan. Closer.

Clara rolled over on her mattress. The shape loomed above her.

"Mum! The monster! Mum!"

Clara blinked. Everyone in the schoolroom stared at her, and drool trickled down the side of her chin.

Rayya's eyes were saucers. Her friend reached over as though to touch Clara's hand, but faltered. Other kids gawped too. Rabbits in front of a baying hound. Some sniggered.

"Mummy!" Tommy rubbed invisible tears from the corners of his eyes. "There's a monster! Help me, mummy!"

A few of the boys around him laughed. Miss Jazrah glared at them

"Thomas!"

"Save me, mummy! Save me from the monster!"

The teacher grabbed her cane and swished it. Tommy covered his mouth with both hands. Mirth shook his body but didn't escape. Miss Jazrah turned to Clara. The end of the cane wobbled.

"Sorry! I'm sorry! I… I just…"

The teacher's expression softened. Clara could only imagine how she must look, if she was getting sympathy instead of a rap on the knuckles.

"Wipe your mouth, Clara."

"Oh."

She brushed her sleeve across her face. More sniggers broke out, but a fresh glare suppressed them. Miss Jazrah put the implement of destruction down and carried on talking about poetry.

"A dactyl consists of three beats. Long-short-short." Chalk scratched the blackboard and shuddered through Clara's skull. "Dum-di-di, dum-di-di. Say it with me."

"Dum-di-di, dum-di-di."

Clara joined the general drone and tried to pay attention. But the lesson dribbled into incoherence. Stressed and unstressed syllables danced around her head until the bell scattered them.

Old Joss walked by the schoolhouse window. He swung his contraption, more like a mace than a handbell, and waved to the children.

"Go on," Miss Jazrah said. "Go play. No murders."

Rayya took Clara's hand and pulled her to the door before the crush. The two girls made their way out into the field.

"I thought she was going to kill me," Clara said.

"She probably would've, if you didn't look dead already."

They sat under their favourite oak, on a blanket of russet leaves. Its trunk hid them from the schoolhouse.

"Take a nap," Rayya said. "I'll wake you up when the bell rings, or if you have another nightmare."

"Thanks. I-"

The thing burst out from behind the tree. Limbs flailed. Teeth snapped. Rayya shrieked. Clara's heart thumped, then her eyes narrowed.

"The monster's come to get you!" Tommy raked the air in front of her face. "Rawr! Monster!"

"Get lost!" Rayya threw a handful of leaves at him, but he swatted them aside and they ended up in Clara's face.

Clara clawed them away.

"Monster!"

Tommy jumped from foot to foot, more like a jester than a beast. Clara sighed.

"Come on." Rayya took her arm.

The girls walked back to the schoolhouse. Tommy capered after them, still hopping about and making finger-claw slashes.

"Monster! Rawr!"

• • •

Fahmaia stood on a hilltop. Sunlight poured down on her, soaked her tresses and lent them its heat. The breeze played with a single lock. It warmed and tickled her cheek.

All the great cities of the world sprawled before her. Colours rioted across Kessalonia, where painted marble made rainbows of its streets. A thousand jewelled minarets glittered beside it in Lakmahd. Each vied with its neighbours for height and splendour. Other settlements surrounded them. They stretched to every horizon. Scrazmar's buildings floated on water, wooden sculptures in the image of marshland beasts. Zerkan's satin tents. Khalib's grand squares and bazaars. The hexagonal heart of Oled-Thar.

Thousands of miles had collapsed in on themselves and brought all these wonders together, so the mawlana might gaze upon each and every one. She thanked Allat for this blessing. To see the world, as only the Goddess had ever seen it before…

Fahmaia shivered.

Something gnawed at the back of her brain. The sun, the breeze, and all those magnificent cities were unchanged. Yet the wrongness spread through her skull. It pressed against her eyeballs.

The universe shuddered.

Fahmaia clung to the vision. She had to stay, had to know what it meant. But her true eyes opened and she was back in her tent.

The mawlana shook. She tried to steady herself, but the palpitations trembled through flesh and blood and bone and mind. She hugged her limbs to her chest. Muttered prayers. Begged the One Goddess to protect her people from unseen horrors.

2

Clara's head slumped. She jerked back, and winced when her skull tapped the wall. Clara forced her eyes open. She refused to fall asleep in the outhouse, and add yet another embarrassment to the tally.

A black speck moved at the edge of her vision. She flinched, went to brush the spider away, but it wasn't there. Her eyes and brain needed sleep. Until then, specks and spiders. Clara sighed.

She picked up the candle and left the outhouse. Evening had already set into the sky. Her light swept shadows from her path. Clara reached the house, joined her mother at the kitchen table, and shivered before the fireplace embraced her.

"Feel any better?" Ella said.

Clara nodded. Her mother thought she was sick, and she hadn't argued. That'd be so much more respectable than getting scared of the dark or screaming at nightmares.

Chunks of lamb, golden potatoes, rivulets of mint sauce stared at her from the plate. Her head dipped and they rushed up to meet her. She caught herself and stopped her face a couple of inches above her dinner. Clara sniffed it.

"Smells great."

Her mother smiled and Clara exhaled. In truth, the aroma did make her mouth water. Stomach and brain had another fight. She was too tired to eat, but too hungry not to. Clara managed the first bite. Then the second. She kept going.

"What did you learn at school today?"

"Nothing."

"Nothing?"

Clara sighed.

"Poetry. Dactyls. Dum-di-di."

She skewered a potato and thrust it into her maw. Ella Mandrake didn't like it when her daughter spoke with her mouth full, so this was usually the best defence against conversation. Sure enough, her mother did all the talking for a while.

"…the pub. And they didn't even order the…"

Clara finished her meal. The aftertaste spread through her skull, warmed her cheeks. But fatigue crept after it. She excused herself and wished her mum goodnight.

Clara Mandrake reached inside and found the strength to close her bedroom shutters, pull her clothes off, and drop them in piles on the floor. Folding them up would've required heroism worthy of an epic poem. She wrestled her way into her nightshirt in the dark. The bed caught her when she fell. A second grappling contest mangled the blanket, wrenched it around till it was on top of her. She huddled. Coolness shifted to heat.

Dark and soft and warm.

Dark.

It was dark, and *it* was there. Its weight pushed all the air in the room, squeezed it around Clara till she swore she'd break beneath it. Her lungs collapsed and pumped and collapsed. Each breath burned and choked her. They tasted of fur and flesh and blood and death.

She couldn't scream. Not this time. Couldn't scream and couldn't bear to look. She curled up, crumpled into a lump of girl and cloth. The blanket wouldn't hide her from the monster. But it would hide the monster from her, and that was enough. She wouldn't see its claws. Its teeth.

Clara screwed her eyes shut and waited to die.

• • •

The last of the morning mist clung to Silas' ankles. He peered into it, frowned, and prodded it with his cudgel. Wisps and nettles shifted around the stick. He felt like a cook stirring his spectral broth. But he stayed low to the ground, poking and prying. And almost missed it all the same.

He pinched a green triangle that was almost identical to the leaves around it. Silas plucked it out, and the rest of the flag emerged from the vegetation. He put it in his belt.

One point for Silas Renshaw.

His lips hurt when he smiled, but he couldn't help it. This game reminded him too much of childhood treasure hunts. He ran the end of his club through the foliage. Autumn had ignited the forest. Last time they played, everything was emerald. Now red and orange, yellow and brown had consumed most of the green. That meant…

A hundred paces. Then another. A twig cracked under his boot. He winced, crouched, raised his weapon. The leaves had hidden it. He'd have to watch out for that. But the air was quiet, save for the trill of birdsong. Nothing rustled in the bushes. So he continued.

There.

Above, at the end of a branch that was like a flaming torch. A flutter of orange a shade brighter than the leaves. There'd only been green ones before, and if he was lucky, some trainees wouldn't expect anything different.

Silas pursed his lips. It was high, but doable. He leaned his cudgel against the tree, rubbed warmth into his hands, and braced himself. Silas jumped. His fingers scrabbled at the bottom branch and he dropped back down, jarred both ankles. His muscles twinged. Stupid. He shook his legs and stretched them out.

He sprang again. His grip closed around the limb and he dangled there. Still too much flab around his middle… But his arms and core were stronger now. He pulled himself up and clambered onto the branch. Silas paused for a moment, lay there like a cat. Drew in the tree's primeval smell. Then he took a deep breath and stood. He swayed. His arms twitched, ready to thrust to the sides for balance. But he kept his footing, and it was easier from there. He climbed from branch to branch and didn't look down. Pretended he was only a few feet off the ground. That stratagem worked until he found himself pressed against the trunk, at the base of the flaming torch which held his prize.

Had it looked that narrow from the ground? Silas' brows knitted. It should be safe. One of the instructors had managed to put it there, and some of them were far heavier.

He crouched, wrapped his arms and legs around it, and slithered. The branch creaked. He stopped, waited. It didn't break, so he slithered some more. Another creak. This time it dipped and his stomach lurched. But he was close now. So close... Silas crawled and grabbed. He took the orange flag, pushed it into his mouth, and clamped it between his jaws.

Victory!

The branch cracked.

He clung on, too startled to drop or jump or do anything else. The branch swung. Silas had an instant to realise it hadn't snapped clean through, that its wound was a splintering hinge. Then he smashed against the trunk.

He fell. His boots landed on a branch and he bear-hugged the tree. Pain hammered in various places, but no broken bones shrieked. He released half his death grip and put the flag into his belt beside the green one.

Silas climbed back down to the branch he'd started on, dangled from it, and dropped to the ground.

"Nice one."

He sprang away from the woman's voice. Jocasta grinned at him. Mud splattered half the trainee's face and a mess of red hair which'd come loose from her ponytail.

"Thought you'd break your neck for a minute there."

"I got lucky." Silas smiled and inched towards the trunk. "What happened to you?"

He kept his eyes on her, but his fingers twitched. They reached out. Then he saw what hung from Jocasta's left hand, and they fell back to his side.

"Had to roll around in the dirt yanking these things off Cardew." She brandished his cudgel by the middle and tapped it against the flags on her belt. "Came off better than him though. He's still lying there. Give me those, and I won't crack your head open too."

"Make it a fair fight?" He nodded at his club.

Jocasta shrugged and held it out to him. He moved. She tossed it aside and swung her weapon.

Silas twisted away. His shoulder screamed where the cudgel clipped it.

"Last chance," she said.

He lunged. She swung.

But he was inside her range, and her arm hit him instead of the club. He clinched. Entangled the limb. Drove the heel of his hand into her nose. Cartilage crunched. Crimson spurted, wine from a freshly tapped barrel. Jocasta crumpled. The strength drained out of her limbs and Silas held back his second blow. He loosened his grasp.

She swept her leg against his.

The back of Silas' knee buckled, twisted. But he kept hold of her arm. He wrenched it towards him, threw his other arm around her neck, pivoted on the balls of his feet. Jocasta flew over his hip and hit the ground.

Silas dropped his knee on her sternum. She moaned and deflated. He snatched the cudgel away. Jocasta squirmed when he went for her flags, tried to throw him off. But he put more weight onto her. She spluttered.

Red droplets spattered her jerkin. He took his prizes. One of them was purple. Where had they hidden *that*? But the mystery wasn't important. He put them on his belt and their eyes met.

The thought passed between them as if spoken aloud. A knock on the head would keep her out of the game, stop her coming after him. Jocasta waited for it and didn't flinch.

Silas sighed. He pushed his weight down on her sternum to keep her winded, then got up. Jocasta grimaced. Or maybe it was a grin. He glanced around, decided he didn't have time to root among the bushes for the other cudgel, and left her there.

• • •

Everything mashed itself together inside Clara Mandrake's head. Doors creaked. Floorboards groaned. Shutters rattled. A horror shifted around inside the wardrobe. The shape loomed beside her bed. Heavy breaths, like a panting dog. Fingers stroked her flesh, and they were soft and warm but chilled her. Clara's skin quivered. Her organs pounded. Heart and lungs and liver and things she couldn't name. They thumped out the same tune that filled her bedroom and her brain.

Clara lay there while the room brightened beyond her blanket, as all these things rose and sank through her memory, and couldn't separate nightmares from reality. Or from madness. Because there was madness too, wasn't there? In the world and inside people's skulls. Like Old Joss' wife, near the end. When she ran through the street in her nightdress, eyes rolling, froth dribbling from her mouth, and screamed that the walrus would eat them all.

Would that be her? Clara Mandrake, the mad girl? Or would teeth and claws rip her apart?

"Clara! Breakfast!"

Her mind was a mess, but her mum's voice made her move. She threw the blanket back. It wasn't an aegis now anyway, and only suffocated her. She looked under her bed but expected nothing and that's all she found. No malevolence thrummed from the wardrobe either. In the morning things were different, and that meant it wasn't real, didn't it? Or the monster only came at night…

Clara opened the shutters and gazed into the mirror on her wall. A pale girl stared back. Colour had drained out of her olive flesh, spilled into the darkness and vanished with the dawn. She looked more like her mother now. But her eyes were even older.

Her mother.

Broken bowl. Spilled porridge. Blood.

Shame and guilt and love churned in her guts. She couldn't let her mum see her like this. Couldn't let Ella Mandrake worry, or question her daughter and hear answers that'd… Make her ashamed of her cowardly girl? Scared of her mad child? Both visions made Clara want to vomit.

So she went to her washstand. Poured water from the jug. Filled the basin and plunged her face into it. She shivered. Fingers on her skin… No! She shoved that away and submerged herself until cold killed the dream. She lifted her head. Droplets rained. Her skin burned. But she was awake.

Clara dressed. This time she brushed her hair.

A speck moved near her head. She tried to wave the insect away, but there was nothing there. Clara wet her fingertips and rubbed them around her eyes.

She ate breakfast. Nodded along while her mother talked.

"I told Sven to stop serving her, but he didn't listen. Then she got up and started dancing on a table, kicking all the tankards over. She caught Dander right on the jaw, and he'll have a goose egg there today. And what do you think Sven did about it?"

Clara shrugged.

"That's right. Nothing. He just left it to the barmaids, as usual. He said he couldn't manhandle a woman. Me and Sasha had to pull her down. Sasha wanted to suplex her through the table."

The thought of the barmaid putting a customer through the pub's furniture shouldn't have been that funny. But laughter burst from Clara's mouth before she could stop it. A rain of egg porridge went with it, and a chunk splatted on Ella's shirt.

"Clara!"

But it had her too now. Both Mandrake women convulsed, and Clara wondered if madness was contagious. Then she realised her mother's laugh was the most beautiful thing she'd heard in a long, long time. She hugged her before she left for school. This time Ella was ready, and her warmth spread through Clara's body right away.

"Don't let Sasha suplex anyone."

They laughed again. Clara left the house with a smile on her face. It burned there and fought the breeze. But it was already fading when she got to the end of the path. Exhaustion came back and hit her like a mace. She traced the carvings on the gatepost, yawned, and trudged down the lane.

If she found a quiet corner, she could sleep forever…

No.

Because sleep meant… Memories surged around her again. A jumble of visions and sounds and things that stank. Clara bit the edge of her tongue to purge them.

Rayya was outside the Shimud house, perched on the garden wall with a piece of parchment in her hands. Cursive script covered its reverse. The missive engrossed her. She didn't notice when Clara stopped a few feet away. Clara opened her mouth, but the greeting died in her throat. A black shape curled over Rayya's shoulder and hung down her front. The serpent twitched. Clara gasped, flinched. Rayya's head jerked up. Clara wanted to kick herself. For a second, the plait had been about to sink its fangs into her friend's chest.

Madness. It turned braids into serpents. Maybe darkness into monsters.

Rayya jumped down from the wall. Her eyes widened and Clara tried to muster up the wakefulness she'd woven for her mother. It fled her body in a yawn.

"Didn't you sleep?"

"Not much."

"Nightmares?"

A torrent of words threatened to gush out. She'd say she didn't know, that maybe bad dreams kept her awake, or a monster tormented her in the night, or else her broken brain saw, heard, smelled, and felt things which weren't there. Then Rayya would help her. She'd... run back inside and tell her parents Clara Mandrake was a madwoman.

"Yeah," Clara said.

"Go home and get some rest. I'll tell Miss Jazrah you're ill."

She couldn't face school. Another day of lessons and loudness. But she couldn't go home either. Couldn't wipe the smile and laughter off her mother's face.

"I'll be fine."

Clara moved before she could protest. Rayya dashed to catch up, then matched her stride.

"Look, you should really-"

"What's the letter?"

"Huh?" She blinked at it, as though surprised to find it still in her hand. "It's from Sachin."

"How's he doing?"

Her friend frowned. Clara thought Rayya might renew the attack or even drag her home by her arm. But she sighed instead, then grinned, as she always did when she had news about her brother. Clara's lips shaped a smile, though it was like carving it in stone.

"His cat... Did I tell you he's got a cat now? He calls her Buskin. That's a type of boot actresses wear. Did I tell you his girlfriend's an actress? Anyway..."

Rayya's voice soothed her. It drifted around her head, fluttered inside her ears and across her eyes.

"...she fell in the mixture and it turned her purple..."

Clara envisioned a purple actress prancing around the stage, till it dawned on her Rayya meant the cat.

"...an apprentice for much longer. His master says he's the best apothecary..."

Specks danced in front of her. Spiders. Clara ignored them. That's what you did with things that weren't real. You ignored them. Until they stepped out of your wardrobe and painted the room with your entrails.

"...came in saying she'd gone blind, but she'd just forgotten to take her sleeping mask off..."

Would her entrails be purple, like the unfortunate cat? Did cats eat entrails? She'd lie there in the corner, gnawing away on them...

Voices sliced her thoughts. They cut into her brain and a headache bloomed around the wound. Their classmates cavorted in the field beside the schoolhouse. Leah and Kasey chased one another in circles, till their speed, their flowing hair and hems, transformed the twins into glimpses of the same girl. Kolbo tumbled like a jester nearby, his face half black, half white with chalk dust. Tommy had Sarah on the ground. He sat on the blonde girl's back and smeared leaves in her face, then looked up, stopped, cackled.

"Monster!" He jumped and waved his arms. "Monster's comin' to get you!"

Clara winced. Her brain was about to burst.

"Monster! Monster! Monster!"

Tommy loped towards her like the hunchbacks in the winter pantomime. The other kids followed. They converged on Clara and Rayya, grinning and giggling.

"Clara's scared of the monster!" Tommy said.

More of them took up the cry.

"Clara's scared of the monster! Clara's scared of the monster!"

Sarah spat out bits of leaf and jeered along with them.

"Clara's scared of the monster!"

"Stop it!" Rayya turned this way and that. Glared at each of them. "Leave her alone!"

Some of them shrugged and went back to their games. Others held their ground but shut up and dropped their gazes.

"Monster's gonna kill you!" Tommy thrust his face close to Clara's. Flecks of spittle wet her nose and cheeks. "Monster's gonna kill you!"

"Go away!" Rayya pushed him aside and pulled Clara past him.

Clara's head hurt too much to speak or think or live.

"The monster's coming! Rawr! Rawr! Monster!"

Clara and Rayya trudged into the schoolhouse.

• • •

Silas' eyes narrowed. So did his enemy's. He tensed. So did his enemy. Silas lunged, dived, and grasped. The squirrel darted away. Silas smacked the earth, grunted, glared. The rodent stared back. Its eyes glittered as it nibbled the brown flag.

His bones ached. But he got up, because he wasn't going to lose to an acrobatic rat. Silas frowned. The squirrel gnawed. Human and rodent watched one another. Silas tensed again, and the squirrel did the same. He paused. Hunters didn't catch squirrels by hand. And after his slapstick endeavours thus far, he felt they were on to something. There wasn't time to make a snare and lie in wait. He didn't have a bow or shuriken. So Silas looked around for a rock to throw. He spotted something else instead.

The animal tilted its head. It gnawed the flag a couple more times, but with less enthusiasm. Silas plucked the sprig of berries from the tree. He tossed it over and it landed inches away from the squirrel. The flag emerged from the rodent's maw. The grey snout twitched twice. It looked at the berries, performed whatever calculations squirrels were wont to make, dropped the piece of cloth. It climbed the nearest tree and the sprig wobbled between its jaws.

Silas picked up his prize and his cudgel. He walked on, added the flag to his belt. Seven. Not bad going. He might even-

Silas rounded a trunk and she emerged from behind another. Lucy's gaze went to his waist and his to hers.

"Good haul," she said.

"You too."

Her flags clumped together. She might have the same as him, maybe more. But it didn't matter now.

He took up his stance. So did she. They both advanced and Silas struck first. Wood clacked on wood. And again. Silas probed her defences, watched for signs of injury and weakness, and knew Lucy was doing the same.

Lucy's right ankle shifted. Only an inch, but Silas was ready. He swung while she was open. Her eyes gleamed. Silas pulled back but it was too late. Her feint became a counterattack and her club smacked his forearm. Pain shot along the bones. His fingers opened and his weapon fell.

Silas threw himself at her, jammed her next attack. Lucy didn't fight for it. She dropped her cudgel and grabbed him with both hands. They clinched, seized neck and elbow. Fought for balance and control. He couldn't shift her. Lucy was built like a boulder. Their eyes met and thoughts merged. Their instructors had taught them the same thing. If an opponent clinched your upper body…

He hesitated.

Lucy's knee exploded in his groin. He doubled over, moaned. She threw her arms around his middle. Her hands locked together, drove up into his gut. Silas dropped his weight. But she heaved him up and over like a sack of grain. His insides lurched. The world flipped round, then bashed his back. Lucy landed on top of him. Muscle and bone ground him into the dirt.

She shifted, moved into a mount. Open hands battered him. Palm strikes rocked his skull and slaps burst every nerve in his face. He threw up his arms, rolled over to shield himself. Desperate. Instinctive. Stupid. Silas knew what was coming, but couldn't stop it.

Lucy's arm wrapped around his neck and squeezed. His head swam. Pressure built against the backs of his eyeballs. He kicked for purchase, but her feet hooked his legs. Stretched them out.

Silas' vision danced and blurred.

He clawed at her arm. It didn't budge. Blackness squirted through his arteries, filled his head. And Silas tapped. His fingertips beat a rhythm on the blade of her forearm. But nothing happened. This wasn't the wrestling ring, and there was no referee to pull her off. Veins swelled in his face. Her grip crushed his throat and he was going to die here in the forest in blood and black and-

Silas gasped. Lungs and brain found air and sucked it in.

Lucy rolled him. He flopped onto his back. Her eyes hardened and sharpened above him. The rest of the world coalesced around them. She held his gaze, raised her fist. Silas lifted his hands, palms out. Lucy nodded. He grimaced as she looted his flags, but didn't move.

She picked up her weapon and looked down at him.

"I beat you. Fair and square. No coming after me, okay?"

"Okay."

Their eyes stayed locked for a moment. They both knew. She might've knocked out one of the others. Dislocated their shoulder. Popped their knee. But Silas' word was good. Silly, noble Silas. He sighed.

Lucy disappeared among the trees.

Silas picked himself up, retrieved his cudgel, and went hunting for flags. Maybe he could still cobble together a respectable score…

• • •

"…anapaest goes short-short-long, short-short-long," Miss Jazrah said. "Anapaest. Say it with me…"

"Anapaest!"

"Anna pissed!"

"Thomas!"

"What, miss?"

Clara mumbled along with the rest of the children.

"Di-di-dum! Di-di-dum!"

The syllables chanted. They drummed into her head.

"Poets sometimes use it for the sound of a galloping horse…"

Miss Jazrah recited a poem. Clara propped up her chin. She needed to rest her eyes for just a minute…

Darkness. The wardrobe door-

Her shin exploded. Her jaw fell off her hand and her eyes opened. Rayya kicked her again for good measure.

"You were falling asleep."

"Yeah. Thanks…"

Her eyes closed. Rayya's shoe scraped the floor.

"Okay! Okay!"

This time they stayed open. She half-listened to the poem about bandits on horses till Old Joss rang the bell.

Miss Jazrah glanced at Clara when the kids got up. The teacher's lips pursed. Clara hurried out before she could say anything. Rayya dashed after her.

"Go home."

"Can't."

They walked across the field, towards their oak. Rayya inhaled and Clara steeled herself for the argument.

"Monster's gonna kill you!"

He ran in front, between the girls and the tree.

"Tommy!" Rayya swerved and shouldered him out of Clara's path. "Bother someone else!"

"It'll rip your face off and wipe its butt with it!"

Sniggers surrounded Clara. A dozen feet clomped after her and each one stamped on the inside of her skull. They were behind the tree now, in its shade. But the din continued.

"It'll eat your guts, crap them out, and eat them again!"

"Ew!"

"Gross, Tommy!"

His audience tittered. Clara and Rayya stopped. There was nowhere left to go. Nowhere he wouldn't follow, with his jeers and stupid face. He posed in front of Clara. Jumped up and down.

"Mons-ter! Mons-ter! Mons-ter!"

"Get lost," Rayya said, "or-"

"Rawr! Rawr! Rawr!" He clawed the air. "Rawr! Rawr! Rawr!"

An inferno blazed in Clara's brain. She shrieked and leapt at him.

"Rawr?"

Her hands closed around his neck. His soft, squishy neck. Her thumbs stabbed the hollow spot in the middle. They dug in and she imagined them bursting through flesh and blood and whatever lay beneath.

"Clara!" Rayya said.

Tommy grabbed her wrists. She slammed the top of her head into his face. He spluttered. She headbutted him again. And again. Impact shuddered through bone. His nose was soft and squishy too.

"Clara! Stop!"

Redness slathered Tommy's face. She liked it better that way. Clara's fingers squeezed and her head drew back for another hit.

Hands and arms ensnared her. Yanked her off the wretched little boy who bled and moaned. Clara thrashed. She dragged the whole pack and they clamoured at her. Tommy lay on the ground. He stared up at the heavens, made idiot sounds. Clara strained against her classmates. She wanted to stamp on his face. Stomp on it again and again till it went squelch and-

Rayya's face flashed past. Her mouth hung open and water glistened in her eyes. Rage drained from Clara's body. She went limp, and the arms fell away.

Tommy groaned.

Clara ran.

• • •

"Mawlana! Mawlana!"

"Look! Mawlana!"

Fahmaia blinked. A maelstrom of dark imaginings held together for a moment longer, then parted to reveal the children who called and cheered and fought. She'd wandered all the way to the training grounds.

"Look what I can do!"

A smile etched itself on her lips. Their joy, their passion, was purer than a prayer.

"Watch us, mawlana! Please?"

"Please! Please!"

Fahmaia laughed and held up her hands before they dragged her by force.

"All right!"

They capered around her, whooping and touching the scriptures on her forearms for luck. A pair of men gasped nearby. Beards and moustaches obscured dangling jaws. Fahmaia didn't recognise them. New converts, most likely. Unlike these children, who'd known her their whole short lives. She'd held them as babes. Whispered Allat's wisdom into their ears when they emerged from the womb.

"Show me what you've learned."

The boys and girls waved their practice weapons. They paired off. Soon war cries mingled with the click and clatter of wood on wood. Fahmaia armed herself in the same manner before she walked among them.

"You're not chopping firewood, Aisha. Smaller motions. Like this…" She cut and thrust at the air. "Wild swings let in enemy blades."

She'd fought alongside many of their parents. It amused her to see the same quirks of martial style pass from mothers and fathers to sons and daughters.

"Good, Shahid! Good! Barzik Khan will be proud."

A blade flew at her face. Fahmaia tapped it aside with her own.

"Careful, Salman! The One Goddess didn't put these scriptures on my skin so you could knock them off."

"Sorry, mawlana!"

A bruise had once taught her never to instruct the children without a weapon in her hand.

"That's enough for now," she said, when their limbs tired and more mistakes crept in. "Eat and drink.

Warriors must nourish their muscles. Even the Khan himself."

They protested, as usual, but did as bidden. Fahmaia swung her sword back and forth while they jogged away. It'd been too long since she last sparred. Perhaps that would help settle her spirit…

She went to the adults' swordplay ground. But only new recruits were at arms there, and that made things awkward. Fahmaia covered her limbs and wrapped her face, to spare them the impiety of striking Allat's scriptures. Yet they still hesitated.

"Anyone?" She smiled her least threatening smile. "I'm not as ferocious as you've heard."

After some moments, a young man stepped forward and she thanked him. They fought. He was too timid. Her mind wandered, dwelt on the dread she'd felt at prayer, and he still couldn't find his way past her defences. She scored a hit to put him out of his misery. Fahmaia thanked him again, put her sword away, and walked the camp once more.

She ate with some of the servants. Visited the invalids. But at last she chided herself and returned to her own tent. She couldn't procrastinate any longer. The One Goddess must have some purpose at hand, and it was her duty to discern it. So Fahmaia lit her incense. Sat cross-legged. Ate more honey, in case that helped. Willed her mind to enter the prayer trance.

And then she was back on the hilltop.

The sun shone and cities sprawled. Magnificent. Glorious. But again a chill fluttered through Fahmaia's bones. Wrongness oozed inside her blood. She whispered holy words. Her markings quickened, spun across her skin in a black blur. And the sky parted.

Two eyes opened in the heavens. They stared down at the world they had wrought and nothing could escape them. A hand descended, cast its shadow over the civilisations below, and Fahmaia trembled. The end time had come. The peoples of the world had angered the One Goddess with their sins, and she would crush them all. The mawlana's scream built in her throat but wouldn't come forth. She flinched. Raised her arms, as though they could shield her from the cosmic avalanche, and prepared to perish.

But Allat's hand didn't smash her and the kingdoms with their teeming millions. It hovered instead. Hovered, and pointed. Fahmaia mustered all her piety, all her courage, to meet the One Goddess' eyes. And she understood.

Her true eyes opened and the vision was gone. For some minutes she couldn't move. The mawlana sat there and shook, as before. But she mustn't succumb to weakness. Not while Allat's message burned within her. The One Goddess was merciful, but only the piety of the Kharjis, Fahmaia's people, could earn that clemency.

The mawlana wiped cold sweat from her limbs. She went outside, took a few steps towards Barzik Khan's tent, and forced herself to look heavenward. A scattering of stars twinkled in the darkness. The prayer trance had carried day into evening. The Khan would be in the pleasure tent, so she went there instead.

"Mawlana!" A guardswoman stopped her outside the tent flap. "The Khan's... He's... Let me tell him you wish to see him! Wait!"

But Fahmaia moved past, and the woman didn't dare block her path.

Young men and women sprawled throughout the tent. Lounged on rugs and pillows. Lay in tangles of flesh. Some of them cowered when she approached, tried to hide their nakedness. Others sat in clouds of shisha smoke and stared through her.

Barzik reclined at the far end of the tent, atop a throne of cushions. A woman anointed his masses of beard with oil. Another did the same to his long locks. Brushes scraped and clinked across his hair, scoured away the dust and dirt. The warlord glanced up. He grabbed the nearest concubine and pulled the young man in front of his loins.

"I've cleaned men's wounds," Fahmaia said. "Your flesh doesn't trouble me."

The warlord sighed and gestured. The concubine scurried away.

"If I'd known-" Barzik said.

"It was too urgent. Allat has spoken."

Barzik Khan dropped to his knees. One of the girls squealed when his hair tore from her grasp. Specks of blood shone in her palm.

"What does she say?"

"A sacrifice." Fahmaia knelt too and took his hands in hers. "A large one, for the sake of the world."

3

Rayya Shimud paced across her bedroom a dozen times. When that didn't help, she sat back down at the table and picked up her quill. But the nib paused on its journey from ink bottle to parchment. Rayya tickled her nostrils with the opposite end instead. It was like rubbing her nose against a kitten, and usually relaxed her. But there was a limit to what feathers, or even actual felines, could accomplish this evening.

She dipped the instrument into the ink bottle again. It rose and fell twice more. Soon there was enough blue on it to write an epic poem. And yet the letter to Sachin lay there unfinished, as it had for the past hour. Rayya forced the nib onto the parchment. She scribbled a couple more words. But how could she write anecdotes about their parents, ask questions about his cat, when…

Clara's face floated in the middle of her mind. No. *Faces*. The first a mask of rage. A visage that belonged on the side of a temple, to scare away evil spirits. But the other was no better. The one which'd been there just before Clara ran. The face of a frightened and broken girl.

Rayya wrote. Words flowed beneath the nib but meant nothing.

A bang rattled the shutters. She gasped. The candle flame wavered, light and dark wobbled around her. Ink fell onto the parchment. Each droplet bloomed into a wound.

The knock sounded again, and this time a voice hissed.

"Rayya!"

She put the quill down. More ink bled from it and drowned her words, but she barely noticed. Rayya ran to the window and opened the shutters.

"Clara! You…"

A gust swept past and leaves tumbled through the air. It froze her face. Clara shivered too. Rayya took her friend's arm and helped her scramble inside, then shut out the cold. The girls rubbed warmth back into their hands.

"Are you okay?"

"Yeah…"

But Clara looked like a sculpture that'd taken a hard blow. Any second now, cracks would creep across her skin and she'd break into a hundred pieces.

"What did Miss Jazrah say? About Tommy?"

"He lied. He said he fell out of the tree."

"Huh?" Brightness flickered in the depths of Clara's eyes. Seeped into her cheeks. She tottered and slumped onto the edge of the bed. "Then…"

Rayya sat beside her.

"After school, he told us he wasn't a snitch. But the twins said he just didn't want the adults to know he got beaten up by a girl."

Clara giggled. The sound meant more to Rayya than all the kittens in the world. It was the old Clara.

"That's why mum didn't know. I thought... I thought they just hadn't told her yet."

"We told Jazrah you were feeling sick and went home. She believed it." Rayya bit her lip. She wanted to stop there. Stop while her friend was relieved and smiling and everything was good. But she couldn't. "Clara... What happened?"

The corner of Clara's mouth quivered.

"I... I don't know. My head just... hurt. It hurt so bad and he was being such a jerk and I couldn't stop, couldn't stop hitting him."

Her body shook. She closed her mouth, tried to hold back the sob, and it exploded from her eyes instead. Tears streamed down her cheeks. Rayya couldn't move. Clara's pain transfixed her. But a fresh sob snapped her out of it. She grabbed a handkerchief and pushed it into her friend's hand. Clara sniffed. Her nose dribbled. She wiped it, and smeared wetness across her face.

"Go home and sleep. You'll feel better after-"

Clara wailed. Her whole face erupted, eyes and nose and mouth. Rayya turned to the door. She didn't know whether to hope her parents hadn't heard or run to them for help.

"I can't! I can't go to bed, because of the monster!"

Rayya's stomach lurched. Or maybe it was the room. Or the whole world. Her friend was crazy. Crazy, like Old Joss' wife.

"Clara, what... what're you-"

"I go to sleep and it's there. In my head. In my nightmares. It's coming for me, and I can't get away. Because it's there. It's right there and... and..."

Oh! Rayya exhaled. Nightmares. She could deal with nightmares.

"It's just a dream. They seem real sometimes."

"No. It was there. In my wardrobe and… and…" She blinked. Blew her nose. Deflated. "It felt… It…"

Rayya couldn't tell if it was epiphany or embarrassment. But the intensity melted from her friend's face, and Rayya jumped into the opening.

"Trust me. Just get a proper night's sleep and you'll be fine."

"I can't. Not there. I…" She grasped Rayya's hand. "Can I sleep here tonight?"

"Okay."

"Thanks."

"No problem. But… Your mum."

"She won't go in my room unless she needs to wake me up in the morning. I can sneak back in early."

Clara's eyes shone, and Rayya didn't have the heart to raise any more objections. Her friend had to sleep. Just one proper night's rest, and maybe everything would be fine. No more tears. No more crazy talk. No more monsters. No more beating Tommy half to death.

"I'll get you a nightshirt."

The girls dressed for bed. Rayya glanced at the ruined letter, sighed, and blew out the candle. She got under the blanket. Clara's heat filled the narrow bed, but it wasn't unpleasant.

She lay there and listened to the rhythm of her friend's heart.

· · ·

"Get him, Silas!"

"Jonas! Jonas! Jonas!"

Figures jostled at the edges of Silas' vision, in the darkness beyond the ring of flaming torches. He tried to ignore them.

Jonas flailed like a marionette at the end of a drunkard's strings. Punches hammered Silas from every angle. Two battered his guard. One pounded the side of his head.

"Jonas! Jonas! Jonas!"

Silas threw a straight right. Jonas darted back out of reach and swung his leg as a parting gift. His shin slashed Silas' thigh. Silas' leg buckled, but he moved with it and stayed upright.

"Come on, Silas!" Jocasta's voice cut through the others.

Jonas held back. Sweat ran down his sinews, and the leather around his fists was several shades darker now. Silas didn't press forward. He took deep breaths, his belly wobbled. The referee coughed and brandished her birch. She wouldn't let them linger.

"Finish him, Jonas!" Lucy said.

"Mess him up, Silas!" Jocasta said.

The trainees on either side of the circle lent their voices. Friendships and enmities meant nothing. If a fighter beat you, you cheered for them. That was tradition. And if someone else beat them, you cheered for that fighter instead. The final match of a tournament was always boisterous.

Jonas moved first. Another low kick. Silas raised his leg to block it on the knee, but Jonas' scarecrow limb flicked in and out, lashed Silas on the inside of his other thigh. He staggered. An overhead right bounced off his forehead. Lights burst in his eyes and mingled with the torches.

He swung back. One of his punches clipped Jonas, and the taller youth backed up again. But Jonas grinned. He could take his time. Pick Silas apart in this contest of fists and feet.

Silas' lungs heaved. He was the better wrestler. If he could get in close, clinch, muscle Jonas around and wear him down, throw some short, sharp blows to the kidneys… His fingers opened and closed. But the referee shook her head. Silas winced. Grappling and other rule-breaking meant whacks from her birch. He couldn't afford to take any more damage.

"Mess him up, Silas! Mess him up!" His half of the crowd chanted with one voice now. "Mess him up, Silas! Mess him up!"

"Jonas, break his face!" The counter-chorus was just as loud. "Jonas, Jonas, break his face!"

Silas snapped a kick at his belly. Jonas knocked it aside but caught the follow-up punch on his cheek. Silas threw everything he had. A barrage of blows. Most bounced off knees, elbows, and forearms. But a few landed.

"Silas! Silas! Silas!"

Jonas backed up, almost into a torch, and had to lunge forward again. His foot thrust at Silas' face. Silas slipped past the side kick. Now! He spotted his target, moved into the punch. Already saw it land in his mind's eye.

Then Jonas' foot hooked round the opposite side of his head. Silas had time to think, "Bloody scarecrow!" before its heel collided with his jaw.

The world spun. Trails of fire whirled around the night sky.

"Jonas! Jonas! Jonas!"

Darkness carried him away.

. . .

The monster loomed over her bed and the wardrobe door opened and the monster loomed over her bed. Warm fingers. Claws. On her cheek. Coming out of the closet.

Clara screamed but it didn't make a sound. She had no voice. No air. A hand pressed over her mouth. Skin. Fur. Fingertips. Claws. They smothered her and she was going to die and-

"Clara." Rayya's breath stroked her cheek and the memory made her flinch. The hand shifted. "You kicked me and started screaming. You were going to wake my parents up."

"Oh. I'm… I'm sorry."

Rayya sighed. Her weight shifted next to Clara as she lay back down.

"The monster again?"

"Yeah. It was here and…" But she realised how stupid that was. Because Rayya was here, not the monster. Clara wanted to curl up and die.

"It's just a nightmare."

"It felt-"

"I know. But there's nothing here. And there's nothing in *your* bedroom either."

"I'm sorry."

Clara tried to stifle the sob. Rayya's arms snaked around her and pulled her into a hug.

"It's okay."

"But it's so real! And I don't know if I'm dreaming or crazy. When I'm there, I hear it. Feel it. When it comes out of the wardrobe it... it..."

"Listen... Tomorrow, we'll sleep in your room. Then you'll know for sure. If anything comes out of the wardrobe, I'll see it. If it doesn't, you'll know it's just a dream. Sound good?"

"Yeah..." She wiped her tears and smiled. "But what if you're crazy too?"

"Then we'll visit Sachin and he can mix us up a crazy girl cure."

"Will it turn our hair purple?"

"Maybe."

"I'd like that."

"Me too."

• • •

Birdsong trilled outside the dormitory windows. Young men shuffled and rolled over under their blankets as the morning music coaxed them from slumber. The door banged open. Feet stamped. Voices drowned out the birds.

"Wake up, you lazy bastards!"

"She's here!"

Silas yawned. An ache throbbed through his mandible and he clamped his mouth shut.

"Stop touching yourselves and get up!"

A phalanx of female trainees marauded through the dorm, kicking beds, snatching blankets. Some of the boys yelled. Others grabbed clothes or hurled pillows. Jocasta intercepted a missile and threw it back. Cardew caught it in the side of his bandaged head and tumbled onto the floor.

Silas swung his legs off the mattress, sat there, and raised a hand to the worst of his bruises before he remembered himself and put it back in his lap.

"The next one's here." Lucy stopped beside his bed.

"Can't be." Jonas vaulted over the adjacent cot and landed next to her. "Too soon. It's only been a couple of days."

"It's true," Jocasta said. "She's in our dorm's guest room. Arrived late last night."

"Who is it?" Silas stood up. His left thigh blared, but he refused to favour it. "Anyone we know?"

The girls grinned.

"Yeah," Lucy said. "Old scarface herself."

Jonas whistled.

"Katrina von Talhoffer. Damn."

A score or more conversations exploded around the dormitory. That name spat from each of them, in such varied tones of awe and admiration, dread and disbelief, it may've belonged to a hundred different women.

"Did she have an apprentice with her?" Silas said. But he knew. The girls wouldn't have invaded with the cockcrow to bring them the news unless…

"No," Lucy said. "Didn't you lot hear what happened?"

"I did." Jonas' chest swelled. He was never short on gossip.

Lucy and Jonas looked at Silas, and Silas was forced to shrug.

"Why? What happened?"

The pair exchanged smirks. For a split-second, Silas saw them as they would've been if they'd never come here. Two kids swapping stories and making mischief behind a village pub, instead of breaking each other's heads.

"Scarface killed him," Lucy said.

"Rubbish." The word squeezed through the bones and bruises of Silas' skull. It sounded weak, petulant in his own ears. His face heated. "A mistress wouldn't…"

"She did," Jonas said. "Or as good as."

The dormitory door opened once more, behind Lucy and Jonas.

"Geoffrey's apprentice told us, when they passed through." Lucy made an obscene gesture and winked. "Cardew got it out of him."

Two figures entered — Master Gunnar and a woman who stood a full head taller. Silas opened his mouth but shut it again. A thousand ideas bounced around his brain. He fixed his gaze on Lucy's face.

"What'd he say?" Silas kept his voice steady.

"There was an encounter, and she ran away while her apprentice was fighting."

"Just left him to die," Jonas said, "to save her own skin."

"She should've been kicked out."

"Hanged, if you ask me."

The silence was a physical thing. It buffeted the dormitory and everyone in it. Colour drained from Lucy and Jonas' cheeks. Silas' heart thudded. His stomach scrunched up into a ball. The two trainees turned, but the faces around the chamber already told them what waited there.

Katrina von Talhoffer's face bore no expression. Her lips were level, and her single blue eye gazed at nothing in particular. But scars twitched below her eyepatch.

"Raise your hands."

Her voice wasn't loud. Or hard. Or fierce. But Silas almost flinched.

"We... We weren't-" Lucy said.

"I didn't-" Jonas said.

"Raise. Your. Hands."

"I'll take them outside." Master Gunnar shifted. His eyes darted from Mistress von Talhoffer to the trainees and back again. "Give them six strokes each for impertinence..."

"No. No flogging." She took a stance and put up her guard. "Raise your hands. Both of you."

Silas had fought Jonas enough times to see it coming. The trainee's leg lashed out, and Silas admired him beyond measure. *He* wouldn't have dared. Not even when the fight was inevitable. But Jonas wasn't a coward.

Katrina von Talhoffer stepped into the kick. Jammed it with her left elbow and jarred Jonas' leg. Her right fist crashed on his jaw. Jonas staggered. He punched. It rebounded off the top of the mistress' head and she hit him twice more. His body twisted, flailed.

More like a scarecrow than ever. He bumped into Silas' bed and went down in a tangle of limbs.

Lucy sprang at von Talhoffer. Her hands snatched, sought purchase, tried to clinch and throw. The mistress headbutted her. Kneed her between the legs. Swept her feet out from under her. Lucy hit the floor and groaned.

Katrina von Talhoffer's eye fastened on her. Silas held his breath. Master Gunnar's hand rose, fell by his side, and rose again. His body jerked in her direction then stopped. But she stepped back, dropped her fists. Everyone exhaled.

"So…" Mistress von Talhoffer's gaze scoured the entire room. "Which one's Lucy Pergan?"

Master Gunnar coughed. It was a few seconds before he pointed. Another moment crawled by.

"Who's your second best trainee?" Katrina said.

"Jonas Andrescu." Again he pointed.

The silence stretched until Silas was sure it would smother him.

"The third best?"

His heartbeat quickened.

"Silas Renshaw."

The finger jabbed from a few feet away, but Silas' flesh throbbed as though it had punctured him. Katrina von Talhoffer turned. He couldn't meet her eye, focused on her patch instead. Its blackness glared at him. Thoughts plummeted into his guts and festered there for an eternity.

She eyed his belly and her lip curled. Silas wished by all things holy and profane that he slept in a nightshirt.

"Very well. Renshaw… Silas. You're injured?"

"Huh?" The pains returned, as though back from a voyage. "I… I'm…"

"He took some hard knocks yesterday," Master Gunnar said.

"Spend today recovering," she said. "Tomorrow, you'll train with me. I'll see what third best is good for."

"Yes, Mistress von Talhoffer. I… I'll…"

But she'd already turned on her heel and walked away.

…

Clara pulled herself up onto the windowsill, lost her balance, and toppled into her bedroom. She landed in a crouch — more out of luck than grace. Things oozed under her hands. She fell backwards and her head tapped the wall.

Leaves. Just leaves that'd blown in because she'd left the shutters open. She gathered them up and dropped the clump outside.

Light hadn't conquered the wardrobe yet. Menace radiated from its crevices, where shadow-spiders blinked in and out of existence. But Clara held her ground and her nerve. Rayya was right. Must be right. And tonight they'd prove it.

Wood creaked. Clara's body twanged like a bowstring. She rolled her eyes, lifted her foot, pressed it down again. Same creak. Stupid, stupid Clara.

She washed her face. Hacked at her hair with the brush. Yawned. She'd love to fall into bed. Snatch more sleep to complete the pieces she'd gathered in Rayya's room. But… No. Not till tonight.

A buzz stopped her on the way to the kitchen. She put her ear to her mother's door. Ella normally went to bed later and woke earlier than she did. Clara couldn't remember the last time she'd heard her mum snore. She wanted to sneak inside, curl up next to Ella Mandrake, and listen to it forever.

Clara took her hand off the doorknob and sighed.

In the kitchen she reached for the woodpile. Things crawled in the shadow of her hand. She pulled it away and they vanished. Just more mind-spiders. Crazy Clara spiders. All those times her mother said little girls needed their sleep, she'd been telling the truth. Tonight they'd fix that. For now... Clara built the fire and opened the tinderbox. She scraped her thumb a couple of times, yelped, but swallowed most of the sound so she wouldn't wake her mum. After a few more fumbles, the flame caught.

Clara watched it for some moments and warmed her hands. Then she went out to fetch water. The full pail yanked her shoulders half out of their sockets. Splashes hit her legs and feet, turned them to ice. But she made it back inside with most of the water, warmed her hands again, dried off, and set to work.

"Huh?" Ella blinked in the doorway, yawned, and rubbed her face. "Clara?"

"Breakfast!"

Clara set the bowl of porridge on the table. The aroma of oats and eggs wafted between them. Her mum stared.

"Breakfast. *You* made breakfast."

"Yep! Oh... There might be bits of shell in it. Cracking eggs is hard."

Ella laughed. Clara beamed. They sat down and ate. Clara waited till her mother looked full, warm, and content.

"Mum… Can Rayya sleep here tonight?"

"If the Shimuds say it's okay." Something crunched between her teeth. Her lips twitched from side to side. "Tomorrow, I'll teach you to crack them properly."

Mother and daughter hugged, and Clara breathed in Ella Mandrake's scent. A smile warmed her face as she left the house. It tingled when she stopped by the gatepost, traced her father's carvings. Clara closed her eyes and a dark shape stood over her bed. A blink banished it. The smile recovered, and widened when Rayya met her in the lane.

"If Tommy says anything…" Clara said.

"Just don't kill him, okay?"

"Not even a little?"

They chuckled.

The other kids whooped and rampaged in the field, as usual. It wasn't cold enough to drive them indoors yet. A few of them watched Clara, including Tommy. His face resembled a chunk of meat from the butcher's shop. But he didn't say anything. Didn't come over. He went back to his conversation, and everyone else did the same.

"Nice one." Leah appeared beside Clara. Or maybe it was Kasey.

"Yeah," the other twin said. "Tommy hasn't beaten anyone up since you battered him."

"Do it once a week. Please?"

The four girls giggled. Tommy glanced over, then looked away again.

Miss Jazrah's lesson flowed in and out of Clara's ears. But Rayya didn't have to kick her awake, so that was okay.

"Clara!" The teacher tapped her chalk on the blackboard. "Is that syllable stressed or unstressed?"

She frowned, stared at the line of poetry above the chalk, and said, "Stressed?"

"Yes. Good."

Her gaze moved on in search of other victims. The lesson drifted along, and so did Clara. The rest of the school day melted away in turn.

"…dress like a witch for the festival." Rayya kicked a pile of leaves. It burst into a cascade of red and gold. The colours clung to their boots as they walked down the lane. "But mum said if a real witch saw me, she'd pull my heart out and eat it."

"Tasty."

"Gross."

"With mint and mustard?"

"Okay. Maybe tasty…"

The Mandrake house was empty. Gloom had gathered in the corners, spilled out over floors, crept up walls, across ceilings. Clara lit a candle and light reclaimed the world around them.

Rayya approached the wardrobe. She inspected it as though for the first time, ran her fingers along its grooves. Clara's heartbeat quickened when her friend grasped the handle. Rayya paused, met Clara's eyes, and waited for her to nod. The door opened. Rayya peered inside.

"No monsters." She closed the wardrobe and smiled.

They sat on Clara's bed and talked. The room brightened with every passing minute. This was *her* room. A place for Clara Mandrake and her friend — not nightmares, madness, or monsters.

"Girls! Dinner!"

Heat hung in the kitchen. It cuddled Clara, snuggled her into smells of ginger, garlic, and roasted duck.

"…turned her purple."

"What's the cat's name?" Ella said.

"Buskin. That's a kind of boot…"

Clara sat there, chewed meat, and nestled within the voices of the two people she loved most in the world. Ella Mandrake laughed. Rayya laughed. And Clara ignored the crazy black things. They'd be gone tomorrow. She'd wake up, rested and refreshed, hug her mother, hug Rayya, and laugh on the way to school about how silly she'd been.

"Clara?"

She blinked.

"Huh?"

"Camomile?" her mum said.

"Oh, sure. Thanks."

The tea added its fragrance to the melange. Rayya wrapped her hands around her cup, shivered despite the kitchen's warmth, and half-swallowed a yawn. A pang hit Clara's heart. Her nightmares had terrified her mother, and last night they'd ruined her friend's sleep too. She vowed she'd make it up to both of them somehow. Maybe she'd bake them a cake. With honey, and bits of eggshell. Because cracking eggs was hard…

Back in Clara's bedroom, Rayya unleashed another yawn. Clara yawned in turn, and the volley went back and forth till each exhalation was half laughter. They put on their nightshirts. Clara climbed into bed. Rayya brushed her hair and gave Clara a look.

"What?"

"If you don't do your hair-"

"Too tired. Tomorrow."

"Come here." Rayya rolled her eyes.

Clara sighed. She sat up. Rayya scrambled into place behind her and went to work with the brush. Each stroke soothed her scalp.

She'd make sure there were no bits of shell in that cake…

• • •

"Fetch us another one!"

Old Joss sipped his ale and tried to ignore her.

"Oi, gorgeous! Another beer!"

His handbell rested on the bar. The entire taproom swam within its metal. It bent and scrunched the traveller into a blob.

"Just a sec, love," Sasha said.

The barmaid deployed tankards from her tray, onto the table next to the outsider's. Joss glanced over his shoulder. The woman was just as obnoxious out of the bell. Good doublet though. Deep, plush blue. A matching sapphire glimmered on her ring.

"Bloody merchants."

He muttered it, but Sven glared at him from the other side of the bar.

"Their coin's always good," the barkeep whispered, "even if their manners aren't. And-"

"Hey!"

Sasha's cry and the clatter of her tray snapped both their heads round.

The traveller's hand clasped the barmaid's buttock for an instant longer. Then Sasha turned. Sven swore and stumbled out from behind the bar. The merchant screamed.

"Oi! Gerroff!"

Sasha wrenched the woman's arm, slammed her chest and cheek down on the table. Sven reached out but thought better of it. Joss didn't think Sasha would toss her boss out the window, but the possibility was there.

"Sasha!" the barkeep said.

The barmaid grunted and released the hammerlock. The traveller clasped her shoulder and roared.

"If that's how you treat paying customers, I'm not staying! Give me back my money."

Sasha snorted.

"This is the only public house in the village, you stupid cow! You'll sleep upstairs or in your wagon."

"Oh…"

The women held each other's gazes.

"Fine. Just bring me another beer."

"No more touching."

"Fine."

Sasha picked up the tray and walked off. Sven returned to the bar and wiped his brow. Joss finished his drink.

"Want another?" the barkeep said.

Joss scratched his beard. Back to an empty house, or another ale… But he knew what happened when he went over his limit. It always ended in tales and tears.

"No thanks."

"Okay. Good night."

"Night."

Joss picked up his bell. His hand shook and the ringer swung. Its clang didn't turn any heads, but raised a small chorus.

"Night, Joss!"

He nodded to the room at large.

"Oi!" The traveller gestured at him with her new tankard. "Take that thing with you to the outhouse too?"

Now heads turned. A mass intake of breath stretched the atmosphere taut. Joss looked from his bell to the merchant.

"Yeah," he said. "Never leaves my side."

She shrugged and drank. Joss opened the door and everyone breathed out.

He plodded down the lane. Steadied his fingers, so the bell wouldn't ring again. Thought about the day he'd first held it. The bright eyes. Sweet grin. Calloused hands.

Leaves crunched behind him. A throat hissed. Joss spun round, and the universe contracted around a face. Their eyes met. The Kharji froze, then the man's arm moved. Moonlight flashed. Joss cried out and his own hand flew up.

Metal clanged on metal.

The Kharji backed up half a step, as though the sound had knocked him away. His heel caught a clump of leaves and he staggered. Joss ran past him. Ran and swung.

"Help! Murder! Help!"

The bell echoed around him. It muffled his footsteps, his heart, his lungs, and they all become one. Candlelight poured out of the pub window, pooled in the lane.

"Help!"

Agony tore through his abdomen. His legs gave out. His knees hit the ground. Crimson glistened on the thing that stuck out of his body. It slid back inside and his innards screamed.

His hands tried to open. Joss clenched one. He slumped on his side but still grasped the bell. His face and the moonlight twitched within its depths. It was beautiful. As beautiful as the day his wife made it for him.

Boots ran past. One pair, then another, then another. Kharjis disappeared into the darkness.

4

"Allatu Akbar!"

"Allatu Akbar!"

Their war cry jumped from throat to throat. The chorus rippled throughout the village of Traverd, and Barzik Khan roared at the heavens.

"Allatu Akbar!"

His warriors dashed in all directions. Flames streamed from their torches, lit their faces, brightened their blades. Pious words flew from every lip.

"Allatu Akbar!"

A woman's boot crashed against a door. It fell inwards, hung off its hinges. She ran inside. Further along, a young fighter slammed her shoulder at another entrance, on the opposite side of the road. She rebounded and snarled. Barzik moved to aid her. But she stepped back, looked up, and threw her torch. It spun end over end, a wheel of fire, and disappeared through the window. She waited, sword in hand. Allat would receive a burnt offering, or else they'd emerge and the sacrifice would spill out in blood. Either would bring glory to the One Goddess.

"Allatu Akbar." This time he whispered, for Allat's ears alone.

A woman screamed. The Kharji hurtled backwards through the door she'd kicked down, landed in a heap.

Her torso heaved and glistened. A figure lumbered out after her. It loomed over the warrior, raised an arm. Muscle bulged and fat quivered. The cleaver caught the moon on its edge.

Barzik roared and charged. His voice stayed the butcher's hand, drew the man's gaze. The warlord wasn't far behind. He thrust his sword at the slab of flesh over his enemy's heart.

The butcher's bulk twisted away. It was a dancer's grace, as out of place on that body as a ball gown. Barzik's sword pierced the air and the cleaver hacked. Steel came down on the mass of beard upon the Khan's chest.

It clinked.

The impact sunk into the warlord's lungs. But not the blade. His beard held that back as though made of mail. The butcher froze. Incomprehension softened his features. Barzik Khan's sword sliced into the side of his neck. Allat's Earring sheared through tendon and bone. The butcher's head flew from his shoulders, crimson sprayed, and his body thumped the earth.

Barzik squatted beside his warrior. He reached to staunch the flow, but their eyes met, a coppery tang flooded his nose, and both knew it was too late.

"Allat has a banquet for you," he said. "Go. Feast. One day we'll all follow."

Her lips twitched, maybe in prayer. Her body shook and breath rasped between her teeth. Barzik Khan closed her eyes. He rose, and his mane settled against his chest and back. The Goddess' gift. Her other blessing glinted in his hand.

The warlord stormed off, to put both miracles to use in her name.

• • •

Miss Jazrah yawned. She put her quill down and massaged her eyelids. Fingertips dampened her skin. She pulled them away, grimaced, and looked around for a mirror. The candlestick was the nearest thing. She held it up, peered at the fish-like reflection, winked each eye. Blue. Miss Jazrah shrugged. It didn't look that bad, and a woman of letters had to expect the occasional war wound. She put the candle back and rubbed her eyes again.

The poem sharpened under her nose. Blots, smears, and fingerprints surrounded its stanzas. The border was quite fetching. Perhaps she'd have the children decorate their own poems that way…

She took up the quill and nibbled the end. Syllables thumped in her head. Anapaestic hexameters were harder to fashion than to read, and she already regretted this plan. But she was in too deep to retreat now. And the poem had to demonstrate every rhythm the children had learned, verse by verse.

Miss Jazrah got up and paced the schoolroom. She passed from candlelight to shadow. Her footfalls rapped.

Ti-ti-tap *Ti-ti-tap* *Ti-ti-tap*

She closed her eyes. Walked between the desks. The pattern rang through her body.

Ti-ti-tap *Ti-ti-tap* *Ti-ti-tap*

Stressed and unstressed syllables arranged themselves in her mind. A word emerged. Another came, couldn't find its place, and sank again. But there were more. Her feet tapped them into being, one by one, until the next hexameter took shape.

Noises floated through the night. They bounced off the anapaests.

Ti-ti-tap *Ti-ti-tap* *Ti-ti-tap*

What rhymed with tongue? Flung. Lung. Dung. Stung! That'd work. And she could-

The bang rocked her thoughts. Her eyes flicked open. She stumbled. The toe of her shoe caught the floor and her feet scrabbled for purchase.

Tap-tap-taptap

Her palms hit the edge of her desk. The flame flickered. Ink sloshed. Floorboards creaked in the hall outside. Miss Jazrah glared. If the butcher's girl and baker's daughter thought they could turn her schoolhouse into a scene of drunken debauchery again…

She set aside the quill and grabbed the inkwell. A bucket of cold water was more appropriate for dogs in heat, but this would have to do.

Wood groaned outside the classroom door. Miss Jazrah pulled the knob and dashed ink into the face of a man in a flowing chemise. They swore in different languages. She backed away. Something clattered on the floor and both his hands clawed at his eyes. Ink dripped between his fingers.

Miss Jazrah turned and ran for the window. The latch fumbled under her hands. It wouldn't budge! It… It flipped aside. She tore the shutters open, flung herself into the night like a woman half her age and weight. The teacher smacked the ground. Gasped.

Rolled onto her back. Stared up at three Kharjis' faces and shrieked.

Their sword points burst through her body.

• • •

Fahmaia's enemy stood in an aura of light. The mawlana glared. The statue gazed back from atop the altar. It wore a smile and nothing else. She advanced towards it, sword in hand. Shadows filled the pews on either side of her. They lounged against the walls, upon carvings of grapes, sheaves of wheat, and other things the darkness hid. The only worshippers this false goddess deserved.

The candles around the statue flickered. Light and dark shifted as though to clothe and unclothe her bosoms. Around the altar's base, an arrangement of pitchforks, hoes, and shovels creaked. Fahmaia stopped. She took up a fighting stance.

"There's nothing of value in our temple."

An apparition flitted in the gloom beyond the altar. It moved into the candlelight and became a man in a nightshirt. Sleeves and hem flapped around his body. The priest planted himself in front of the idol.

"I'm not a robber. I'm here for the good of the world, not wealth."

His cheek twitched. Fahmaia stepped into the light and their eyes met. The priest didn't cringe or gawk at her markings. That made *her* hesitate instead. A smile crossed his lips and he looked a decade younger.

"Many gods have power." He crouched and reached for the altar without turning. "They don't all require murder for their miracles."

"There are no other gods. Only the One Goddess."

He stood, and held a pitchfork across his body as though it were a halberd.

"Please, leave." The priest put one leg forward. His weight shifted onto the balls of his feet. "I don't want to defile her temple."

Fahmaia went for him. He thrust. Four prongs shot at her face. The mawlana sidestepped and cut. Her blade sliced at his forearm, struck the sleeve, and clacked against it. Fahmaia's jaws clenched. Who wore armour under a nightshirt?

The priest swung his weapon round. The side of the pitchfork's head bashed hers. Fahmaia's legs wobbled and feet danced. Lights bloomed before her. A blur flew between them. She threw herself sideways. The pew hit her hip and knocked pain through her pelvis. She hacked at him, to keep him at bay while her vision settled. Metal clinked on metal. He twisted his weapon, trapped her blade between its tines. The snap echoed through the temple. Steel clanged and clattered on the floor. Fahmaia blinked at a stub.

Four spikes lunged to skewer her.

The mawlana twisted. Cloth ripped, heat tore across her side. But the prongs went past and didn't impale her. Fahmaia's left arm whipped around the pitchfork's shaft, clutched it to her body. Her right darted. One of the priest's hands shot up, snatched at her wrist. But the broken sword bit into the side of his neck. Fahmaia twisted it, widened the wound. His fingers squeezed and scratched her skin. Crimson spurted, through the light and into the darkness.

He collapsed. The priest's eyes trembled. A pair of dice shaking in a gambler's hand. Then they were still and the rest of him stopped too.

Fahmaia squatted over him. His nightshirt was coarse between her fingertips, closer to sackcloth than silk. She pulled the sleeve back. An ornament of some kind? No… It had the texture of tree bark, but it *grew* around his forearm. As much a part of his flesh as the script which flowed upon her own.

Above her, the idol gazed into nothingness. The mawlana's eyes narrowed. Djinn and demons had power. Sorcery, to reward the fools who worshipped them.

Fahmaia stood. She placed her hands, threw her weight against the statue. Stone grated. It toppled. The false goddess shattered on the temple floor.

…

Dark figure. Wardrobe door.

Wardrobe door. Dark figure.

But she wasn't alone with it this time. Shouts and screams. Feet pounded. The whole world was in chaos. Had the monster scared them all? Did it matter? They couldn't save her, and she couldn't save them.

A bang shook her bedroom.

Clara struggled, but it had her. Pinned her down. She couldn't sit up. Couldn't… Merciless limbs melted into a clump of bedclothes. Rayya turned beside her, murmured something, yanked the blanket and tightened it across her friend's chest. Clara's eyelids quivered. Dream fragments fluttered away like moths, but the noises remained. The wardrobe swam in the shadows.

Still shut. But that bang... Boots stomped somewhere beyond her bedroom. The front door... It was the middle of the night! Who'd-

"Clara! Run!"

"Mum?" Clara wrestled with the bedding. "Mum!"

"Huh?" Rayya grappled with it too. "What's-"

Ella Mandrake's shriek tore through the house and her daughter's soul. Clara's limbs quickened. They shoved, kicked. Bone bashed bone and Rayya yelped. She had to help her mum!

The next crash was so close it was inside Clara's skull. Firelight growled and threw redness into her room. A man and woman followed. His torch painted their faces, transformed them into demons. Both held swords.

Rayya screamed and scrambled. She tumbled off the opposite side of the bed. Blankets and legs snagged Clara and she went over too. They fell in a tangle, between the bed and the window.

"Mum!"

Clara threw everything off. She stood and shouted and the Kharjis came. The woman put her boot on the mattress. Blood glistened on its toe. Ella's scream echoed in Clara's brain.

"I'm sorry, child," the woman said.

The Kharji's legs tensed to launch her. The man moved towards the foot of the bed. His torch roared and burned and their swords were made of fire.

The wardrobe door opened.

5

Rayya Shimud knew she'd gone mad. The floorboards beneath her feet, the pain where Clara kicked her, the scent of burning, were too real for nightmare. So this must all be insanity. The Kharjis with their flames and bloody swords. Ella Mandrake's scream. Clara standing there, a statue-girl. Crazy Clara who believed in the wardrobe-monster. And if Clara was crazy, so was she. Because she saw it too.

The man spun round. The woman turned, one foot on the bed, one still on the floor, like she was posing for a portrait. It squatted inside the wardrobe, stayed there for half a second. Then it sprang, all purple fur and spindly limbs. And claws. Bright pink claws.

Swords slashed. The monster howled. Fingers raked.

Blood and madness painted the room.

But Clara didn't move, didn't even blink. And Rayya couldn't either. Mad statue-girls, watching murderers and monster fight. Rayya screamed. Clara Mandrake came to life and grabbed at the shutters.

Claws tore the woman's face. The Kharji shrieked.

"Rayya, go!"

Rayya couldn't turn round. Couldn't even scream again. The Kharjis and the monster whirled in a tempest of salwars and steel, fire and fur.

"Rayya!"

Clara yanked her. Heaved her. Rayya was half out the window before she knew what had happened. She pulled herself the rest of the way, dropped down. Leaves crunched and squished. Chilled her soles.

Her parents! She had to tell her parents!

Rayya ran. Down the path. Into the lane, where a stone bit her foot and she stumbled.

"Rayya, wait!"

But she couldn't. She needed to get home. Her mum and dad would protect them. They'd know what to do. More stones dug and gouged. She didn't slow down. She ran towards the brightness and the crackle-growl noise. Towards the bonfire that didn't make sense, because it wasn't the festival…

She stopped. Her insides sank. They fell through her body and the earth below.

Her house burned. Fire blazed across the roof, hurled smoke into the sky, and cast its devil light over everything. The garden. The gateposts. The two heaps that lay beside them, at the Kharji's feet. Her sword was almost black.

Clara screamed in her ear, but the words bubbled. Underwater sounds that made no sense and never would. Fingers crushed Rayya's hand. They pulled and her arm shot after them. The rest of her followed. Her legs worked on their own, and she ran with Clara. They hurtled off the lane, over the leaves and grass, towards the trees.

Towards the shadow that became a Kharji.

Rayya's arm jerked and she staggered. The Kharji charged. Clara turned and spun Rayya right round. They ran back towards the lane. Where the woman waited with her sword.

The girls stood there, between the woman and the footfalls that pounded behind them. Rayya's fingers hurt. She didn't know if she squeezed Clara's hand or Clara squeezed hers, but she couldn't let go.

That black sword floated towards them. The footsteps slowed, but they didn't matter anymore. There was only the sword.

It wavered. The edge tilted. The woman screamed. The monster roared, and slashed her again. She fell onto her knees, cut at it to fend it off. But the monster mauled her and half her face flapped.

Clara whirled Rayya around again. The other Kharji was in front of them, but he stared over their shoulders. They ran and he did too. He stormed past, towards the monster and the shrieks and the butcher shop sounds. The girls sprinted for the woods.

Rayya's foot landed on a root and it should've hobbled her. But the pain was dull and faraway. So was the cold that lashed her through the nightshirt. Her legs too. They pumped and so did her lungs, but she felt neither till her chest crunched inside and she stumbled instead of running.

Their hands parted. Rayya heaved air into her body and Clara gasped too. They both shook. Somewhere, a dozen yards or miles away, things shouted and crashed and blazed.

"Need… Need to hide," Clara said.

She dashed off and Rayya groped after her. But Clara didn't disappear. Her nightshirt flitted through the shadows, this way and that, until she cried out. She took hold of Rayya again. Her hand burned. Cold throbbed through the rest of Rayya's flesh.

"In there. Go on!"

She drove Rayya to the ground and scrabbled beside her like a dog burying bones. Then Rayya saw it, in the mound at the foot of the tree. Among its roots. A gap. Clara pushed her and Rayya scrambled. Wood scraped her skull. The bottom half of her face gouged the earth. Dirt and grit smeared her lips, invaded her mouth, her nose. The taste of soil smothered her. She tumbled into a space, bigger than she'd expected. Things caught in her hair, tore at her nightdress.

Clara slithered in and swept her arms outside the hole. Leaves rustled. She drew a heap of them towards her, then another. The moonlight faded. Darkness enveloped them.

They huddled and Rayya clung to Clara's heat. Her jaw shook. A million things burst in her brain and her eyes burst too. She bawled, but strength flooded out with the tears, drained her in seconds. Sobs racked her body. Water stung her cheeks.

Clara held her.

• • •

The moan carried far. It reached Fahmaia even amid the exaltations to Allat, the fire's roar, and the last of the screams. A human throat cried animal pain. It twanged inside her heart, drew her footsteps. The mawlana grimaced and vowed she'd find whichever warrior had done this. These villagers must die. But that didn't mean the One Goddess' followers should leave them to suffer. Fahmaia took out her knife.

She rounded the burning building and the moan came again. This time it mangled the first words of a prayer. Fahmaia's knife slid back into its sheath.

The air reeked of blood and waste. Two lumps lay on the grass, and for a second she couldn't tell which still lived. Wounds lacerated their flesh. Gore littered the ground around them. No blade did this. Fahmaia crouched and her gaze swept the trees, but there wasn't any sign of a bear or other beast.

"…lana…"

Red fingers groped at her face. She took them. He tried to grip her but his digits trembled. She squeezed so they wouldn't slip away.

"Girl…" The warrior's other hand quivered, pointed, then slapped back down. Something squelched beneath it. "Gir…"

His lips widened, closed, twisted. He tried to talk again but breath, blood, and soul came out together. Fahmaia set his hand down.

"Allat welcome them both," she whispered.

The mawlana looked around. One warrior's sword had fared no better than her own, and half a blade glinted in the grass. The other weapon lay intact. But the woman's bowels had spilled across its handle, and she couldn't bring herself to touch it. No matter. Fahmaia doubted the blade could overcome a bear's savagery. She'd have to trust in the One Goddess.

The mawlana entered the forest. She imagined the young woman blundering among the trees while fear drove her on, scrambled her thoughts, hammered her heart.

Fahmaia Hashad's knife would grant the girl a swift end.

...

The girl was close. Her scent hung amid the aroma of dead and dying leaves. His claws tingled. Fur bristled along his forearms. His wounds widened. A dozen slits vomited blood onto his purple hide.

Xerachus loped through the forest, but his left leg buckled and autumn crunched under his knee.

The monster forced his senses beyond the pain, shut out the smell of girls and guts. He found it in a tree. An opening two feet higher than his head. Darkness beckoned, where the moon couldn't trespass.

He climbed. His injuries howled, but he scrambled up the trunk and didn't gouge its bark. No sign, if anyone came. Xerachus poured himself into the hollow, among odours of bird and squirrel. The dark embraced him. It enveloped his essence and soothed his mind. He sloughed into slumber.

Xerachus dreamt of meat that quivered beneath his claws. Of gasps and screams and slaughter. He dreamt of Clara Mandrake.

...

Rayya's body was cold against hers. Clara clung to her. Their faces brushed and her friend's tears wet Clara's cheek. Rayya Shimud was a snow-girl, melting in her arms.

Another girl wept too. Grief broke her bones, ground her organs to mush. But she was buried somewhere. No water fell from Clara Mandrake's eyes.

The monster lunged through her brain, the only vibrant thing amid the numbness. Its claws sliced. Blood and bits rained on her bedroom floor. Her bedroom. Her bedroom in her home, where her mother…

That faraway girl bawled.

Clara tensed. Her muscles clenched, arms tightened. Rayya cried out but the yelp broke into sobs.

"Shhh!" Clara said.

Rayya groaned and wept and wouldn't stop. Clara put her hand over her friend's mouth. Rayya twisted, pulled away. Then she froze. Sobs still shook her, but the hand silenced them. And the other noises grew louder.

Thuds. Rustles and crunches.

Their hearts beat together.

The boots stopped. Leaves choked the hole and blinded her, but Clara knew the Kharji was there, right outside. They were going to die. The Kharji would drag them out of their den, pin them to the ground, hack them to-

More thuds. Rustles. Crunches. They faded into the forest.

• • •

"Allatu Akbar!"

The soldier saluted Barzik Khan, thrust her fist to the heavens, and belched. She blushed. Her face softened into one ten years younger. The warlord laughed.

"The One Goddess provided for us." He accepted the wine bottle, glugged its sweetness, and passed it back. "Your stomach praises her generosity."

He wandered through the square, where his warriors gathered. A few called to him and he returned their greetings.

"Khan! Khan!" A youth held out a bloody blade. The boy looked barely old enough to shave. "See?"

"Your first?"

"Yes, Khan."

Barzik ruffled the youngster's hair.

"Remember them in your prayers tonight. The One Goddess judges them now."

Some offered beer, wine, or chunks of roasted meat. He declined each with a smile and a shake of his head. Plunder was Allat's gift. Fighting earned refreshment. But a leader couldn't fill his belly or cloud his head just yet, and he'd already slaked his thirst.

Barzik squatted in front of two girls. One had her salwar pulled up to her knee, while the other wrapped a length of cloth around the calf below.

"Is it bad?" he said.

"No," the wounded woman said.

"Yes," the other said. "But she'll be fine if she doesn't put it through another door."

"It was locked."

"Next time, use this." The Khan clapped her on the shoulder. "But Allat bless your ferocity."

At the edge of the square, a Kharji lay beside a villager. Four eyes stared at the stars. Barzik sighed. The man's family would have to mourn without a corpse. But the Goddess' edict was clear. Martyrs must lie where they fell, so she might gaze upon them in that state of perfect grace.

"Barzik."

"Mawlana?"

He turned, and her breathlessness made him reach for his blade. But no enemies appeared behind her.

"One escaped. Into the forest. A girl."

She wiped her brow and swept stray hair behind her ear. The script quickened on Fahmaia's skin, rushed around her face.

"The sentries?"

"An animal attacked them. She must've got past while they fought it."

Barzik spat. Saliva splatted on the toe of his boot.

"Then the sacrifice…"

"It isn't complete. The whole village must die."

"I'll gather the warriors. We'll sweep the countryside and finish it."

Fahmaia shook her head and pointed to the horizon. Reds and pinks bled into the blackness.

"You should return to our brothers and sisters. Break camp, as we planned. If the infidels retaliate… Our leader and best fighters can't be spread across the fields and forests. I'll gather some warriors and find her myself."

She moved, but he caught her arm.

"Mawlana…"

Barzik Khan gestured at her waist. Her gaze followed his to the empty sheath.

"It broke. I'll borrow a weapon."

"Wait." He unbuckled his sword belt, brought the scabbard to his lips. "Take Allat's Earring."

Her eyes widened. Her hand hovered above it.

"This belongs to the One Goddess," he said, "not to me. And your deeds are her will."

"Thank you." She fastened it at her side. "I'll pick my warriors and find her."

"Allatu Akbar."

"Allatu Akbar."

They clasped hands, then she jogged away.

Barzik prayed the Goddess would forgive them their failure. And he prayed for the girl, whom the mawlana would soon cut down.

Part 2

Orphans' Road

6

Silas straightened his shoulders, sucked in his gut, and clasped his hands behind his back. Minutes passed. Morning light drifted across the floor and wall. His posture threatened to give way, but Silas held it in check. When Katrina opened her chamber door, she wouldn't find him slacking and slouching like a wastrel.

Another minute crept by. Silas' muscles ached. He gave in, and paced the corridor. But his footsteps echoed. Each one announced him to the world — Silas the trespasser, slinking through the girls' dormitory. He stood to attention again.

Should he just knock? What if that enraged her? A trainee demanding a mistress' presence, as though her time belonged to him instead of the other way around. What if she told him to raise his hands, and punched him up and down the corridor for his impudence?

Silas waited. The door waited too.

What if he was *supposed* to knock? This could be a test. Katrina von Talhoffer wouldn't want a coward for an apprentice. A weak, snivelling wretch too timid to even announce himself.

He cleared his throat. He cleared it again, just to be sure. An attack of morning mouth wasn't going to garble his words. Not today, of all days. He raised his hand. Paused. Maybe the door was about to open anyway…

Silas Renshaw knocked.

"Mistress von Talhoffer? I…"

The door creaked. It gave way a few inches.

"You… You said we'd train today?"

No eye glared in the gap. Silas pushed the door. He regretted it in the same instant, tensed for a barrage of words or fists. But the door swung inward and the room lay empty. There wasn't even any baggage. No clothes or weapons littered the floor or table. A few creases in the sheets gave the only sign anyone had slept in the chamber.

Silas frowned. Was he late? Had he spent too long in his dormitory, waiting for her to send for him? Was Katrina fuming somewhere, wondering where that flabby fool of a trainee had got to?

He went outside. Deserted, just like the dorms. The others were off on their run. But hooves clopped through the stillness, and Silas headed towards the noise. He found a stablehand walking one of the stallions. The girl glanced at him.

"Er…" Silas groped around for her name. "Morning… love."

She stared. So did the horse. Silas resisted the urge to kick himself, and ploughed on before she decided to do it instead.

"Do you know where Mistress von Talhoffer is?"

"Her with the…?" She put a hand over one eye.

"Yeah."

"Went off with Master Gunnar and the rest of them. All the masters and mistresses."

"Huh? Why?"

"If it's not about the horses, they don't tell *us*, do they?"

"Oh. Right. Thanks."

The horse neighed. Silas stayed away from the animal's hindquarters as they trotted off, since he was still due a kick.

He walked the academy's grounds, unsure whether he should find Katrina or do some arms drills until she summoned him. Voices and the clang of iron drew him to the forge. A few of the servants gathered there, amid the heat and sparks. Their conversation died out when he approached. A couple of them nodded, and he nodded back. The blacksmith tapped a horseshoe into existence.

"Um…"

Silas looked around, but knew none of them by name. Some of the trainees referred to the smith as Double Black, on account of his profession and complexion. But if he didn't relish that nickname… The blacksmith's muscles rippled. Metal glowed and gave way beneath his blows.

"Mates…" Silas said. He mentally added a few more kicks to the tally, but they didn't lynch him. "Any of you know what the masters and mistresses are doing?"

"Meeting," a woman said.

She chewed on a bit of salted beef, and Silas waited for some seconds before he realised she was done talking.

"You not heard about Traverd?" the smith said.

Silas shook his head.

"Kharjis attacked. Last night." His hammer thudded. "Killed everyone. The whole village."

The smith held his gaze and didn't blink. Silas couldn't think of what to say. An entire village... gone. Slaughtered!

"Silas?" a girl's voice said.

"Yeah?" He turned around, glad for the excuse.

A young woman stood a few yards away from the forge.

"Helen!"

Silas swelled. Finally! Someone whose name he knew! Now these people would see he wasn't some stuck up twerp who thought servants were nameless, interchangeable, and... And everyone was staring at him, because he'd yelled her name like a battle cry.

"That's me." The maid curtseyed. She lowered her head, but it didn't quite conceal her smirk. The others sniggered. "You're to go to the quartermaster for weapons, before-"

"Oh. Sure." Silas hurried past her.

"...you leave."

"Yeah. I'll..." He stopped, turned. "Leave?"

"I've packed your clothes and supplies on the horse, but the quartermaster-"

"I'm leaving? Where am I going? I don't..."

She shrugged.

"Ask Morris. He might know."

"Morris..."

"The quartermaster."

"Right..."

His head spun. Leaving! Were they kicking him out? Had Gunnar and Katrina talked about what he did in the dorm, and decided…? But that didn't make sense. Not if they wanted him to collect weapons. The quartermaster wouldn't give sharp objects to rejects, so they could carve people up on their way out the door.

Morris loomed above his counter in the armoury building. Racks of swords, axes, and spears gleamed behind him.

"Morning, Silas."

"Uh… Morning." The greeting was so mundane, incredulity echoed around his skull. "I'm… Helen said I'm leaving."

"That's right. Here you go." He placed a bundle on the counter. "Something sharp, something blunt, and a sturdy belt."

Morris gestured, so Silas strapped the belt around his waist. The sword and iron bludgeon settled into place. Their weight dragged at him, but he was used to this. Weapons always felt heavy when you first put them on. It made sense, and right now it was the only thing that did.

"Where am I going?"

"Heard what happened? In Traverd?"

Silas nodded.

"The militia sent a bird. Message said they want one of our lot there. Katrina's going."

"And me?"

"You're her apprentice, aren't you?"

Apprentice. The word was heavier than the weapons.

"But… We haven't even trained together. We were going to…"

"You'll learn on the road. That's the whole point of apprenticing."

"But…"

"Don't keep her waiting. Usual place. Good luck, mate."

He held out his hand. Silas shook it, then made his way back towards the dormitories. By the time he got to where the horses waited, he barely noticed the sword or bludgeon at his sides.

Katrina von Talhoffer sat atop her steed. She looked down at him.

"Do you know where we're going?"

"Traverd."

"Good. Mount up."

Silas climbed into his saddle. A breeze swept through the space between the dorms. The other trainees were still off on their run. No… Not *other* trainees. He was an apprentice now, like Cryze. His innards scrunched up. No one was going to see him off. This was it. He'd be gone by the time they returned. No goodbyes, no hugs or kisses or exhortations. He wouldn't have to face Jonas and Lucy…

He looked at Katrina, tried to find something to say. But she just rode off. So Silas followed, and the clatter of hooves drowned out his thoughts.

• • •

When the darkness softened, Clara thought her eyes tricked her. But the roots, the barrier of leaves, the ice-girl who shivered in her arms, all took shape amid the shadows. Night should've lasted forever. How could there be anything after that? Yet day had dawned, and the universe swept her along.

"Sa…" Rayya's voice rasped and died. She shuddered, fought for breath, and tried again. "Sachin… Need to tell Sachin…"

A splutter stole the rest. It rattled in her throat, and the vibrations passed from her body to Clara's as though they could carry her meaning. Rayya coughed, wheezed.

"Water," Clara said. Then, after a few moments, "We're near the river…"

Rayya went still. Silence hardened around them. If they left their hiding place, if they went out there…

"It's okay," Clara said. Stupid words. Things would never be okay again. But she forced them out, and kept going. "They're gone."

She reached for the leaves. Rayya snatched at her arm.

"We have to." Clara clasped Rayya's hand, held it for a second, then moved it off her forearm. "You need water."

Rayya groaned but didn't stop her. Clara brushed aside the heap and marvelled that something so flimsy had shielded them. She peered out at the new universe that'd come into being, then crawled through the gap. Things poked her skin, dug at her bones. But they didn't matter. She turned around on her hands and knees, and helped her friend scramble out into the daylight.

Rayya toppled. Clara clutched her fingers and steadied her.

"Can you walk?"

She nodded. Clara kept hold of her, but she didn't crumple. They padded through the forest, moved from trunk to trunk, bush to bush. Their necks jerked at every sound. But no footsteps pounded. No voices cried out. They'd left those things in the night. The burning, bloody night…

Water burbled. It grew into a rush that swallowed their footsteps by the time they glimpsed it through the trees. The river smothered Rayya's groan. Clara caught her when she fell, took her weight. Rayya clung to her and trembled. But even that was weaker than before, as though her body was too exhausted to even shake or sob.

Clara half-carried her into the nearest bushes and sat her down.

"It's okay. I'll bring you the water. It'll help."

Rayya's head moved, and it may've been a nod. Clara squatted beside her. It was like looking into a magic mirror, one that reflected the girl inside Clara Mandrake. The tired, shattered child. But somehow the skin and muscles wrapped around her could still go on. So Clara stood. Shoots stroked her cheeks, caught at her nightgown. She rustled through them and made her way down the slope to the bank.

Cool air enveloped her. Mud squelched underfoot, colder still. But her flesh burned. Maybe she had a fever? Didn't matter. Rayya. Water.

She scoured the bank for a minute or so before she found the right plant. The one the children all called cup-blooms. What was their proper, grown-up name again? She'd have to ask her mother. Oh…

The inner Clara wailed. The outer Clara took hold of its flesh and pulled. It tore. She grunted and seized its neighbour. This time she grasped it lower, a few inches down the stalk. She yanked. The stalk gave way, and the cup-shaped end stayed whole.

Clara padded and squelched her way to the water's edge. White flecks sprayed her shins, then splattered her face when she crouched. The river rushed by but left its blood on her cheek.

Blood…

She dipped the cup into the flow, turned it when the current tried to snatch it away. Clara drank. It tasted of nothing, though cup-blooms usually made everything sweet. But it spread through her body and quenched the distant thirst. She filled it again for Rayya.

Then Clara looked up and saw her, across the silver-blue expanse. A black woman knelt on the opposite bank and drank from cupped hands. She glanced up too. Breath hissed through Clara's lips. She wasn't black. Snakes writhed around the woman's arms and face.

Clara stood. So did she, and a sword swayed at her side.

A Kharji.

They stared at one another. Clara inhaled. The snake-woman couldn't get her, not with the river between them. She'd have to work her way around…

Clara Mandrake turned and ran. Water sloshed over the cup-bloom's lip and splashed her wrist. Mud caught at her toes. She grabbed a tuft of grass with her free hand, scrambled up the slope, sprinted.

"Rayya!"

Rayya Shimud's head snapped up and she yelped. "Whuh?"

"Drink. Fast." Clara thrust the cup-bloom at her friend. "We need to go."

• • •

Katrina von Talhoffer signalled. Silas shifted his weight back in the saddle and coaxed the reins. His horse slowed to match the steed in front, and the drumming of hooves broke into a clip-clop. Silas held his breath. Maybe he could stay behind her, see out this walk-rest in silence, then-

She waved him forward. He sighed and nudged the animal's flank with his thigh. It turned, sped up.

"Other side."

"Oh. Yeah…" Blood rushed into Silas' face. "Sorry."

He aimed the horse in the other direction, and came alongside her on the left instead.

"In combat, you can fight on my blind side if you want. But talking in the saddle's easier this way."

"Sorry, Mistress von Talhoffer. I… I didn't think…"

"Katrina. You're an apprentice now, not a trainee."

"Right. Sorry."

Katrina. It clopped around his brain in time with the hoof beats. First-name terms with Katrina von Talhoffer! Cardew, Jocasta, and the rest would gawp when he addressed her in front of them! But Lucy and Jonas headbutted their way into his thoughts. Their glares melted his pride to sludge.

"Gunnar said you come from noble stock."

"Uh… Yeah…" He met her gaze, then looked away.

"Raised on fine dinners."

His cheeks pulsed, and all of a sudden he was that fat trainee again — the one the others mocked, till he threw a couple of them around.

"We had good cooks."

"The academy must've been a shock."

"I wasn't expecting banquets."

"You impressed him."

"Mas… Gunnar?"

"He didn't think you'd last a day."

"My family's rich, not weak."

Silas winced, and wished he could cram the words back into his mouth. But Katrina gave the slightest of nods.

"You're a third child?"

He managed a smile.

"My brother gets the title and the estate. Most of the rest goes to my sister."

"So you chose the academy."

"Yeah."

"If you're looking to bring a bit of glory to the family name, you won't find it in our work. Most days, we ride down dusty roads and talk to superstitious fools after something's scared them in the night. It's almost always a cat."

She turned and spat.

"When there *is* a real encounter, there's a good chance we'll die in pools of blood and shit."

Katrina fell silent, but her words echoed in Silas' head all the way to Traverd.

• • •

Their eyes met across the water. The girl stood there, barefoot. Only a nightshirt shielded her from the cold that rose off the river. Fahmaia thought of the laughing, boisterous children in the Kharji camp, and cursed herself. The poor thing must've shivered for hours.

The girl scurried up the slope. Hand and feet scrabbled in the mud like a mouse's paws. Fahmaia longed to go to her. One stroke of the blade, Allat's will and the mawlana's pity. But water rushed between them and the girl disappeared into the wood.

Fahmaia mirrored the child and made for the trees. Her muscles ached. Wounds throbbed. But her legs pumped, and she flew over the red-gold forest floor. If she cut across to-

"Help!"

The cry stole her speed.

"Goddess! Help!"

Momentum carried her forward a few paces, then died. Sayeeda's voice. One of her handpicked warriors. It came from deeper in the forest, the opposite direction. Fahmaia glanced towards the river. Her quarry was so close…

"Help!"

The mawlana swore. She couldn't abandon a fellow Kharji. And the girl wouldn't get far unshod. Her legs protested, tried to cling to their repose. But Fahmaia ran and they found the strength to propel her.

Sayeeda yelled again. This time a roar drowned out the woman's words.

Fahmaia froze at the edge of the tableau. Sayeeda clung to a branch high above. Crimson slathered her thigh, smeared the wood beneath her. And enraged the beast below.

The bear looked up at its prey. It bellowed again. The sound reverberated from tree to tree and through Fahmaia's bones. Those bodies at the edge of Traverd…

"Help!"

Sayeeda's eyes fastened on the bear. If she saw the mawlana, if she shouted to her instead of the forest and Allat, she gave no sign. Fahmaia's hand went to her belt. She'd seen a bear fight a lion. Even that fierce feline hadn't stood a chance. If the creature struck her, it'd shred her innards, tear her limbs off, crush her skull.

She drew her sword. Another blade might only nick its hide, scratch a slab of muscle, and doom her. But she wielded Allat's Earring now. Maybe, just maybe…

The bear rose onto its hind legs. Its fur rippled, frame stretched. It planted its front paws on the trunk, as though it would climb or else shove the tree and send it crashing to the ground.

Sayeeda was silent now. Fahmaia didn't look up, but imagined the woman's eyes on her. She crept forward. If she struck fast, before it knew she was there, and thrust deep into its vitals…

The bear's nose twitched. Its bulk twisted round and thudded back onto all fours faster that she'd have dreamt possible. Their eyes met. Fahmaia clutched the sword, braced for slaughter, and wondered which of them would die.

But the bear just stared, and she realised it was looking at her markings. The animal sniffed again. Its muzzle shifted from left to right, then scrunched up. The expression was so similar to a quizzical child's that she almost laughed. It took several steps backwards. Its eyes and nose pointed at her face for some seconds, even as its hindquarters turned, and only spun away at the last moment. The bear ran off.

Fahmaia exhaled and thanked Allat.

Sayeeda clambered down from the tree. She tried to put weight on the injured leg, and it buckled. Fahmaia took hold of her and examined the wound. Blood seeped along the woman's leg, soaked into the shreds of cloth at her knee.

"Thank you, mawlana. I…"

"Give me your shawl."

Fahmaia took the garment and bandaged her.

"We'll find one of the others," the mawlana said. "They'll take you to safety."

"But…"

"You're no good to the Goddess if you bleed to death."

"Forgive me, mawlana. I should've heard it coming. I should've…"

"Allat filled this world with creatures stronger and deadlier than us, to teach us humility. It's not your fault."

Fahmaia took Sayeeda's weight and they plodded away on three legs. She glanced in the direction of the river.

No, the girl wouldn't get far…

• • •

"The village is still burning." Silas pointed.

Tendrils of smoke rose over the treeline and seeded the sky with a second layer of cloud. He tightened his grip on the reins, prepared to send his steed into a gallop. But Katrina forestalled him with a gesture.

"No. Even the worst militia would've put a bucket brigade together by now. Those'll be pyres."

"Oh."

The road turned, took them into the outskirts of Traverd, and the world changed. Houses lay in ruin, like the stones of an ancient graveyard. Bits of door and shutter littered the ground or dangled from hinges. Some buildings were roofless, save for crowns of blackened thatch. A couple had collapsed into heaps. They might have been the dwellings of a long-forgotten people. But crimson painted wood and stone.

Silas swore under his breath.

"Kharji raiders usually take what they want," Katrina said, "kill whoever gets in their way, and go. Same as any other bandits. But this…"

He nodded without looking at her. A small red handprint marked a door frame, low down. He tried not to imagine, but couldn't help it.

A man in a yellow-brown tabard sat on a garden wall. He stared into space, scratched the stubble on his chin. Katrina stopped her horse and called to him.

"Where's your commander?"

"Huh?" The militiaman didn't look at them.

"Your *commander*."

His gaze crept upwards, but only as far as her horse's face.

"The square. She's in the square."

Katrina rode on. Silas gave him one last look, then followed.

The breeze shifted. It brought the smoky-sweetness of summer roasts, of pigs that'd glistened on spits and made Silas' mouth water. But another smell followed. His brain recoiled and stomach churned. Memories of feasts dissolved.

People moved around the square. Streaks of dirt and ash smeared their militia tabards. Voices blended with the buzzing of flies. Silas slapped one insect away from his face. But they weren't interested in him. Most swarmed around the piles of dead, revelled above them in mad spirals. A couple of militiamen drove them off with flaming torches. They rallied and made a battle of it.

"Urgh!" A young woman stumbled from an unfinished pyre, squatted down, and vomited. She groaned, then threw up again.

"Oi!" An older woman laid more kindling atop the heap. A foot poked out from the pyre's layers, and she pushed it back under a drape. "If you want to chuck up, go some'ere else. Respect for the bloody dead!"

Her tabard had a crest stitched onto the back. The world's worst griffin, if Silas had to guess.

Katrina dismounted. Silas did the same, and grabbed both sets of reins while Katrina approached her.

"Captain?"

"What?" The woman wiped her brow with her sleeve, brushed back a tangle of brown and grey hair. She looked round. "We're…"

She stared. Silas couldn't blame her. Katrina's scars might've intimidated a hardened general. After a moment, she barked a couple of orders, then came over.

"I'm Katrina von Talhoffer. This is Silas Renshaw."

"From Tensia?"

"Yes, we came from the academy. You're the one who sent the bird?"

The woman nodded and wrestled a glove off her hand.

"Cap'n Gertrude Sarminder."

They shook.

"Come wi' me. I'll show you what we found."

She walked away, shouting instructions as she went. Katrina followed and beckoned for Silas to do the same. He glanced around.

"Here." The young woman was back on her feet. She followed his gaze, winced, and wiped vomit off her chin. "I'll take 'em."

"Thanks." Silas handed over the reins and jogged after them.

Leaves blanketed the lane, and even they were tainted. Blood and gore smeared autumn hues. Silas stepped between the clumps. Captain Sarminder led them to a wreck of a house, little different from the others they passed. The women went into the garden. Silas paused, and examined the carvings on the gatepost. Two symbols marred the stone. One was a… tree? Maybe a human figure. The other was a collection of blobs and lines. Perhaps an animal of some kind. What had these meant to the folk who'd lived here? He'd never know, because Kharji blades had cut them down. Now their secrets, their family lore, burned atop pyres. He touched the images and sighed.

"Silas."

"Oh. Sorry."

He joined Katrina and the three of them went inside, through a kitchen, into the hallway. A red stain covered a section of floor, almost from wall to wall. Silas grimaced when the captain trod on it. He almost expected a phantom to shriek and curse.

"Body here," Sarminder said. "Nowt special about it. Run through wi' a sword, poor thing. Lasses took it 'fore they found the others. Told them to leave those ones be."

She moved aside and gestured at the doorway at the end of the corridor. Katrina went through. Silas and Sarminder followed, into the stink of immolation.

"Knew at once these weren't killed wi' no blade."

"No," Katrina said.

She crouched beside a wreck that'd once been a bed. There wasn't room to pass her, and Silas didn't want to. He swallowed the moisture in his throat. Fire had charred the two corpses on the floor, but couldn't disguise what claws and teeth did to them.

Katrina brought her hand to her face, as if she wanted to cover her eye and blind herself to this butchery. Instead, she lifted her eyepatch. Silas and Sarminder gawped. The captain turned to him. He fought the urge to shrug or gesture, tried to keep his face neutral. What the hell was his mistress doing?

"Yes." She put the patch back down. "There was an encounter here. Are these the only ones?"

"No. Two more, ou'side."

Silas met Katrina's gaze but she went past without a word. He traipsed after them once more, and wondered if he'd imagined it. But the militia captain's reaction belied that. If anyone here was mad, it wasn't him…

The stench was worse near the edge of the forest. Guts befouled the air. Black shapes undulated around them, as insects crawled over one another and vied for their share of the feast.

Katrina squatted and lifted her eyepatch. This time there was no bed or wall to keep him back. Silas moved around the corpses, avoided the filth, and faced her. He gasped, fell backwards. His rear end hit the ground but he didn't feel it. He couldn't look away. Couldn't close his eyes. The scarlet iris and crimson sclera glared at him, held him — a bloody island in an ocean of gore.

She stood. Silas flinched. But she didn't speak or glance at him. Katrina strode into the wood. Silas scrambled to his feet. He ignored Sarminder's look. His mentor's eye glowered in his brain, but he was an apprentice and he had a job to do. She drew her sword. He did the same and his heartbeat quickened. The captain's sword hissed out of its sheath beside him.

Something rustled. He spun round, levelled his blade. A bird sprang off a twig and flapped away. Silas chided himself under his breath. But Katrina hadn't noticed. She paced ahead of them, first in one direction, then another. Her eye… eyes… scanned the ground. She stopped, lowered her patch, and grunted.

"The trail disperses. It's too faint to follow."

A dozen questions battered Silas' brain, but none found his tongue. Katrina turned to Captain Sarminder.

"We'll have to get our horses and search the countryside for any sign of it."

The captain snorted.

"Like tryin' to find a needle in a bloody hayloft."

"Maybe. But needles don't leave tales of missing farmhands and mangled corpses in their wake."

• • •

The forest thinned. Clara strained her senses, groped for signs of pursuit. An animal chittered — impossibly close. But it was just the sound of Rayya's teeth, chattering as she shivered. Clara threw her arms around the ice-girl.

"H… How're you so hot? Are you sick?"

"Don't know."

She rubbed Rayya's limbs, her cheeks, her hands. The girl's body creaked as though her legs would snap beneath her. Clara wished they could stop, huddle. That she could keep her friend warm and safe. But the Kharjis… That snake-woman… She nudged Rayya onward, guided and supported her.

Clara's stomach bubbled. When had they last eaten? A lifetime ago. Hunger seemed an alien thing. But when she spotted the bush, she broke off two sprigs of purple berries and passed one to Rayya.

"Eat."

Rayya just held it. Blinked at it. But Clara plucked a couple, put them in her own mouth, and she did the same. Their bodies burst between Clara's jaws. Blood prickled her tongue. Gore stuck to her teeth. She didn't want the rest, but forced herself to eat until Rayya was done.

"More?"

Rayya shook her head. A purple-black droplet trickled down the side of her chin. Clara wiped it away.

They stopped at the edge of the wood, as though they'd reached the end of the world and found an abyss instead of a field, a road, and a cottage. The house's shutters were closed against the daylight. Clara chewed her lip. At this hour, that probably meant…

"There'll be clothes inside," she said. "Maybe food."

"Doesn't look like anyone's home. And even if they were, we don't have any money."

"We'll take what we need."

"Clara! We… We can't…"

But even as she spoke, Rayya shivered. She shifted from foot to foot and her whole face twitched. Clara's own soles ached, but she didn't know if it was sympathy or true pain. Perhaps they were the same thing now. She moved towards the cottage. Rayya didn't argue.

A garden gave onto the back of the house. Weeds sprawled in its flowerbeds, entangled the stalks. The girls crept between them and Clara stood on tiptoe at a window. She put her eye to a gap in the shutters. A bedroom. A wardrobe…

Purple fur. Pink claws.

…with four boots lined up in front of it. Small ones.

"Wait here," she whispered.

"Why? Where…"

Clara jogged to the nearest tree and returned with a stick in her hand. She fumbled at the window for a few minutes, but it wasn't hard. The latch flipped open. Doors and shutters… She'd once believed people were safe behind them. Now she knew better.

She pulled herself up and dropped into the gloom.

"Stay-"

"No." Rayya came up behind her, and Clara had to hold her arm to stop her tumbling back into the garden. "If you're going in there, I'm going with you."

Clara helped her inside and had never loved her more.

Dust coated the sill. It bore the shapes of their hands and knees. A grey layer smothered the table too, and the mirror frame that poked out behind a drape. In the corner, no creases marred the blankets on the bed. Clara's forearms tingled.

Both girls moved to the wardrobe. Clara hesitated, but an inner voice chided her. Did she think every wardrobe in the world had its own monster? She opened it. Just clothes. Kid clothes.

Rayya reached for a jerkin.

Wood creaked.

The bedroom door flew open. Clara hissed. Rayya yelped. The woman roared and swung her weapon at Clara Mandrake's skull.

7

Ghadi's hand froze. The poker hovered overhead. The olive-skinned girl moved in front of the other child. Her eyes glistened at the corners but gleamed and didn't blink. Behind her, the other girl trembled. Ghadi lowered her arm and the poker dangled from her fingers. She'd been ready for robbers, not a pair of frightened kids in nightshirts.

"Where'd you come from? What're you doing in my house?"

The one with the plait burst into tears. She held herself, bawled, and shook. The girl in front didn't quiver, but tears crept down her cheeks. Questions could wait…

"Here."

Ghadi backed away into the main room and beckoned. The girls didn't move. She followed their gazes. Embers glowed in the hearth and lent the room a little warmth, but didn't part the shadows. What child would follow a stranger into her lair?

In the corner, Yallis coughed. Ghadi went to the crib and stroked the baby's cheek. Floorboards creaked as the girls inched towards the room. A smile creased Ghadi's lips. Dangerous lairs didn't have babies in them. She moved to the hearth.

"I'm Ghadi," she said, as she built the fire.

After some moments, the olive-skinned girl said, "Clara. This is Rayya."

Light and heat reclaimed part of the room. Ghadi surrendered the space in front of the fire and sat by the crib. She rocked it with one hand, gestured with the other.

"Go on. Before you catch your deaths."

Clara went to fireplace. She waved Rayya over, but didn't take her eyes off Ghadi. A rat, ready to flee or bite. Rayya crumpled onto the rug. She sat there, hugged her knees, and shuddered. Clara squatted beside her.

"Are you hungry?"

"Yeah," Clara said.

Ghadi got up. She paused, then lifted Yallis and held the baby against her shoulder. Yallis coughed. Ghadi rocked her on the way to the kitchen. She worked one-handed, put bread and a lump of cheese on a plate. After a moment, she added a chunk of sausage.

Rayya didn't look up when she went back through. But Clara accepted the plate and murmured.

"Thanks."

Ghadi put Yallis in her crib and sat. Clara picked at the food first, passed morsels to Rayya. Soon both girls were eating. Ghadi didn't have the heart to interrupt them. They sat in silence until the plate was empty.

"What were you doing, going around like that? Where are your parents?"

Rayya's eyes met hers, then dissolved in a flood of tears. Clara clasped her friend's shoulder.

"Kharjis attacked our village." She rubbed Rayya's cheek. "We ran."

Ghadi didn't want to say the words, but she did.

"Your families?"

"They... They killed my mum. And Rayya's mum and dad."

Rayya's sobs hung in the air between them. Clara caressed her hair, hugged her.

"Do you have anyone else? Anyone who can take you in?"

"Dad died when I was small. Mum was my only family."

Rayya wiped her face, swallowed one last sob, and blew her nose. Life and light gathered in her eyes.

"Sachin. My brother. He lives in Lemstras." She turned to Clara. "He'll look after us."

The fire crackled. Clara and Rayya looked at one another but said nothing.

"I'll help you on your way," Ghadi said. "As much as I can. But you can spend the night here first."

"We can't..." Clara glanced at Rayya and fell silent.

"You need sleep." Or you'll collapse in the road, she thought.

Clara gave the smallest of nods.

"You can take Kahla's room."

"Is that your baby?" Rayya said.

A thousand things whirled around Ghadi's brain.

"Yes," she said at last. Because that would always be true.

She went into the room with the open shutters. Its own fireplace was a tiny thing. But after she lit it, warmth and brightness softened the chamber. Ghadi blinked at objects that now seemed... different. She ushered the girls inside. If she focused on them, she wouldn't have to think and remember.

"I'll bring some hot water, so you can get clean." Ghadi looked at the wardrobe, touched her tongue to her teeth, and mustered up the words. "You can take whatever clothes you want."

The girls thanked her in near whispers.

Ghadi sat up beside the crib as the gloom deepened. Creaks came from beyond the bedroom door. They matched the ones in her memories. She wiped away a tear, held her daughter's hand, and thought long into the night.

• • •

A twig cracked. Hands went to hilts, then relaxed when Jamsheed emerged from the darkness between the trees. He looked at Fahmaia and shook his head.

"I didn't find her, or any sign."

She nodded, sighed. He joined them at the campfire and warmed his hands.

"All of you, get some sleep," Fahmaia said. "I'll take the first watch. We'll wake early and keep looking."

Her half dozen warriors curled up beside their weapons. Wood crackled. Snores mingled with the sounds of fire and forest. Fahmaia murmured a prayer. Flames danced to the same cadence, till she didn't know which followed the other.

The girl scurried among the words. Their eyes had only met for an instant, with such distance between them. Yet her gaze fastened in Fahmaia's heart.

One of the sleepers stirred.

"Mawlana?" Jamsheed's whisper drifted amid the sparks.

"Yes?"

He sat up, and Jasmina twitched nearby. She mumbled something in her sleep. Jamsheed winced. He crawled close to Fahmaia and knelt there.

"I…" His jaw worked, as though it gnawed meat from a bone.

"Don't be afraid. You may ask whatever you wish, and it'll be between the two of us and Allat."

He nodded but didn't look at her.

"I killed an infidel, in the attack. She came at me with an axe and I cut her down."

"You did well."

"But…" Firelight washed one cheek, shadow the other. They stole the years and made him a boy. "But the one we're hunting… The girl… If I find her, I don't know if… She's just a child."

"Yes."

"Forgive me, mawlana."

"I understand." She touched his knee. He flinched at first, then his muscles loosened, deflated. "Do you remember the tale of the prophetess and her daughter, at Mount Garwud?"

"Of course. Allat asked for a sacrifice…"

"Sacrifices are meant to be hard. If they weren't, they'd be meaningless gestures — not true tests of piety. The One Goddess knows best. Trust in her, and know she'll never despise you for your doubts. All you endure in her name will be repaid a myriad times over in the next life."

"Thank you, mawlana."

His jaw worked again, but he went back to his place by the campfire and lay down. After some minutes, his breathing deepened.

Fahmaia prayed.

• • •

Moonlight mottled the road and silvered their horses' manes. The animals trod the shadows without slowing, but every so often their nostrils flared, and the smell of their sweat thickened. It was a good, clean scent. Meadows and leather. Silas had always loved it. But any horseman knew what it meant.

He tried to catch Katrina's eye. Did she plan to ride all night? Darkness swallowed the landscape, hid any tracks or signs they may've found. A dozen corpses might lie in those fields. Unless that red orb of hers saw in the dark, like a cat's… And if so, she didn't bother to unveil it.

The road wound past a copse of firs.

"Good," she said. "I knew it was close."

Light poured from windows. A sign dangled above the building's door. Even from here, there was no mistaking the drumstick and the mug of ale.

"Oh…"

Silas tried to bite back his surprise, but it was too late. Katrina von Talhoffer slept on rocks and devoured live rodents. That's what the trainees said. They'd never believe she scoured the countryside for beds and decent meals.

"Inns are good places for information. If local labourers or passing travellers spot something strange, they talk about it in the public houses. Especially if the story's interesting enough to earn a drink."

Two young men sat on a bench across from the inn. A lantern swayed above their heads and glinted off the bottle they passed back and forth. One of them gulped down a mouthful of liquid, coughed into his fist, touched his cap.

"Take your 'orses, miss?" He jabbed a thumb at the outbuildings behind him.

"Yes," Katrina said.

They dismounted. She passed each stableman a coin, then removed a pack from her horse. Silas checked his own baggage. He found a knapsack with a change of clothes and a few other things he might need.

The taproom was bright and boisterous after their nocturnal ride. Patrons chattered at the tables. Some whispered, others roared. Two drunks laughed and tussled in the far corner. One put the other in a headlock and dug his knuckles into the bearded man's bald pate. His opponent retaliated by tugging his ratty ponytail. It was like being back in the dormitory…

"Oi!" An elderly woman waved them over from behind the bar. "No weapons in here. Causes too much trouble when the ale starts flowin'. If you're stayin' the night, you can stow them upstairs. Otherwise you'll have ta leave them outside with the stablehands."

"We'll take a room," Katrina said.

"One bed or two?"

Silas spluttered. Both women stared, and he pretended to cough.

"Two then?"

"Yes. And we'll eat."

"The rabbit's good."

Katrina nodded.

"And a couple of ales."

Money and a key changed hands.

"Third door on the left."

Katrina gestured to Silas.

"Bag and belt."

He unstrapped his weapons and handed them over, along with his pack. Katrina slung the gear over her shoulder. She disappeared upstairs. Silas stood around and fiddled with his sleeve.

"Want your one now?" The landlady nodded at an empty tankard.

"Please."

She reached for a spigot, opened it, and filled the vessel without looking. Dark liquid wobbled just below its lip.

"Thank you."

He wrapped his hand around it, wedged his fingers inside the handle, sipped. Bittersweet with a hint of apple. He took another drink and smiled at the landlady, but she was busy wiping down the bar and didn't notice.

Silas wandered among the tables. If Katrina was right, maybe…

"…so the bloke says, take my wife while you're at it!"

"I told him horses kicked. Wouldn't listen. No kids for him!"

"…pig crap all over…"

"She said it come from Oled-Thar. But I touched it and the paint were still wet! So I says, if that's from Oled-Thar, me mother's a…"

"…frogs in the well…"

"If she prefers blondes, I know a cracking lass from over in..."

"...husband ran away with a..."

"...donkey..."

"Oi! Who nicked me beer?"

Silas sipped, frowned, sipped again. None of these titbits would impress Katrina with his initiative and intelligence-gathering. He'd have to strike up a few conversations and ask around... A redhead's eyes met his. She beamed at him.

"Hi," he said. "I'm-"

"Oi!"

Someone smacked into his back. He spun, tried to recover his balance. His tankard swung. Ale sloshed. The bald drunkard roared and clutched a handful of jerkin.

"Watch where you're goin', you pile of hog crap! I'm bloody soaked!"

"Sorry, mate." Silas held up his empty hand. "I wasn't-"

"Don't take that from this tubby bastard!" The one with the ponytail nudged his friend. "Kick his arse!"

"There's really no need for that. How about I-"

"Really no need! I say, there's really no need!"

Silas winced. Did he sound like that? If so, he'd want to thump himself too.

"Go on, Lucas. Smash the posh wanker's face!"

Lucas' eyes and scalp reddened.

"Bash him in!"

The bald man shoved. Silas took the impact, stepped back a couple of paces.

"Mate, let's just-"

"You want some?" He advanced, shoulders swaying, and puffed his chest out. The other drunk's grin hovered behind him.

"No! I'm-"

Lucas' fist flew at his face. Silas caught it on his forearm. His right hand twitched around the tankard's weight. One good hit with that... No. He couldn't bludgeon an unarmed drunk in a bar fight. Silas opened his grasp. The handle snagged on his bunched fingers. He swore.

The drunk's second punch rocked his skull. Silas staggered away and flailed. The damn thing wouldn't come loose! Lucas' arm wrapped around Silas' head, yanked him forward into a front headlock. Bone and muscle pressed against his neck. The tankard fell away, clattered on the floor. Lucas tightened his hold. His friend's laughter pounded in Silas' ears.

"Choke the posh boy out! We'll drag him to the outhouse and shove him down the crap-hole!"

Gunnar's advice echoed through Silas' head, chided him. He knew what to do. His fist clenched, opened, clenched again. And Lucas shifted, shielded himself with his thigh before Silas could punch or grab him there. He squeezed and Silas was back in the forest. His vision wobbled. Lucy-Lucas had him. His eyes bulged. Lucy, Lucas, Lucy... The universe was laughing at him, just like the other drunk.

The universe could go to hell.

He threw his arms around Lucas' waist. The drunk twisted, but Silas locked his grip behind the man's back. He bent his legs. Popped his hips. Lucas howled and flew overhead.

Silas gave him an extra heave, put him all the way over instead of spiking him on his skull. It was a bar brawl, not a massacre. Lucas' back hit the floor. He roared. Silas lay beside him and gasped.

"Posh wanker!"

The other drunk stormed towards him. His boot drew back. Silas put his arms up, tried to guard his head. But a hand snatched the drunk's ponytail, pulled him backwards before he could kick. He squealed. Katrina's boot hooked his legs out from under him. He landed on his butt, sat there, and swore.

Silas got up. Lucas did the same, and his torso heaved.

"He spilled his drink on me!"

Katrina went to the bar. The landlady passed her a tankard, and she held it out to him.

"Here. You can take this one internally."

"Oh."

He took it and, after a moment, glugged.

"Oi!" The other one sprang to his feet. His mouth snapped at her like a dog's. "Try me when I can see you comin', you one-eyed bint!"

Katrina held his gaze. Her lip curled.

"My companion and I are monster hunters. We kill things that'd eat the two of you."

The man sneered, but it quivered at the edges. He looked to his friend, looked back at her, and snorted. The drunks slouched across the taproom. Katrina glanced at the landlady.

"Two more ales, please."

They took a table. Katrina said nothing. A boy brought their food over and they ate in silence. Lucas shot him the occasional look from the other side of the room, but there was no fire, no glint in his eyes. When Silas nodded at him, he nodded back and raised his tankard.

Katrina led him up to their room. She'd left his bag and weapons by the further of the two beds. He went to them and rummaged in the pack. When he stood up, she was half-undressed. The marks of blade and tooth and talon decorated her skin like constellations. He turned his back and changed.

Silas lay in bed, closed his eyes. But too many things tumbled through his mind and they opened instead of sinking. Darkness thickened on the ceiling.

"Who first taught you to fight?" Katrina said.

He tensed. He'd been lying there for hours, hadn't he? Was she awake this whole time?

"My family's duelling master."

"I thought as much. Noble duels have too many rules. You need to break those habits, stop shying away from 'dirty' tactics. There are no referees in our fights."

He waited. Steeled himself for whatever came next. But no more words parted the shadows, and his eyelids grew heavier until they sealed shut.

• • •

Blackness filled Clara's bedroom. It drifted before her like silk. A silhouette stood beside her bed, darker than everything else. The wardrobe door opened. Her brows knitted. The figure reached for her. She waited for claws to shred her face, but warm fingers stroked her cheek. Clara shivered.

"You're not-"

But the bedroom was gone now, and her words melted away too.

"Do you like it?" Ella Mandrake said.

Clara sat with her at their kitchen table. Wisps of steam rose from a plum cake and played around her mother's eyes. Clara chomped down on the chunk in her hand. Hot, sticky, magnificent sweetness burst inside her mouth.

"Needs more eggshells."

Ella laughed. Clara laughed too. They stood and hugged and Clara knew, but clung to her all the same. The world faded. She tried to linger, plunge back into its depths. Her lids fluttered.

Rayya's eyes shone, inches from her own. Red lines bled across their whiteness but they were dry. She touched Clara's cheek and whispered.

"There really was a monster."

"Yeah."

"Or we're just a couple of crazy girls. Crazy orphans…"

They hugged beneath the blanket. Rayya was warm now. The ice-girl had melted, but Clara's friend was still there.

The clothes from the wardrobe fit well enough. They dressed in what they'd picked out, and the garments hung like armour after so long in just nightshirts. The boots were a bit big for Rayya, but they found woollen socks and the padding did the trick.

Ghadi had bowls of soup ready in the main room. Steam snaked around her face, framed her smile, and Clara wanted to laugh or cry but did neither. The girls thanked her and drank. It was thin, yet filled Clara's body. Spices lit fires along her tongue that tingled instead of burning.

Their hostess held her baby. The infant coughed, and Ghadi rocked her.

"There's a town called Hogmire." Her eyes were still on the child, and it sounded like the first line of a lullaby or nursery rhyme. But she turned to the girls and said, "Have you heard of it?"

"I think so," Clara said.

"Yeah. Miss Jazrah, our teacher, comes from…" Rayya bit her lip.

"It's a couple of days north if you follow the road outside. My cousin, Jarbul, lives there. He runs The Cracked Crown pub." Ghadi laid the infant in her crib and sat beside it. "Tell him I sent you and ask him to put you on a wagon that's heading to Lemstras. Lots of merchants from Hogmire trade in the city. He'll find one easy enough."

The baby coughed again. Clara wanted to ask if she was okay, but something glimmered in Ghadi's eye, weighted the edges of her smile, and drove the words back down.

"There are farms on the road. Travellers can get a spot in the hayloft and a good meal at some of them, in exchange for an afternoon's work. You'll come to one today, before it gets dark. Marvin and Isley Darthun's place. The gateposts outside their farmhouse have roses carved on them. They're friends. They'll take you in for the night if you say I asked them to."

She went over it again, made the girls repeat the name of her cousin's pub and the mark on the Darthuns' gateposts. Clara and Rayya thanked her, though it didn't seem enough. Clara wished she had something to give the woman. Money, or food, or… anything. She finished her soup. Stood. Glanced at the bedroom with its dust and drapes. The baby coughed in her crib. When Ghadi rose, Clara threw her arms around her. Ghadi hugged her back. Squeezed her tight.

"Thank you so much," Clara said.

Ghadi just nodded, but her smile grew. She saw the girls to the door, wished them luck. Then Clara and Rayya took to the road.

• • •

The aroma captured Silas at the top of the stairs. For an instant, the scent of meat brought back Traverd and its pyres. But even those horrors couldn't eclipse the glory of bacon. Other smells joined it. Bread fresh from the oven, eggs and mushrooms atop bubbling grease.

Trainees didn't starve at the academy — the masters gave them all they needed to fuel hard exercise and build strength. But there was a difference between nourishing and tasty.

His mouth watered. He sprang down the steps to the taproom. A waitress hurried by, and bore things far more colourful than the blocks of porridge they ate for breakfast at Tensia. Katrina was already there. She sat in a corner and watched the room.

"That's him," the redhead said when he passed by. She leaned towards the girl next to her, but the whisper carried at least a dozen paces. "He nearly put that sloshed tosser through the floor."

Both women gazed at him, and Silas' back straightened. His gut withdrew into a semblance of flatness. He strode to Katrina's table and sat down. Her eyepatch fastened on him. That hidden eye bored into his thoughts, glared at his pride. Silas deflated, looked away, and gave thanks when the waitress came over and set plates down in front of them. Katrina's eye and patch focused on bacon, eggs, devilled kidneys, and a slab of bread. She began her assault. He did the same.

"I wasn't born with my eye like this…"

Silas closed his mouth and stifled a splutter. Yolk oozed against his teeth. Katrina pursed her lips and looked over his shoulder.

"Yes?" she said.

A woman stopped at their table, planted her feet, and crossed her arms.

"You two the monster hunters?" Her forearms bulged like ham hocks.

"We are. Katrina von Talhoffer and Silas Renshaw."

Katrina held out her hand. The woman grunted, spat on her own palm, and shook.

"Marwa Fazan."

Silas offered a handshake too, but she re-crossed her arms without looking at him. He picked up a piece of bread instead.

"How can we help you?" Katrina said.

"By telling my husband he's a fool who needs some sense knocked into him."

"Not our usual line of work…"

Marwa snorted and scratched at her collar. The skin beneath the garment was a shade or two lighter than her face and hands.

"Someone killed one of my cows. Carved up its hide too, the little bastards."

"Little bastards?" Silas said.

"Two of the farmhands' kids are gone. You ask me, they did the cow in and ran off." Her fingers curled into rocks. "Workers these days have no respect for our property, and their brats have even less. We feed them, give them a roof over their heads, and they…"

The farmer's knuckles twitched.

"Their parents are crying about a monster attack. They expect me to believe a beast came along, tore up the cow, then snatched their scum kids. But my husband's a gullible sod. And those layabouts, Lucas and Jacar, said there were monster hunters at the inn. Now I won't get any peace from the lot of them till you've come and poked around."

Katrina's eye flicked to Silas. Her expression didn't change, but he understood. Monsters didn't keep livestock. If something dragged off a pair of children, it was already too late for them.

"We'll investigate the matter," she said.

"Mind, I won't be conned out of my gold. Plenty of charlatans pass through here, and they get nothing but bruises from me."

"Our order has its own sources of wealth. We don't charge for our services."

Marwa snorted again.

"Heard that one before. Work's free, but a few chickens go missing… Well, hurry up then. If I'm not there, the whole farm'll be going to ruin."

They wolfed down the rest of their breakfast and went for their weapons.

· · ·

Jasmina approached the cottage door. She looked to Fahmaia. The mawlana stepped over a bed of plants, inhaled their perfume, and leaned against the wall some paces from the entrance. Even with her markings covered, it was better this way. Masked women didn't inspire trust.

Fahmaia gestured and Jasmina knocked. The door opened.

"Hello?" A woman's voice. She sounded young.

"Hello…" Jasmina's face crumpled. "Have you seen a little girl, wearing a nightshirt? My daughter… She's… She's touched in the head. She ran off in the middle of the night. I… I've been looking everywhere, but…"

The mawlana winced. Jasmina was a far better warrior than an actress.

"Oh, the poor thing!"

But maybe the world was full of bad acting, and no one who didn't know her as well as Fahmaia could tell the difference…

"I'm sorry. I haven't seen any strange girls around here."

"Okay. I'm… I'm sorry to trouble you."

"I hope you find her."

"Thank you."

Jasmina walked away and the door closed behind her. Fahmaia joined her in the road.

"Keep trying?" Jasmina said.

"Yes. A small child without proper clothes on her back doesn't sleep under the stars or live off the land. She must've tried to find shelter somewhere…"

8

"Scum." Marwa Fazan spat. It splattered on the pink and red tangles that festered beside the tear in the cow's underbelly. "Nothing but scum. In my mother's day, she'd've tied them to a tree and whipped the skin right off their backsides."

A fly landed on the animal's eye, walked a circle, then flew off again. Silas' nose wrinkled. Death and manure battled for supremacy.

"These wounds…" Katrina crouched on the other side of the cow, by its spine.

Across the field, Lucas and Jacar leaned on their hoes and watched the monster hunters work. Silas tilted his head to them. Lucas touched his cap.

"Oi!" Marwa stomped towards the pair. A cowpat burst under her boot. "Don't stand there gawping! Get back to your work or I'll send you both packing!"

The men lifted their tools onto their shoulders and plodded away.

"These aren't slaughter marks." Katrina waved her hand over the animal's flank.

The lacerations crossed one another again and again, like the patterns of scar tissue on Katrina's body. But each group was spaced out across the cow's side.

Katrina put a fingertip into one of the cuts, traced its line.

"Rougher and more jagged than you'd expect from steel."

"Nails?" he said.

"Perhaps. But I've never heard of a monster carving symbols into its kill. And those guts haven't been snacked on."

She flipped her eyepatch up. Marwa barked out a syllable, then clenched her jaw. Katrina's gaze roamed back and forth. Both eyes were open, but she squinted — favouring the right.

"There are traces from a monster, but they're faint. Much fainter than I'd expect."

"Is it the same one? From Traverd?"

"I don't know." She looked up at him, then at Marwa. "We'll speak with the farmhands. The parents."

"Can't. They're off looking for their brats. Asking around the other farms. Shirking their work, as usual…"

"A monster may've snatched their children," Silas said.

"Rot. Utter rot. *They* did this…" She nudged the carcass with her boot. "…then ran off. Probably made shivs out of stone or bone, like a pair of criminals."

Katrina rose, and replaced her patch.

"How old are they?" she said.

"Lara and Hedmud's girl, Lotti's eight. Jost, Parvi and Kikos' boy, a year older."

"Show me where they sleep."

"Over there." The farmer pointed to a far corner of the field, then went off in that direction.

It resembled a heap of kindling from a distance. A bonfire waiting for the touch of a torch. But as they drew nearer, the spurs of wood became walls and a slanted roof. Marwa kicked the door open. The inside smelled of dung, sweat, and the heaps of straw Silas first took for a makeshift carpet. But each one bore the impressions of a sleeper's body.

"There's no bar or bolt for the door," Katrina said. "It wouldn't have needed to smash its way in. But monsters aren't master burglars. If one came through here and snatched two children, it would've woken their parents."

"That proves it! Nothing took the brats. They had their fun with my cow, then-"

"Do the children work?" Silas said.

"I don't allow freeloaders on *my* farm. Unless you count that husband of mine…"

"Milking the cows?"

"Yeah…" Her sneer faltered.

"Early in the morning. So they may've been outside when it came."

Katrina's eyebrow arched.

"There's a farm on my family's estate."

They went back outside. Katrina tapped her patch.

"I'll try to pick up the trail. You look around, search for any other evidence."

She strode back towards the carcass. After a moment, the farmer stomped after her. Silas pivoted on the spot and took in each direction.

Most creatures would've torn their victims apart in the field, gobbled up whatever they wanted on the spot. But this one was cunning enough to whisk them away before anyone saw…

He made for the nearest trees. Brambles girded the border between farm and woodland. He paced their length, scoured every inch till he spotted it. Silas plucked it from a barb. He turned around, ready to jog back to Katrina with his prize. But she was already there. Both eyes met his.

"The trail?" he said.

She nodded.

"It leads here. What do you have?"

He passed her the thread. She ran it between her thumbs and forefingers.

"Good quality," Silas said. "It didn't come from a farmhand's clothes."

"Nor a monster's hide."

Katrina put on her gloves and pushed her way through the brambles. He followed, low to the ground, and watched for anything her strange eye might miss. They didn't have to go far.

"The masters said some monsters use tools…"

"They'll throw a boulder to crush your skull. And I saw one rip off a crab's claws, then use them to pry open the shell so it could get at the meat." She toed the edge of the rut. "They don't drive carts. But…"

She touched the scars beneath her eye.

"There're monster traces here. Faint, just like in the field."

"Could anything else make those? A person?"

"If they came in close contact with one. Splashed with its blood in battle… Stepped in its crap… They might carry it for a while. But…"

She frowned, pursed her lips, then shrugged.

"We can follow a cart's tracks easily enough. Get the horses."

∙ ∙ ∙

A crow flew overhead. It matched their route, as though it followed a doppelganger road in the sky. Clara craned her neck and watched it glide. Was it homeless too? Maybe they'd travel together. Other animals would flock to their side and they'd all make their way to Lemstras, turn up on Sachin's doorstep like a travelling menagerie.

The crow arced away to the west. Perhaps it had a nest after all.

They walked past trees where the last leaves clung, and others still dressed in green. Squirrels clambered among them in search of food or places to hide. Sheep lazed in the fields. Cows chewed the cud and lent their fragrance to the breeze. Traverd belonged to another world, one far away and long ago.

And the monster... It belonged to no world at all.

Rayya's fingers touched hers. Clara held them and they cooled her. Perhaps she had a fever, or else that distant Clara burned inside her, along with everything she'd once loved. What would be left when they were ashes? She squeezed Rayya's hand.

The ground rumbled. Wheels rattled behind them. The girls moved to the other side of the road as the cart neared. The horse stopped next to them, blew a raspberry with its nostrils, pawed the ground. It was a stocky thing, and the driver looked almost as broad across the shoulders. She scratched at a crop of iron-coloured hair. Her lips made a chewing motion. But another rumble and clatter came from the opposite direction, and they sealed together without saying anything. The woman stared at the approaching vehicle.

This wagon was larger. Clara and Rayya stepped off the road, onto the grass verge, so it could pass by. But its driver pulled back on his reins and his pair of horses stopped alongside the other animal. Barrels sloshed. The man and woman held each other's gazes. Neither blinked.

"Lencia." His face resembled a chunk of bark. He might've been the same age as Clara's mother, or ancient as Joss.

"Manesh."

She twitched the reins. The horse blew one more raspberry. Its hooves clopped and the cart trundled off. Manesh's head swivelled. He watched over his shoulder until she cleared a rise and vanished. Then he looked down at the girls and his expression softened.

"Good morning."

He raised his hat a couple of inches off a crown of white hair. They replied with one voice and it came out as a chorus.

"Morning."

"Where're you two headed?"

"Hogmire," Clara said.

He whistled.

"That's a long walk. Wish I could offer you a lift, but…" He pointed his thumb at the barrels. "These've got to get where they're going."

He glanced over his shoulder again. His brow darkened.

"You girls keep your distance from Lencia."

Clara and Rayya looked at one another.

"Hope you have a good journey," he said.

"Thanks," Clara said. "You too."

He set the horses going and his cart rumbled down the road.

• • •

Fahmaia squatted beside the graves. Jasmina walked a couple more steps towards the house, but halted when she noticed.

One mound was longer than the other. Two chunks of night-black stone looked upon them. These were hefty, unsculpted things, but their planes and angles were beautiful all the same. The mawlana doubted they'd been quarried anywhere in the region. Their inscriptions sprawled, scrunched, and tilted. No craftsman had engraved those letters. But they too were lovely, and Fahmaia touched them.

The mawlana nodded to her companion. Jasmina approached the door, and Fahmaia took up her place near a shuttered window.

Jasmina knocked. After some moments, the door opened. Another passed before a woman spoke.

"Yes?"

"Hello… Have you seen a young girl… with olive skin, lighter than mine? She's wearing a nightshirt… My daughter. She's… touched. She ran off last night, and I… I… Have you? Have you seen her?"

Seconds crept by.

"No. I'm sorry."

Jasmina glanced at Fahmaia. The mawlana was already moving to the doorway.

• • •

"Fancy," Katrina said.

"Yeah…" Silas said.

He'd been to grander country houses. The Renshaws had one of their own. Still, the building beyond the gate was a place to host banquets and garden parties, not monsters, kidnappers, and cattle-mutilators. But the cart's tracks scarred the dirt where it had turned into the grounds.

They dismounted and tied their horses. Katrina lifted her patch, while Silas examined the bronze plaque on the gatepost.

"Monster traces. Still can't tell if it's the one from Traverd."

"This's a Harvishti family crest."

"You know who lives here?"

"No. Some of the Harvishtis come to my family's feasts and balls, but not these ones." He pointed to either side of the emblem's shield. "There's usually a wyvern and a bear. Some of the flourishes are missing too. This belongs to a lesser branch. Oh… I just meant…"

"A lowly noble family. Not good enough to associate with the Renshaws."

"No! I… I mean, yes… But…" He looked away, and indicated something else on the device. "A minor lord and lady live here."

"Then let's meet them."

She tried the gate. It wasn't locked, and the two of them approached the front door. Katrina replaced her eyepatch before she knocked. Silas breathed easier. He hadn't dared point that out.

Some seconds passed. She beat her fist on the door. Then a third time, as though clubbing it to death. At last it opened.

"Yes? May I help you?"

The man wore a butler's uniform. He glanced down, brushed crumbs off his belly. A few more hid in his moustache.

"We're looking for two missing children," Katrina said. "We believe someone brought them this way."

"Children? I assure you there are no children here, madam."

"How about a cart?"

"Excuse me?"

"Has anyone from this household taken a cart out today? To the nearby farms?"

"They have not. Now, I'm afraid I really must return to-"

"We want to speak to your employer, and the other servants. One of them might've seen something."

"That's entirely out of the question. The household's in the grip of a rather unpleasant illness, and I fear I'm the only member out of bed."

Katrina's eye glimmered.

"You're a poor liar for a servant. I've always heard you lot are good at that, whenever you have to explain where the jewellery or silverware's gone."

The butler flinched. His back straightened, and he transfixed her with a look that would've done credit to a duke.

"Leave my mistress and master's property at once, before I have you chased off."

"Look," Silas said, "we're sorry. But please understand, there are children's lives at stake and we can't just-"

Katrina punched the man. Her knuckles caught him on the chin and his eyes rolled back in his head. He collapsed in a heap. Silas gawped. She stepped over the butler, into the hallway.

"Draw your weapon. He didn't lie to us and try to send us away for nothing."

Silas' hand went to his bludgeon. But Katrina drew her sword and he did the same. His heart pounded. Bloodshed? Here? This was a noble family's house, not a cave in the wilderness!

A drawing room opened off the hall. No fire burned in its grate, and the candles weren't lit. Armchairs, couches, and tables wallowed in shadow. Rugs smothered his footsteps. The silence comforted him, but only at first. Where was everyone?

The dining chamber lay empty. They moved through a study, into a library. Hundreds of tomes mingled on its shelves. His mother would've torn through the place and arranged them by colour or size. Perhaps *this* family kept books for reading…

They returned to the hall. Katrina glanced up the staircase, where more shadows waited. But she went forward instead of ascending. The gloom was softer at the rear of the hallway, beneath the stairs. Katrina eased the door open. A set of steps led down, and a light burned at the bottom. She adjusted her stance as she took them — readied her sword for battle in those confines. But nothing appeared to test its point.

Silas had seldom been below stairs, where servants had their quarters. But he'd expected more… stuff? They passed rooms with bare mattresses. No belongings graced tables, shelves, or the corners where a maid or manservant might've thrown their clutter. Only one room looked lived in. A candle flickered over a plate containing two whole biscuits and one half-eaten. Nightclothes lay atop the bed.

Near the end of the passage, Katrina froze. She gestured before advancing. Her boots crept, and he did his best to match their tread. At first he took the sound for a trick of the wind. But after a few more steps it shifted, into… voices? Chanting?

The corridor turned. A hole gaped in front of them, where a section of wall had swung outward. Beyond it, flames lapped at stone. Candles dripped in a sconce and illuminated another set of stairs.

Silas tensed. Secret doors weren't unusual in these houses. A couple of centuries prior, the Renshaws, Harvishtis, and other families had stashed their loot where the tax-collectors wouldn't find it. He'd played in such places as a boy, while adults told stories of their past. But now? After missing children and a mangled cow? While that chant flittered in his ears? His fingers tightened around the sword.

The voices grew as they descended. What language was that? Its tones and cadence reverberated from the stone and prickled his skin.

Four figures stood in torchlight, backs to the stairs, and bent their heads over a slab. Paint adorned the walls around them. Those symbols were more elegant, but not that different from the ones on the cow's carcass.

"Stop! Stop!" A woman said, and the chant died. "Harold, we told you not to come down here during-"

She turned and her jaw hung open. The others whirled around. For an instant they all just gawped. The woman and the man next to her were middle-aged. The other two, a boy and a girl, might've been a couple of years younger than Silas. Both had the man's round face and the woman's upturned nose.

Their daggers matched too. Four blades, made of bone.

"What the hell is this?" Katrina said.

"We…" the woman said.

"We're…" the man said.

They exchanged glances. The boy glared at Katrina.

"You're trespassing." He took a step towards her. "This is our home, and we have every right to peacefully practise our religion here."

"Those knives don't look very peaceful."

The boy held out his left hand. Scabs and scars laced its palm.

"We shed our own blood. That's no crime."

"And you two don't look much like peacekeepers anyway," the girl said.

"We aren't," Katrina said. "We're-"

A roar bellowed through the chamber. Katrina's head snapped to the right. A passageway led from the room, and she moved towards it. The boy darted forward and stabbed at her neck. She jerked round, slashed him. The other Harvishtis cried out. He rolled on the floor and screamed.

"Kill them!" Red droplets spattered the stone around him. "Kill them or we all hang!"

The man charged at Silas. Eyes shone, mouth twisted. They flew towards him, more terrible than the dagger. He backpedalled. His blade flashed before he knew he'd swung it. The knife hit the floor and the man staggered away, clutched a forearm.

Someone shrieked. A blur in the corner of his vision. Silas spun round, tried to bring his weapon up to parry, to shield his face, to...

Impact shuddered along his forearms, into his shoulders and chest. The girl gasped. So did he. She looked down at the sword, where it joined her dress, then up at him. Their gazes locked. Her eyes trembled. She fell backwards and dragged him with her. Silas planted his feet. She slid off the blade with a wet, butcher-shop sound, and thumped the stone.

Redness slathered steel. Dark things stuck to it. Bits of... of...

Noise droned around him. Something moved nearby. The red... The bits...

His mind locked but his muscles didn't. When the man leapt at him, screeching, clawing, the sword hacked. The man thrashed on the floor. Brown fingers grasped his throat, tried to hold it together. But blood gushed and his arms fell away. Hands slapped stone, then just twitched. Father and daughter lay side-by-side.

"Silas."

Pierced, torn, broken.

"Silas!"

Katrina shook him.

"Huh?"

"Come."

The woman and the boy sprawled behind her. Neither moved. Katrina went past him, towards the passage. He was with her, halfway along the corridor, before he felt his legs under him. Next to a door. A bar and bolt held it closed, but there was a window at eye-level. Katrina peered between its rods, then stepped back so he could see. In the cell beyond, two children lay in darkness. Silas' throat squeezed shut. They were too late. They'd... But his eyes adjusted and air flowed back into his lungs. Their limbs twitched. Chests rose and fell.

Katrina threw the bar aside, drew back the bolt, and opened the door.

"Hey." Silas shook the girl's wrist. "Lotti?"

Katrina touched the boy's eyelid.

"Drugged," she said.

Silas set his sword down, put his arms under the child.

"No." Katrina held his shoulder. "Not yet. Leave them out of harm's way."

A roar tore through the corridor outside, rebounded from wall to wall. She went to it. Silas picked up his weapon.

Further along, the passage stank like an overflowing latrine. The stench grew as they neared the door. This one was larger than the cell's. A slab of metal, with three bars and several bolts. An iron plate sealed its window. Katrina undid the latch and slid it back. Her features set, eyes hardened. She stepped aside. Silas took a deep breath. The air assaulted his throat but steadied him.

They had countless diagrams at the academy. Paintings. Stuffed corpses masters and mistresses pointed to as they lectured, and gooier ones they dissected. But a single glimpse made all of them meaningless.

A monster. A living monster.

Katrina said nothing, and Silas pulled himself together. He wasn't there to gawk like some labourer or shopkeeper. Training... Assess the threat. It was a hulking beast, maybe a few inches taller than Katrina and broader across the chest than both of them put together. Dark green scales covered its body. A metal collar held its neck. Chains clanked and rattled. They ground against the brackets which fastened them to the wall, but the Harvishtis or their minions had done their work well. That steel might've lasted for decades…

"Ready?" she said.

How could he ever be?

"Silas? Are you-"

"Y… Yeah. Yeah."

"Pincer. You're left, I'm right. You know what to do with scales?"

He nodded. Katrina began on the bars. Silas' hands helped her, while his mind played out a dozen victories and a million deaths. The door opened and the monster's roar battered his bones. It lunged. Jaws snapped, fingers raked. The chains' links rang out as one. The monster growled, strained against them. Lumps of muscle bulged under its hide. But it came no further.

Katrina circled to the right. It went for her, and again the collar thwarted it. Her eye flicked to him. Silas went to the left. Something cracked underfoot and he sprang back. Other things scattered around his boots. He tried to keep his eyes on the monster, but he had to know…

Bones. A small skull lay on its side next to his foot.

Heat built up in his eyeballs, as though they'd explode and his brains would spew through the holes. He was going to kill this thing.

Silas trod through filth and debris. A bone crunched. The monster bellowed. Its head twisted towards him, then its body jerked round and launched itself. Silas backed away. He swept his blade in front of him, swung it back and forth like a kid waving his first toy sword. Yellow eyes glowered at him. Its mouth opened and slivers of flesh flapped between a million spikes. The chains pulled taut. The monster's thews shuddered. It kept going for him, but couldn't get any closer.

Katrina struck.

It howled, spun round, clawed at her. She leapt backwards. Her left hand gripped her blade partway along its length. Black blood spattered the floor around the creature's feet.

Silas matched her half-sword grip. He lunged, brought the point down into the monster's back. The tip pierced its scales, penetrated the meat, and the creature's whole body quivered. The monster rounded on him. But he was ready. Silas darted away and Katrina struck.

It attacked her again. But its movements were slower now. Ichor poured down its hide, ran along its thighs. She hacked at its hand. Three green fingers fell among the bones. The monster didn't howl this time. It made a noise that was either a moan or a hiss.

The rest was butchery.

They each attacked when it was open, and their half-sword techniques punctured it again and again. It staggered between them like a drunkard, went for one then the other, but got nowhere near either. It tried to spring at Silas and fell onto its knees.

Katrina drove her sword into the base of its neck.

The monster flopped forward. Its chest crashed down onto blood and bone and filth. It didn't even twitch.

They stood there for some moments. Katrina was a statue, but Silas' chest heaved. He gasped, tried to pull air into his lungs, and couldn't quite fill them.

"Congratulations," she said. "Your first monster kill."

First monster kill. First *monster* kill. First kill…

The girl's eyes flashed in front of him. Silas doubled over and threw up. He spewed until there was nothing left, and still kept going.

"Better?" Katrina said.

Silas looked up, tried to talk, then dropped his head and vomited again. His stomach dredged up more from somewhere. It gushed from his mouth, squirted through his nose.

Katrina waited for him to recover and didn't say a word. In the corridor, Silas fumbled with his scabbard, tried to aim the sword's point into the opening.

"Clean it first."

"Oh… Yeah."

"Here…"

She walked back down the passage, past the cell where the children slept, and wiped her sword on the woman's dress. Silas stared. Katrina looked at him. He squatted down and cleaned his blade on the dead man's doublet. His chest convulsed. He gulped. But nothing came up his throat. The weapon slid back into his scabbard, and it was impossible that the world had changed so much and so little between drawing and sheathing.

"Can you manage?"

Silas nodded. He thought he'd be shaking, but he wasn't. So when Katrina took the farmhands' boy in her arms, he lifted the girl. Lotti murmured something and pressed her head against his chest, but her eyes didn't open.

Upstairs, Harold, the butler, still sprawled where they'd left him. But he groaned and moved when they approached. Katrina set the boy down on a rug. Silas did the same.

"Wha…"

The butler's eyelids quivered. Katrina shook him until they opened.

"Huh? Whu…" His eyes focused on the face above, then on the rug where the children lay. He squealed. "Wait! Don't… Don't kill me! Please! I'm just a servant. I've never hurt anyone!"

"Talk, if you want to live."

"Lord and Lady Harvishti…" He looked past her, towards the stairs. "Are they…?"

"Dead. And their children. Fear us, not them."

He exhaled.

"They're… They were… Chidna worshippers. She's supposed to be the mother goddess of monst-"

"We know who Chidna is. What did they think they were doing?"

"His lordship believed if they made the right offerings, performed the correct rituals, she'd bless the family with power over her offspring."

"The cow on the Fazan farm…" Silas said.

"The young master and mistress were in… high spirits. They went out to mutilate cattle as a sacrifice."

"And snatch children."

"The boy and girl caught them in the act. And since the thing below eats…"

"They thought they'd silence the witnesses by feeding them to it," Katrina said.

"A ghastly affair. I assure you, I warned Her Ladyship and His Lordship that they'd bring ruin to the house, but they wouldn't listen."

"Nobles…"

"Quite."

She helped him to his feet. Harold straightened his uniform.

"If you require a formal statement, I'll gladly denounce them in writing and explain how they threatened me into silence."

"And loot the silverware on your way out."

"Ha! Oh, I don't know about-"

Her hands closed around his throat. The butler wheezed and his eyes bulged. He grabbed her wrists, but Katrina's grip didn't budge. One hand went for her face. Fingers gouged at her eye. She drove his head backwards and it thudded on the doorframe. It struck again, and again. Katrina yanked him back and forth like a hound shaking a rat, and battered his skull against the wood.

Cracks gave way to squishier sounds. His arms dangled and legs crumpled. She tossed him aside. Crimson oozed down the doorframe.

Katrina von Talhoffer picked up the boy. After a moment, Silas Renshaw lifted the girl. They carried the children back to their horses.

• • •

Barbs of ice ripped through Ghadi's stomach. She tried not to look down. If she did, if the masked woman noticed, somehow that'd make it worse. But she couldn't stop herself. A sword hung from the woman's hip, and even inside its sheath the blade promised slaughter.

She was dead. The Kharji would draw it now, cut her down. Because they were the ones from Traverd. Had to be. And one more life would mean nothing to them. Two lives...

"Is the girl here?" the masked woman said.

The other Kharji moved back, left the two of them facing one another in the doorway.

"I told your friend..." The words came out steadier than she thought possible. "I haven't seen a girl. I haven't seen anyone."

"Yes, I heard what you said. But I'd prefer the truth."

Ghadi put her hand on the door, shifted her weight. But the Kharji placed a foot over the threshold before she could slam it shut.

"Truth?" Heat rushed through her body, blazed inside her eyes. "I haven't seen any child of *hers*, and that's true enough to tell the gods."

"No, I suppose you haven't. She isn't Jasmina's, but we still need to find her. Where-"

Yallis coughed. The masked woman looked over Ghadi's shoulder, and fire turned to stone in her breast. Ghadi ran to the hearth, seized the poker, stood between them and the crib.

The Kharjis came through the doorway.

Yallis coughed again. It became a splutter. Ghadi wanted to turn, touch her, comfort her. But if she took her eyes off the intruders…

"She's ill," the masked woman said. The tenderness in her voice shocked Ghadi more than any rage or malice could've done.

Jasmina stayed by the front door. The masked Kharji crossed the room, looked into each doorway, and stopped outside Kahla's chamber.

"I'm sorry. You've already lost so much. Did illness take them too?"

"Yes. Please, go. Just go."

The woman unwound the cloth from her head. Ghadi made a sound and bit the side of her tongue, but didn't feel the pain. Black script flowed upon the Kharji's skin. Living tattoos.

"May I see your baby?"

The poker shook in Ghadi's hand. A string of curses and profanities massed in her brain, but she held them back. If she refused… She'd fight. They'd kill her. Then Yallis would die at their hands, or starve while Ghadi's corpse rotted on the floor.

"I swear by Allat, I won't harm her. You see I've been marked by the One Goddess. I'd never break an oath sworn to her."

Ghadi shifted, gave her space to see into the crib. But she drew back the poker and took aim. If the woman went for Yallis, she'd smash her temple.

The baby spluttered again. Then came a sound Ghadi hadn't heard for a long, long time. She stole a glance. Yallis gazed at the markings on the Kharji's face. Another giggle became a rasp.

"I know that cough," the woman said. "And that ashen colour in her cheeks. We saw it in our camp, last year."

She looked Ghadi in the eye.

"Tell me about the girl, and I'll cure her."

The Kharji was lying. It *had* to be a lie, a monstrous one to make a mother talk. She didn't have to choose. But... That script danced on the woman's cheeks, across her brow, faster than before. She had power. Her goddess had power. And Ghadi knew *she* was the liar, not the Kharji. Because she wanted it to be true. By all the gods and demons and everything in the whole wide world, she wanted her daughter to laugh and play in this house, not lie outside with her father and sister.

"How? How will you cure her?"

"A few herbs, a few mushrooms, and Allat's favour. If you agree, I'll send Jasmina to gather the ingredients."

"Cure her. Cure her first."

The Kharji held her gaze for several seconds.

"Very well. Though if you refuse to talk after that, I'll have to compel you."

Ghadi said nothing, but the woman went to her companion and murmured. Ghadi caught snatches, the names of flowers and fungi. Jasmina nodded along to each instruction. Then she left. The marked Kharji shut the door behind her.

"My name's Fahmaia. Fahmaia Hashad."

Yallis coughed.

"Ghadi."

The two women stared at one another for a time. Ghadi didn't want to speak, but she had to know…

"What do you want with th-" She stopped herself before she said *them*. Did they know about Rayya? Were they looking for her too? "…the girl?"

"It's Allat's will. Terrible things will befall the world if we don't find her."

The woman looked at her, waiting. But Ghadi found no words. Yallis wailed and Ghadi put down the poker. She picked her baby up, cradled her, whispered sweet words for minutes or hours. When the door opened again, the sky was darker.

Jasmina unslung a bag from her shoulder and gave it to Fahmaia.

"May I use your kitchen?"

Ghadi nodded. Fahmaia left, and noises came from the next room. The tap of cupboard doors, the slosh of water in a bowl, and countless other once familiar sounds. Ghadi was a ghost, haunting her old home while a new inhabitant cooked a meal in the place she'd fed her family.

Fahmaia returned with a clay bottle. Ghadi flinched when the Kharji reached for the baby in her arms, and Fahmaia paused until she nodded. The woman tilted the bottle. A few drops fell into Yallis' mouth and the baby smacked her lips. The Kharji bowed her head, closed her eyes, and spoke words

Ghadi couldn't understand. Her markings quickened, whirled around her face. Ghadi's vision spun. She looked away and the world settled.

Yallis' chest rose and fell. She sucked air deeper than she had for many days, then laughed. A clear, musical laugh. Ghadi's eyes stung.

"How can it work so fast? She only just drank."

"This is Allat's blessing. The drug will take time to complete its work." She tilted the bottle one way, then the other. "You'll need to give her the rest over the next few days."

"Thank you." Wetness blurred the room and the woman and that bizarre script. "Thank you."

"Now you must fulfil your end of the bargain."

Ghadi's face burned. A mass blocked her throat, filled her mouth. But Fahmaia held the bottle before her.

"The girl was here. I gave her food and clothes and sent her on her way."

"What's her name?"

"Clara. I don't know her second name."

"Where did she go?"

Ghadi's mind raced. A dozen falsehoods crawled onto her tongue, but how could she deceive this woman with sorcery crawling across her skin? Fahmaia would *know*. Somehow she'd sense the lie and draw her sword, or just leave with that medicine. But…

"Lemstras. She wants to go to Lemstras."

"That's over the hills, to the east?"

"Yes."

"Why there?"

"She knows someone in the city. He might take her in."

"Do you know his name?"

"I…" She frowned. What had Rayya said? She groped for it, but nothing came. "I don't remember."

She braced herself. If the sword flew from its scabbard, she'd shield Yallis with her body…

"Thank you." Fahmaia put the bottle on the mantelpiece. "Give her this over the next three days. One dose each morning, one in the evening. Try to give her the same each time, but it won't harm her or stop it working if they aren't exact."

Jasmina opened the door. The Kharjis left, and closed it behind them. Ghadi watched it for a full minute. They were really gone and she was alive. And Yallis…

The baby dozed, but a smile curved her lips. Her lungs drew breaths into her body and sent them back out into the world without a single cough or splutter.

Ghadi sat by the crib and cuddled her child.

Clara… Her eyes burned and blurred again. Tears trickled down her cheeks. That poor, hurt girl who'd thanked her and hugged her… Perhaps she'd be safe. Maybe Ghadi had done enough. The girls were on their way to Hogmire, after all. A roundabout route for anyone going to Lemstras, especially without transport to ease part of the journey. And the Kharjis knew nothing of that. They'd head east instead, wouldn't they? A shorter, quicker path. But one that went through places the locals shunned and only travellers strayed.

They might never make it to Lemstras. And if they did, it was a big city, with peacekeepers. Kharjis couldn't raid it and murder people in the street as they'd done in Traverd.

Ghadi clung to these things, and hoped one day she'd forgive herself. When Yallis woke, when the baby looked up at her and those brown eyes sparkled, it was easier to believe she might.

9

Clara stood on tiptoe. The stepladder creaked under her and she went still. But it didn't topple over, so she reached up into the yellow leaves, palmed an apple, and twisted till it came off the spur. She placed it inside the basket.

The movements were natural, as though she'd always known them. Clara picked several more before she remembered.

"Don't pull them off. Twist them, or you might break the spur."

"If you drop them in like that, they'll bruise."

Her mum wore a brown and yellow dress that day. She'd matched the trees.

Clara plucked another, turned it in her hand. A white thing wriggled in the fruit's flesh. And another. More. She watched the maggots gnaw and burrow for a while, then tossed the apple away.

Did Rayya's mother teach her too? Flame-coloured branches hid her friend's face atop the other ladder. Any tears spilled in secret.

She filled the basket and brought it down. Rayya descended before Clara had a chance to go back up with an empty one.

"Thirsty?"

"Sure," Clara said, though the dryness at the back of her throat was a faint and trivial thing.

"Where'd she say it was?"

"That way, I think?" Clara's arm swept to encompass almost a quarter of the horizon.

They made their way through the orchard, across a field where two goats chewed a boot, to a collection of pens and outbuildings. A girl came along from the opposite direction. She stood there, a white bundle in the crook of her arm, and waited for them.

"You the ones doing apples?"

"Yeah. Clara."

"Rayya."

"Tammie." Her smile plumped up her face. It could've belonged to a kid their own age, though the body beneath it was too sturdy for that. "Need something?"

A head popped out from her bundle. The chicken's orange eyes stared at them for a second, then scoured the ground instead.

"Mrs. Darthun-" Clara said.

"Isley. She lets everyone call her Isley."

"Isley… said there's a well, if we wanted a drink."

"I'll show you. Lemme just sort this 'un out."

"Thanks."

"Thank you," Rayya said.

Tammie sat on a stool and put the chicken down. It pecked at the dust. She reached behind her seat, picked up a butcher's knife. The chicken looked up and she struck. Its head flipped over three times before it landed. The bird ran in circles, while blood spurted from its neck.

Rayya went pale and turned away.

Clara squatted down. Droplets sprayed her upper lip. She wiped them away, and a metallic tang filled her nostrils. The chicken almost stepped on its own head.

"Dumb things," Tammie said. "Don't even know when they're dead."

The farm girl grinned, so Clara smiled for her. But it wasn't dumb. You lose everything and you keep on running anyway, go through the motions until…

It flopped on its side. Tammie picked it up by its legs but left the head lying there. She stood up, nudged it with her boot.

"The dog'll have that. Loves crunching 'em." She walked away. The chicken swung at her side, and crimson circles spattered the ground behind her. "The well's over here."

They went past a pigpen. Sows wallowed in mud and watched the girls go.

"Ducks are worse," Tammie said. "They can fly away after you do them. Just fly off, without their heads. Can lose your dinner that way if you're not careful."

At the well, Tammie turned the crank one-handed until the bucket came up. She nodded and the girls grabbed the tin cups which rested there. Rayya dropped hers into the hole, yelped. But Tammie tugged a length of twine and it jumped back out. The farm-girl caught it with the same hand, while the chicken flopped in the other.

"That's why we have these." She passed the cup back to Rayya and touched the threads. They went from the cups' handles to one of the canopy's struts. "Marvin kept knocking 'em in."

The girls drank. It tasted... different. Denser than the water in Traverd. But it was good all the same and washed the dryness back down Clara's throat.

"Better get this 'un plucked. See you."

She skipped towards the farmhouse. The chicken danced beside her. Clara and Rayya made their way back to the orchard, where the air was light and fragrant after the pens.

Clara climbed her ladder. She plucked apples, but thought of decapitated ducks. Maybe she and Rayya could be like them. They'd fly away to someplace good, instead of blundering around in stupid circles till they keeled over.

"It'll be dark soon."

Clara blinked away ducks and chickens. She bobbed under the branches. Isley Darthun stood below, amid the baskets and their blood-coloured mounds.

"I don't mind. I can pick more..."

"These'll do just fine."

Clara frowned. Those few piles of apples didn't seem like much in exchange for a place to sleep. But Isley steadied the ladder and she climbed down.

"We're eating soon. Do you like chicken?"

"Sure," Clara said.

Behind Isley, Rayya grimaced.

The dining table at the farmhouse stretched almost the full length of the room. Clara, Rayya, Tammie, and the Darthuns clustered at one end. Farmhands revelled at the other. Their laughter and the smell of wine mingled together, warmed and blurred the edges of the world.

"Ley says you're on your way to Lemstras." Marvin pushed a nest of ginger curls back from his face with one hand, ate a drumstick with the other, and chewed as he spoke.

Rayya and Clara looked at one another. Clara blurted the words out before her friend could speak or the silence could stretch.

"Yeah. We're going to visit Rayya's brother."

"Oh, that's nice," Isley said. "Is your family from Lemstras, Rayya?"

Clara held her breath. Would her friend burst into tears? If she did, they'd have to tell the truth. About fire and swords and Kharjis and their parents. The laughter would die. Everyone would avert their eyes, murmur sympathies…

"No," Rayya said. "Sachin moved there to take up an apprenticeship. He's an apothecary…"

She smiled. Her leg shook under the table. Clara pressed her thigh against Rayya's, shared her warmth, and it stopped. Rayya's smile and voice grew steadier too.

"…and it turned her purple!"

The Darthuns laughed. Tammie grinned over the chicken bones. Clara ate everything they pushed at her, though her stomach protested and threatened to burst. A piece of gooey blackberry pie shut it up.

"There are blankets and pillows in the hay barn," Isley said. "If you need anything else, just come up to the house."

"Thank you," the girls said together.

They walked beneath an indigo sky. Stars sparkled like gemstones. Rayya was a step or two ahead, and Clara couldn't see if her smile had slipped. But there were no sobs.

They got ready for bed, and made themselves comfortable in a corner behind piles of hay. Rayya only said a few words. She wished Clara goodnight, then huddled in her bedding.

Clara lay awake amid hay-hills and rustic smells. Wood creaked in the wind, but the barn had its own noise that was nothing like her wardrobe's. She closed her eyes though her mind didn't close with them. Clara turned one way, then the other.

After a while, perhaps hours, she said, "Rayya?"

The darkness swallowed her voice and didn't yield any other. Clara sighed. She pulled her blanket aside, fumbled with her boots, and put them on.

Maybe a walk would help her sleep…

• • •

Stars twinkled, celestial wounds that seeped into the sky. Xerachus' wounds leaked too. He should stop, return to the dark, finish healing. But he loped onward. Clara Mandrake was out there and he'd find her.

Mandrake… Claws and blood.

Xerachus padded through meadows that stank of sheep dung. Some of the animals watched him from a distance. Easy meat. He could leap upon them, tear them apart in an orgy of woollen gore. Feast. But… Clara Mandrake. He'd devour flesh later.

The breeze changed and he sniffed new scents. Blackberries, apples, cows, chickens… All the food and filth of farms. But there was something else... Ah! Xerachus ran towards it. Pain spread through his wounds, ensnared his limbs. But he didn't slow and the smell strengthened with every bound.

There!

A figure stood in the starlight, its back to him, head tilted towards the heavens as though reading their secrets. That familiar odour hit Xerachus in waves.

His eyes flashed. Claws twitched.

He crept forward and a growl rumbled through his teeth.

...

The growl trembled through Clara's bones. Her muscles tightened. The monster had chased her through her dreams and found her. Should she turn around? Or she could watch the stars and hope its teeth and claws were swift.

Maybe it'd tear her head off. Would she fly away like a duck or scurry around and thump the ground like a chicken?

Another growl. Closer this time.

Clara turned.

Jaws widened and saliva glistened. It barked at her, the biggest hound she'd ever seen. Eyes and teeth gleamed. It wore a collar. A farm dog, out in search of foxes to rip open.

It barked again, snapped at her.

Clara's eyes burned. Stupid animal! She'd strangle it like she strangled Tommy, smash its head on the ground, gouge its eyes, tear its stomach, eat its innards.

All this burst through her brain and came out in a snarl of her own.

The dog cringed, whimpered. It backed away and ran off into the night.

• • •

The man tensed. He spun round. His eyes met Xerachus' and widened into moons. He screamed, but pink claws slashed his throat and the noise drowned in a gurgle. Blood spurted from the wound, spat between his lips.

He fell in the dirt and Xerachus stood over him till he was still.

His claws shone. Life and death dripped from them. They were broader than they'd once been — no longer the needles that could penetrate a nose or ear, pierce a brain, and leave a corpse almost unmarked. That throat would shriek like a mouth, tell others he walked the countryside. Unless…

He dropped down, straddled the corpse, and bit into its neck. His teeth tore at the wound, mangled flesh. The man tasted foul but they always did. He sat up. The throat was a mess now. An animal could've taken him, a wolf or feral dog. It'd do.

Xerachus stood. Blood trickled down his chin, and along his limbs as well. He growled. His wounds gaped, soaked his fur.

He sniffed the air. Clara Mandrake was on the wind, faint but sharper than before. Xerachus longed to press on and find her. But his strength would bleed away into the fields, and even if he reached her he'd be in no fit state to deal with her.

Another smell came, weaker despite its nearness. He loped towards the house and its open window. Beyond it, a boy lay with blankets bunched halfway over his face. They muffled his snore.

Xerachus watched him for some minutes. Then he skulked away, towards the rear of the cottage. A shed stood near the outhouse. Dust and cobwebs laced its crannies. The door opened to his touch, and darkness greeted him. Xerachus melted into its embrace.

...

"…and the monster…" Katrina lunged and swiped her fingers above a girl's head. "…attacked!"

The child cried out, and even a few adults gasped, flinched — as though Katrina might leap off the table and strew the taproom with their bones. But the girl's eyes gleamed. Her shriek gave way to a grin.

"We drew our swords…"

She brandished one of the fire irons. At least she wasn't waving sharp steel over their heads, Silas mused. He bit into the lump of cheese at the end of his knife. Fruity flavours crumbled between his teeth.

"…and thrust!"

Katrina gripped the middle of the poker and performed a half-sword technique on her invisible foe. The whole inn cheered — the audience that clustered around the makeshift stage, the drinkers who lounged in the corner where Silas sat, even the landlady behind her bar and the waitresses who walked among the tables.

He gobbled his cheese and glared. What the hell was she doing? Katrina von Talhoffer, up on a table, entertaining a taproom like a bard or wandering storyteller! Had the battle at the Harvishtis' house driven her mad?

The young woman's eyes swam before him. His arms shuddered, as they had when she… she… He bit down on the flat of the knife. How could Katrina make them cheer about that?

A tankard thudded on the table in front of him. Liquid sloshed inside.

"On me." Lucas sat beside him. He brandished a mug of his own, and his beard glistened.

"Thanks…" Silas picked it up. Ale burned its way down his throat.

"Did it really happen like that?" He waved his mug towards Katrina, who continued to slaughter imaginary enemies.

"More or less."

"Nice one."

Silas murmured more thanks, but the dead girl's eyes were back. He took another drink and tried to focus on Lucas' instead.

"How're Lotti and Jost doing?"

"Marwa's going easy on them. She brought them food and said they should just rest for a bit."

"Good."

"In a week or so, she'll go back to treating them like crap. That's how she is."

"They're little kids. They shouldn't… They… They deserve better."

"Aye." Lucas gulped his beer. "They do. Maybe things'll get better for them. Maybe they won't. But they aren't monster food. And that's on you and her."

Applause shook the taproom. Katrina jumped down and passed the poker to a waitress. Hands patted the monster hunter's back as she came over. Behind her, the audience fragmented and conversations sprang up. Lucas clasped Silas' shoulder and walked off. Katrina took his seat.

Someone brought her an ale. A few more followed, along with grins and praise. Silas avoided their eyes. Drank. When the last beer-bearer left, and the two of them were alone in the corner, he glowered at her.

"We killed people. *I* killed people."

"I know." She sipped a drink.

"You made it sound like a… a… Like it was good! A fun little story to excite people in the pub!"

They drank in silence for a minute or two.

"Stories are important." Katrina waited for him to meet her gaze before she continued. "They make what we do real."

"It was real when we killed the Harvishtis. It was real when you grabbed the butler and-"

"Not to them." She nodded towards the middle of the taproom, where men and women chattered. "Our order needs them. They're our eyes and ears. We don't have enough people to scour all the lands till we find monsters. We need them to send for us if they think something's lurking in the bog or the woods. They have to know who we are, what we do, and trust us to kill the things that want to kill them."

She drained her tankard and Silas did the same. They both reached for fresh ones.

"And this will protect us, if the Harvishtis try to cause trouble. Any peacekeepers who come here will find the whole county's on our side. Every farmworker for miles around will tell them how the Harvishtis fed children to a monster and tried to murder us."

"They only believe that because you told them."

"What matters is they believe it. In a few days, the story will be truth and they'll tell it as if they saw it happen with their own eyes. Speaking of which…" She tilted her tankard towards the door, where a band of drinkers stormed off into the night. "I reckon they're on their way to the Harvishtis' place."

"They want to see the bodies." He winced. "The bones. The dead monster."

"And burn the place to the ground, probably."

"But…"

"People need vengeance. And when it's too late for a lynching, this is the next best thing."

They drank for a time. Silas imagined the mob barging into the country house. Would they desecrate the corpses? He tried to push those images out of his brain.

"I was telling you about my eye, before Marwa Fazan came to us."

"Huh? Oh, yeah."

"Eighteen years ago… I would've been a little older than you, I think…"

Silas tried to calculate, but the numbers drowned in his drink.

"We tracked down a monster. A fierce, cunning thing. It killed Robyn, my mentor, and almost did for me too." She caressed the scars below her eyepatch. "The healer said my eye was infected. He wanted to cut it out, but I wouldn't let him. The infection… the corruption… took the eyeball and left the rest of me alone."

"Now you can see where monsters have been?"

"Their traces are…" She gulped down a mouthful of ale. "It's like being a dog, I think. They can smell the world and know what's passed through a place. Like that, but I *see* it."

Silas didn't know what to say, so he concentrated on his ale for a while.

"We still have to find the thing from Traverd," he said.

"Yes. We'll carry on asking around tomorrow. If we can't learn anything at the farms and country pubs, we'll head for a town. Hogmire, maybe."

Two children played near the fireplace. One was the girl from Katrina's audience, and she mimed a half-sword thrust. A boy clutched his phantom wound, collapsed, and writhed around on the rug.

Silas sighed and drank.

• • •

Allat's eyes shone brighter than the summer sun. They lit the hilltop and Fahmaia's skin baked in their heat.

"Forgive me, Goddess. I've failed you."

The mawlana braced herself. Those cosmic orbs would blaze, and she'd burn in hellfire while a million souls cursed her name. For she had doomed and damned them all.

But tears the size of oceans glistened in the Goddess' eyes. Allat's sorrow was worse than wrath. It shivered through Fahmaia's bones, and she welled up in turn. Humanity had sinned. Failed. The One Goddess wouldn't rage or revel in mankind's destruction. She wept for what she must do.

"Forgive me…"

Fahmaia knelt and the heavens opened. Allat's voice sounded, not in thunder but a whisper that drifted into her ears.

"Wake."

Fahmaia's eyes opened and the Goddess' were gone. She gazed at another pair instead, white in a night-dark face. The man crouched before her. One of his hands reached for her sword, the other clutched a dagger.

She twitched. His eyes flicked up. The knife glimmered and came for her.

10

The dagger froze. Moonlight caught its point and danced in the stranger's eyes. He gawped at Fahmaia's face. The weapon moved again. She kicked out. Both heels thumped his chest, knocked him back on his rear.

"Enemies!" Fahmaia let loose a noise like a hawk's cry. The Kharji danger signal tore through the night and her voice chased it. "Enemies!"

Bodies stirred nearby, dark shapes crawled onto the hilltop. She clutched at Allat's Earring. Her foe dived forward, seized the middle of the scabbard, yanked the weapon away. But her fist closed around its handle and she pulled. The sword flashed. His dagger thrust.

The mawlana hacked his elbow and the man screamed. Blood spurted from his stump. She slashed him across the chest and his life gushed out. Its warmth splashed her face.

"Allat!" Jamsheed struggled on his back, wrestled with the woman above him. "Goddess, help me!"

The woman tore her arm free, raised her club. Fahmaia cut and Allat's Earring sheared through her head. Half the woman's skull slid away. Lengths of hair fluttered in the moonlight.

Figures dashed across the hilltop. Kharji war cries bellowed in their wake. The mawlana's warriors stood in good array now, dishevelled as they were. Their enemies scrambled back down the hill.

"Allatu Akbar!" Jasmina ran after them, waved her sword around her head. It became a beam of pure silver. "Unbeliever scum!"

"Jasmina, wait!"

Fahmaia tried to catch her arm but missed. Jasmina charged down the hill, and a couple of the others moved to follow.

"No." The mawlana waved them back. "Stay here."

She sprinted, and was off the hilltop too fast to know if they heeded her. Shadows hurtled away below — as though they'd routed the darkness itself. Her foot caught on a rock. She lurched, scrambled, almost tumbled. But Fahmaia found purchase at the last moment and leapt onto the ground beneath.

Steel glinted ahead, vanished, glinted again. Jasmina still swung her sword, and it flashed like a sentry's signal. The mawlana flew towards it.

"Stop!"

"Argh!"

Something splashed. Fahmaia grabbed an arm, pulled the woman backwards. Jasmina's leg broke free with a second splosh. Stench wafted from the water. Rotten eggs and decaying vegetables.

"We can't blunder through a swamp in the darkness." Fahmaia drew her further back. Ahead, silhouettes disappeared and footfalls faded after them. "They know where to tread. We don't."

Jasmina panted. Water dripped from her leg.

"Sorry, mawlana. I-"

"Let's get back to the others."

They found them tending to their wounds. Two bodies lay in the camp, but neither wore Kharji garb.

"Who was on watch?"

"Samir," Jamsheed said. "He took over from me."

Only four warriors sat or squatted on the hilltop. Fahmaia pursed her lips. Jamsheed followed her gaze.

"Should I… Should I search for him, mawlana?"

"Tend to that cut. I'll look. Jasmina, dry yourself and help the others."

Fahmaia lit a lamp and shuffled down the slope in its glow. She paced around the foot of the hill, walked almost its full width before she found him. Samir lay in a heap. His head lolled, limbs straggled as though in the middle of a swimmer's stroke. An arrow protruded from his chest. Its end dangled from the shaft, half its fletches gone.

She extinguished the light and the shadows took him back. Fahmaia moved away. The archer would've fled with the others. If they still watched, they'd had ample time to hit her already. But still…

The mawlana went back to her warriors. They clustered together in the middle of the camp and five faces looked up at her. She shook her head.

"An arrow."

"Shall we go get him?" Parmeen said.

"No. He died a martyr, doing the Goddess' will — as surely as if he fell in Traverd. Let him lie there, so Allat may look down upon him and smile when he meets her."

Fahmaia went to the woman's body. Goo pooled where the top half of her head had been. Cords hung from her belt, and the dead man carried the same.

"They killed our sentry," Fahmaia said, "but they may've wanted the rest of us alive."

"Slavers?" Jasmina said.

"Maybe. I've never heard of a slave-trade in this part of the country. They'd have to sell their captives far afield, or to those willing to risk the consequences…"

She gazed into the night. Had the girl made it past? Or had they fallen upon her, bound her, carried her off the path and into their swamp?

"There's a tattoo." Jasmina raised the dead woman's wrist.

The design was obscure at first. A collection of shapes on the light-brown skin of her forearm. Fahmaia tilted her head, and they became triangle teeth inside an open maw. She went to the man's body, paused, then found his severed forearm. The tattoo was harder to make out on his black flesh, but it matched.

"A bandit symbol maybe," she said.

She tossed the limb off the hill. With her warriors' help, the corpses tumbled after it.

"I'll keep watch for the rest of the night," Fahmaia said. "Sleep if you can. Tomorrow we'll find who did this, and take the Goddess' vengeance before they harry us again."

...

"Stop staring and eat your breakfast, silly boy." Isley Darthun looked from the dog to Clara. "I don't know what's got into him. He must've taken a liking to you."

"Yeah…" Clara Mandrake forced a smile.

The dog lay in the corner and stared at her while Isley joined them at the table. Marvin shovelled bacon, eggs, and toast onto his plate.

"Go on," Isley said, "before he gobbles it all up."

Clara and Rayya claimed their portions, then waited for Isley and Tammie. Marvin looked at the girls and spoke through the wedge of toast in his mouth.

"Dun wait. Breakfast's quick round 'ere."

The table was half-empty. The farmhands were probably already in the fields, hard at work. Clara stared at the food and her lips twitched.

"We can pick more apples. To pay for-"

"Dun-" Marvin coughed and swallowed. Isley rolled her eyes at him. "Don't be silly."

"You've got a long walk ahead of you." Isley glanced at Clara's plate, then smiled at her. "Make sure you eat enough. You'll need your strength."

Clara bit into a piece of bacon and moved its salty sweetness around her mouth. She tossed the end of the rasher to the dog. After a couple of seconds, he sniffed it without taking his eyes off her. Then he devoured it. He continued to watch her, but that was okay.

Isley went into the kitchen when they were done eating. She came back with a pair of bags that hung from cords.

"Some lunch for the road."

The girls thanked her and slung the provisions over their shoulders. In the doorway, Isley frowned at a grey sky.

"It'll rain today. If you want to stay till it passes…"

"Thanks," Clara said, "but we need to get to Lemstras."

She took a step, paused, and looked back.

"Ghadi…" She bit her lip.

"I should see how she's getting on. She always likes my plum cake…"

They both smiled. The girls walked to the road, and it carried them away from the farm.

Rayya was silent for some time. Should she tell her about the dog? It was on the tip of her tongue, but she bit it back. What did it matter? Just a silly animal…

A droplet plinked on Clara's nose. One landed in her hair, then another. Soon drizzle misted the fields on either side. The girls sped up. The rain quickened too, pelted their faces and shoulders. Puddles rippled in the road. Rayya's stride lengthened, as though she could break through to the other side of the water. Clara matched her. It became a jog.

But when Rayya's pace lapsed into a brisk stride again, then a slow one, the rain still endured. It cooled Clara's skin. Rayya hugged herself and rubbed her upper arms. A drop exploded on her brow. She flinched and lowered her head.

Clara shielded her eyes. No buildings sat in the downpour. There was nothing around them but meadows and…

She touched Rayya's shoulder and tilted her head towards it. Rayya nodded. They ran off the road, jumped over a patch where mud oozed in gashes. Water dripped from the fir trees' needles. It sunk into their hair and dribbled down their faces. But at least the copse kept some of it off them.

They sat and sheltered there while the world drowned.

• • •

Rain lashed the swamp, scoured its surface. But it didn't wash away the smell of decaying plant life. That thickened, as though the raindrops were made of the same foul water that undulated on either side of them.

The earth squelched under Fahmaia's boot. She moved into the middle of the narrow strip, and the ground yielded less. Behind her, Jasmina blasphemed. The mawlana sighed but didn't chastise her. This place would've tried the patience of the ancient prophetesses.

Fahmaia's foot sank. She stopped before the rest of her weight went into the step, then waved the others around that patch. They'd found the bandits' escape routes easily enough in the light. But the rain ate into them by the minute. At this rate they'd soon have to swim…

The spur of earth snaked through the swamp. Ahead, where a line of trees cut across it, the ground rose. Once they got there, they'd be-

She spun away an instant before she understood why. Her arm swung out, hit Azim on the chest, and knocked him back. He swore, then a second time when the arrow hissed into the water. The others yelled and drew their weapons. Fahmaia broke into a run.

Her boots slashed the mud. The woman up in the tree fumbled with another arrow. She shifted on the branch she straddled, corrected herself. Rain beat down on her through the foliage and Fahmaia prayed it would ruin her draw, her aim…

The shaft flew. Fahmaia leapt aside. The ground slid away underfoot, spilled her towards the churning swamp scum. She scrambled, waved her arms, threw herself forward. The balls of her feet caught something solid and pushed against it.

Fahmaia rushed towards the trees. Narrow, mossy trunks. Was that woman a bird to perch up in one's branches? Stratagems flashed and clashed before her. If she made it past, the archer couldn't hit her. But the next arrow might take one of the others…

Allat's Earring caught the raindrops on its edge.

This wouldn't work. Couldn't. But it was too late to stop.

"Allatu Akbar!"

She swung the sword like a cavalrywoman slashing mid-gallop. Blade met wood. Then Fahmaia was on the other side of the trunk, and her speed drained away in a few more paces.

The din of rain and swamp water swallowed any creak. The tree topped without a sound, but the archer yelled. She plummeted from its branches — little bigger than a child, though it was a woman's face that flashed by and disappeared in the splash. Branches crashed down after her. Green things on the surface surged in all directions, sloshed over her warriors' boots. They backpedalled in the mud.

Fahmaia gazed at her sword. She'd seen it go through flesh and bone before. Even the leather armour around an enemy's breast. But *this*… Barzik Khan only wielded the weapon in battle. He'd refused to sport with it in camp and try its edge against wood or stone.

"No mortal man should put the One Goddess' miracles to the test. I put my faith in them instead."

Jasmina and Jamsheed stood by the water, blades in hand. But the archer didn't emerge. After a few moments, Fahmaia beckoned for them all to join her. Whether the woman had swum away underneath, drowned in the murk, or met a creature's teeth, that was in Allat's hands now.

The Kharjis pressed on through the swamp.

• • •

The apple yielded with a sweet crunch, and its juices mingled with the tang of preserved pork in Clara's mouth. Rayya nibbled away on a slice of meat. Rain danced and shimmered across the landscape like ghosts.

Clara gnawed the last bits off the core and tossed it among the trunks. A red squirrel stole it.

"Do you think he knows?" Rayya said.

"Huh?"

"Sachin. About…"

"Oh…"

Clara tried to hold it all in her brain. Distances and routes, peddlers and mounted couriers. The ways knowledge might spill from Traverd into the world beyond. But how could she? She'd never even been past Ghadi's house before, and that was so close. She and her mother could've come through the forest with hampers, visited that kind woman and her baby, given her food and laughter and…

"Maybe," she said. "I don't know."

"If he's heard, he might think I'm dead too."

Rayya sighed. Clara pulled her close, and Rayya rested her head on Clara's shoulder until the heavens quietened. Then she stood up.

"Let's go. Before it gets bad again."

They abandoned the copse and slogged through the field. The muddy patch was almost a bog now. They went around it, back to the road. Rayya's stride ate the ground. Her pigtail swung from side to side.

They splashed through the smaller puddles, jumped or skirted bigger ones. Clara's legs pumped to keep up but her lips took on the ghost of a smile. When Rayya had a mission, she launched herself at it. If storming down the road kept tears from her eyes, if she imagined her brother weeping just ahead, so be it. Ducks, not chickens.

Lightning split the sky and seared the corner of Clara's vision. The world rumbled. Rainclouds burst. It cascaded down, drummed against the road. Cloth clung to Clara's skin. Hair plastered itself over half her face.

They ran, threw themselves into the tempest. But it battered them. Rayya moved close, shouted.

"Need to find-"

Thunder stole the rest. Clara nodded anyway.

Fields rolled away in each direction. No trees stood against the deluge. Not even a bush or hedge to crouch beneath. They went on, and the rain washed them down the road.

"There!"

Beyond Clara's mask of hair, Rayya pointed. Clara slicked it back, splatted it atop her head. Rayya was already sprinting. Clara tore after her.

The buildings stood far back from the road, and looked as half-drowned as the two girls. Water sloshed down their slates. It poured from a dozen places in miniature waterfalls. But smoke climbed out of a chimney and motes of light glowed behind shutters. They zipped past a barn, beyond the stable, towards a farmhouse.

Clara knocked on the door. They both panted.

Lightning flashed. Harsh brilliance painted everything, and Clara blinked again and again to dispel it — but afterimages stuck to the inside of her eyelids. She raised her fist to knock again.

The door flew open and a voice boomed with the thunder.

"What do you…? Huh."

Phantoms flashed around a burly torso, broad, hard features, and a tuft of grey hair. Lencia stared down at her. The woman from the road looked at Rayya, then her eyes swept the space above their heads. She chewed.

Lencia stepped back and waved them in. The girls looked at one another.

"Hurry up. Letting the cold in."

They entered and she shut the door. A bolt thudded into place behind them.

• • •

The scream echoed through the dying rain. Fahmaia moved towards it and her warriors followed. If that was the girl's voice, if the bandits were hurting her… The mawlana's eyes narrowed. She gripped her sword, tore through the tangled foliage.

Men and women cried out. Were those empty noises, or words from a tongue she didn't know? Wrongness thrummed in each sound or syllable.

Trees encircled a clearing and a cluster of huts. Fahmaia crept among their trunks. The others did the same, quiet as mountain cats. She rounded one of the hovels and the central space lay open before her.

A naked man sobbed and clutched the red stump at the end of his elbow. He let out a squeal that might've come from a wounded pig. Men and women in rough garb jeered at him. They shoved him towards a cage where a few people lay or squatted. All were undressed. None were intact.

Another of those alien cries reverberated through the clearing. This time it came from a single throat. The man brandished a sword, raised it aloft as he roared, and his belly undulated as though it yelled too. A forearm rested on the wooden block in front of him. Burnt flesh capped its end.

Invisible insects crawled along Fahmaia's limbs.

The sword came down. It rose and fell again before the first thunk faded. Two new scars marred the wood. Wisps of steam drifted from five severed digits, but no crimson trickled. The swordsman gathered the fingers in his fist. Some yards behind him stood a totem pole, a stack of five faces that were mostly jaws and teeth. He laid a finger in each maw.

Fahmaia turned and Jamsheed's gaze met hers. His eyes flashed, muscles rippled. She nodded. There was no sign of the girl, but…

The mawlana gestured, gave the others a moment to prepare, and charged. She was on the first idol-worshipper before the woman looked round. Allat's Earring slipped through her back and pierced her heart.

Shouts rang out, and this time she understood them. The bandits, the blasphemers… whatever they were… scrambled. An axe flew at Fahmaia's face, spun end-over-end. She cut it out of the air, lunged, and opened the thrower's chest.

Jasmina grabbed the squealing man. She dragged him out of the way, then thrust at the nearest foe. Metal clanged.

"Allatu Akbar!" Jamsheed vaulted the chopping block and went for the swordsman.

Fahmaia moved to support him, but a spear point thrust at her face. She twisted, lopped one way then the other. The weapon's head and the woman's fell in opposite directions. Just an instant of steel and slaughter, but Jamsheed had already closed with the swamp priest.

The young Kharji struck. The idol-worshipper jumped away, gulped. His cheeks puffed and a torrent of bile spewed out. The goo caught Jamsheed full in the face. He stumbled backwards, shouted for a split-second, then sputtered. The stench hit Fahmaia like a slab of spoiled meat. Her gullet convulsed and she didn't know if she'd vomit too. But she ran towards them, yelled a war cry to draw the priest.

He didn't even glance at her. His sword slashed and the blow spun Jamsheed around. The Kharji's neck gaped. The smell of cooked flesh wafted as he fell.

Fahmaia chopped at the priest. Allat's Earring came down to split his skull, part his brain. His sword flew up. The blades clashed.

"Allat!"

"Grush-ka's balls!"

Clouds of dust drifted between them. A million grains slipped through Fahmaia's fingers and the idol-worshipper's. She blinked at her palm, turned her hand. Grey powder seeded the damp air. It puffed and bloomed.

Impossible...

The priest hurled himself at her. But without his sword he was just a fat fool, and she was the mawlana. Her first strike crumpled his throat. The second broke his nose. She knocked him down and went to where Jamsheed lay. Filth covered the young warrior's face, trickled into that second mouth. Fahmaia picked up his sword.

Her enemy crawled towards the totem pole. Blood poured from his nose. Red fingers reached for the lowest visage. Fahmaia stabbed him through one kidney, then the other. She glanced over her shoulder. But the fighting was done, and the others stood near Jamsheed's body.

A layer of dust coated the dirt. There was some on the priest's hand, where it mingled with the blood and formed clumps. She put down the sword and found traces of it in the grooves of her palm. All that remained of her holy weapon and the idol-worshipper's sinful relic.

His djinn... demons... false gods... How had their gift, their sorcery, destroyed a true miracle? Only by the One Goddess' will. Allat's displeasure...

Fahmaia strode to the cage. The one-armed man stood near it, but didn't look at her. He stared at his stump and sobbed. The others lingered inside, though the door was wide open. Two flinched from the mawlana, a man and a woman. The third lay on her back, gazed at nothing, and mumbled. Her limbs ended at knees and elbows.

"Was there another prisoner? A child?"

The man shook his head. Both his forearms were gone.

"No." The woman's voice rasped from her noseless face. One of her hands was missing its digits. "No kids."

Fahmaia sighed. At least Clara hadn't fallen into their clutches.

"What was this?"

"They gave our fingers to…" The woman tried to point. She faltered for a second, then used her other hand. "Ate the rest. Said it'd make them strong."

"Because you still lived…"

She'd heard of such things. The abominations false gods and their worshippers inflicted on the world. Now Allat would destroy it all, unless…

"Are you strong enough to walk?"

"I… I don't know."

Azim and Parmeen helped her from the cage. Maalam guided the man out. Jasmina murmured to the other man, who was sobbing again. Fahmaia waited till they were at a distance before she went inside and crouched by the last prisoner.

"Can you hear me?"

The woman's lips moved. Fahmaia put her ear beside them, but there were only noises. The mawlana's knife ended her suffering.

"What shall we do with them?" Jasmina said, when she emerged.

"Search these huts. Give them clothes, food..." She grimaced. "If they want to come with us, we'll take them to Lemstras. Otherwise, let them go where they wish. The way we came should be safe enough now."

"Yes, mawlana."

Jasmina carried her commands to the others. Fahmaia gazed up at the clouds. Allat had punished her, reclaimed that great gift. But her markings moved and the world lived. The One Goddess was merciful. There was still time to find the girl, make the offering, and spare all of creation from her wrath.

But first, a token of their piety...

"Find axes or maces." She pointed at the totems. "Destroy them."

• • •

"Come." Lencia waited by the hearth. Flame and shadow shifted on her face. "Dry off."

Clara almost grasped Rayya, held her back. But Rayya shivered and Clara stood still while she entered the firelight.

"Clothes are soaked." She chewed every time she spoke, as if her jaws worked away at a lump of gristle. "Should take them off, 'fore you catch a cold."

"Oh..." Rayya looked at Lencia, then down at herself. "Yeah..."

Clara's neck itched. The woman was right, but she wanted to shout, stop her friend, and didn't know why. Rayya peeled off her clothes. They splatted on the floorboards by the rug, and the girl stood there in her undergarments.

"Those're wet too."

"I… They'll get dry." Rayya moved closer to the fire, angled her body towards it.

Lencia shrugged. She looked at Clara.

"Go on. You'll catch a cold else."

"I'm okay."

"And drip water all over my house."

"Oh…"

Clara undressed and dropped her clothes on the pile. Lencia gathered it up in her arms, glanced at the fire, then went to a rack in the corner. She hung each garment and dragged the contraption closer. The scrape juddered through Clara's bones like fingernails on the school blackboard.

"Hungry?"

"No," Clara said.

"Yes," Rayya said.

"There's stew. Get dry. I'll bring some."

"Thank you."

Lencia went into the next room and closed the door. Clara joined Rayya at the fireplace. Heat touched her flesh and made no difference.

The woman came back in with a tray. Two bowls steamed on it, and the air smelled of offal. Rayya took one and thanked her. Clara didn't want the other bowl but lifted it anyway.

"Thanks," she said.

Lencia put the tray on a table. The wood was almost as thick as a tombstone, but she gripped its edges, her forearms bulged, and she hefted it. Its legs thudded down near the hearth. Clara's shoulders tensed. Lencia picked up two chairs and swung them over, then a third. She sat at the head of the table.

"Can't eat standing up, like horses."

One chair was right beside them, its back to the fire. The other stood on the other side, a mile away. Lencia watched them. Clara let Rayya take the nearer seat, and forced herself to leave her friend's side. She walked around the foot of the table, took her place. Lencia's eyes lingered on Rayya.

"Eat up. Warm your insides too."

Rayya put a spoonful of stew in her mouth. Clara did the same. A kidney disintegrated between her teeth and she wanted to spit it back out. She swallowed. Bitterness oozed down her throat. What herbs were those?

"It's good," Rayya said, after a few spoons.

Clara blinked at her. Rayya's eyes and smile shimmered. Clara shifted her lips from side to side. Had her own taste buds burned away along with everything else? She took another mouthful, but it was just as bad. Her stomach churned, bubbled. Clara smiled at her hostess anyway, though the woman didn't even look at her.

"Where were you two going?"

"Hogmire," Clara said.

"Lemstras." Rayya burped and covered her mouth. "My brother lives there. I need to tell him our parents are dead. Kharjis killed them."

Clara's jaw hung open. Rayya's voice didn't change. She might've been talking about apples or the weather, and gobbled more stew.

"Poor thing…"

Lencia stroked Rayya's cheek. Clara's own flesh tingled there, and she shivered. But Rayya didn't flinch.

"Poor, poor, thing."

Lencia pushed her chair back. Wood grated, and vileness sloshed around Clara's belly.

"Come, sit with me."

Rayya's smile levelled, but she didn't resist when Lencia touched her arm and coaxed her. She sat down on the woman's thigh.

"Rayya-"

Clara's stomach convulsed and she gasped.

"Poor little girl..."

Lencia stroked the other cheek. Her fingers crept lower, and Rayya tried to shrug them off. The woman's grip tightened. Rayya frowned, mumbled something. She twitched, but there was almost no strength in it.

"Hey..." Clara pushed against the table, stood. Her innards clenched. She doubled over like someone'd punched her. "Get off..."

Rayya struggled. Lencia squeezed an arm till Rayya's skin whitened, but her other hand caressed and probed. Clara staggered at her. She held on to the woman's forearm.

"Let her go!"

Lencia's arm tore free, seized her hair. Clara yelled. Lencia wrenched her around and her scalp screamed.

Broken bowl, spilled porridge, blood...

Clara flew across the room. The wall smashed her shoulder and skull. She lay there on all fours.

Blood! Blood! Blood!

"Clara..." Rayya thrashed. "Clara!"

She scratched at Lencia's face. The woman swore, turned her head away, but Rayya's nails gouged and red streaks glistened. Lencia roared. She heaved Rayya up, slammed her to the floor. Rayya moaned.

Clara's stomach bubbled once more. Then it blazed. Liquid fire. The inferno devoured her innards and incinerated the pain, the vileness.

Lencia pinned Rayya down. One hand held her throat. The other stroked her thigh. Rayya twisted, bucked. Lencia's bulk crushed her against the floorboards. Clara hurled herself at them. Her fists hammered the woman's shoulder. Lencia backhanded her, knocked her spinning. Clara's hip banged into a cupboard. Her hand swept across its top, scattered objects, toppled them, and bashed something. A stone mortar. Fire licked along her sinews and raged inside her right hand. Her fingers wrapped around the pestle.

Lencia's hand scuttled up Rayya's leg.

Clara smashed the side of her skull. It rocked away, then jerked back around just as fast. Crimson bloomed on her cheek. Bloody eyes glowered. Lencia went for her but Clara Mandrake didn't care. She hit out a second time and the woman's head snapped backwards. A third. A fourth. Lencia was on her back now. She rolled onto her hands and knees and Clara brought the pestle down on her spine. The thud echoed through the room but Clara didn't feel it. There was only fire, in her hand, her stomach, her eyes.

Red dribbled between Lencia's lips.

"Clara!" Rayya's voice burned away too.

The pestle landed again. Blood splashed Clara's face.

"Stop it! Clara! Please! Stop!"

She hit the woman three more times, and didn't know if she splatted blood or bone or brain. Clara dropped the pestle. Her hand throbbed. Rayya wept.

"Clara... You... You..."

Clara reached out to touch her, hug her, but Rayya flinched from scarlet fingers.

"It's okay."

"You killed her."

"She was hurting you."

"But..."

A coolness spread through Clara's head, drove the flames down into her body, towards her red right hand. Thoughts cleared and sharpened. Sound returned to the world around them. Rain drummed on the roof, logs crackled in the hearth. If things could go on after Traverd, why should they stop for this worthless woman?

"No one'll come here tonight. Not through that. And tomorrow we'll be gone."

Rayya's eyes widened.

"Go to the bedroom. I'll get rid of her."

"How-"

"You won't have to see her again."

When Rayya was out of sight, Clara stood above Lencia and watched blood pool around her skull. Did that faraway girl care? Clara didn't know, so maybe that meant she was gone forever. The fingers of her right hand opened and closed. An itch nibbled away at it. Fire-insects boiled her blood, gnawed her bones.

Clara lifted one of Lencia's legs under each arm, put her back towards the front door, and dragged. The body shifted a couple of inches and Clara grunted. How long would it take to get her outside, heave her into a well or the stables? Minutes? Hours?

The kitchen was closer.

Clara knelt down, turned the corpse. It flopped over. Knuckles rapped the floor. Something squelched. She pushed, pulled, and rolled Lencia through the doorway. Clara kicked the door shut behind her, just in case Rayya emerged from the bedroom across the way. She slumped against the wall. Her limbs and back ached, but they were dull pains. The blaze in her hand eclipsed them. Had she broken something?

A light burned on the kitchen table. Clara sat on the bench beside it, and examined her digits one by one. She paused. The pot of stew lay at her elbow, and something hid behind it. A blue bottle. She picked it up, pulled the stopper out, and sniffed. Her vision swam. Her fingers opened and a blue blob hit the table, rolled off. Glass smashed a million miles away.

Clara shook her head until it cleared. The odour hung in the air, but her senses held and thoughts hardened. Her eyes flashed. That bitch! Clara's hand shook. She'd lift the pot, bring it down on Lencia's head. Bash and grind till the woman's brains smeared the floor and-

Her fist clasped shut. Joints locked in place, fingers bored into her palm. She fought to unclench them but they wouldn't budge. The inferno doubled, trebled in a ball of bone and tendon. Clara's fingers snapped open. That hellfire shot along them, into the tips. Skin tore. Blood spurted and something else came out amid the crimson. Something black.

Clara's mouth held a scream, but she swallowed it. Her hand didn't hurt anymore. Pain and fire had spurted out too, and not even a tingle remained to show where they'd been.

Clara Mandrake spread her fingers in the lantern's light. Five black claws gleamed.

• • •

Xerachus stirred. His nose twitched. Even in the darkness of his dreams, that shift in the far-off scent ignited his brain.

Clara Mandrake…

Torn flesh knitted itself back together, inch by inch, hour by hour.

He had to find her.

11

"Kharji! Murderer!"

Rashida Al-Taquba froze. Quietness detonated around her, silenced the voices of merchants hawking their wares and customers haggling them down from outright robbery. The woman glared at her.

"My cousin's dead. You burned his house down, with him and his family inside."

"What? No! I never-"

"We've all heard what you did in Traverd. You and the rest of your-"

"I haven't left the city in months. I had nothing to do with-"

"Murderer!"

The woman shoved her. Rashida stumbled backwards. Her heel caught on the ground and she tottered, but her other leg found its footing.

"Oi! Get your filthy hands off the imam!"

Rashida sighed. A young man and woman jumped up from the stoop where they'd been lounging. Empty wine jugs rolled on the ground behind them. Neither wore Kharji garb, and Rashida didn't recognise them from her congregation. But their eyes gleamed. Snarls twisted their mouths.

People drifted closer. Some blinked at the commotion. Others glowered and lent their shouts.

"Bloody Kharjis!"

"Leave her alone!"

"Rip her head off!"

"Wait!" Rashida held out her hands. "Listen, I'm sorry for your-"

"Murderer!"

The woman whirled, her fingers opened and closed. They snatched the nearest weapon.

"Hey!" The fishmonger grabbed but missed. "Give that back!"

She brandished the trout, swung it round, hurled it at Rashida. The imam swivelled at the waist and it swam past her face. The blacksmith caught it in hers instead. She roared and vaulted over a collection of hammers, chisels, and tongs. Rashida thanked Allat that the smith didn't grab one of those on her way.

"You hit me!"

"I was aiming for her!"

A dozen more voices joined the din. The Kharji drunks threw the first punches, and others followed. Fists, feet, and missiles rained everywhere.

"In the name of the One Goddess, please-"

"Screw your goddess!"

Two bodies barged past Rashida, locked in a clinch. The inebriated Kharji woman took a kick that launched her over the fishmonger's table. A few wise words weren't going to fix this… The imam hastened away.

"Murderer!"

"Argh!"

Hands grabbed Rashida's turban from behind and snagged her hair with it. Rashida writhed. The turban came free. She spun around, seized it. The other woman's eyes blazed.

"Let go!"

"Kharji filth! Hanging's too good for you! We should burn you like you burned my cousin!"

Rashida yanked but the woman's fingers tightened and crumpled the turban's folds. Grime smeared its white cloth. They tugged back and forth, shouted till their words lost sense. Then the male drunkard slammed into the woman. She let go of the turban, Rashida backpedalled with it, and the two combatants rolled around in front of her.

The imam raised her hand, opened her mouth. The man and woman thumped each other's ribs. Rashida turned away. An elbow whacked her in the face and sent her spinning. She almost dropped the turban, crushed it in her grasp to keep hold of it. Her other hand went to her cheek. It came away red. She pressed down on the wound and ran.

A pair of peacekeepers charged past her. One's shoulder clipped her, but she recovered and kept going, careened through the streets of Lemstras like a lunatic. Faces flashed past. A few grinned. Shouts echoed behind her but the city swallowed their words.

She reached the masjid and panted outside it for a while. Rashida realised she still clutched her turban. She winced at its state, but put it back on her head and arranged it as best she could without a mirror.

The imam entered Allat's house, quickened her pace. It was almost empty at that hour. If she made it past the main prayer area, got to her study, she could-

"Imam Rashida!"

"What happened?"

Rashida Al-Taquba stopped and sighed. Two young women knelt nearby. Both sprang out of the prayer pose and rushed towards her.

"You're bleeding!"

Fatima pulled a handkerchief from her sleeve and handed it to the imam. Rashida dabbed her cheek, grimaced, and pressed down on the cut.

"Who did this?" Yasmin's fists clenched.

"A woman. In the market. Her-"

"Take us there. Point her out and I'll smash her nose."

"I'll break her back." Fatima mimed something that might've been a wrestling hold.

"Don't be foolish. We can't attack infidels in the street like common criminals."

"Allat would want her punished," Yasmin said.

"The One Goddess can see to that herself."

"Barzik Khan wouldn't let her get away with this," Fatima said. "Or the mawlana. They'd cut her down, like the infidels in Traverd."

"Did you hear about that, Imam Rashida?" Yasmin's face lit up. "They put the village to the sword and torch…"

Rashida pursed her lips.

"Don't believe infidel rumours. The Khan's a pious man. He wouldn't go to war unless the non-believers provoked him. And the mawlana communes with Allat herself…"

"But-"

"No! There must be no violence in Lemstras. Our brothers and sisters here are merchants and craftsmen, not warriors."

"Imam, we can't-"

"Finish your prayers. Now."

The imam went into her study and shut herself inside. She turned her injured cheek to the mirror, touched it, and swore.

Rashida Al-Taquba prayed that when the day came, when Allat visited her judgement on the unbelievers and crushed them all, that wretched woman would die in particular agony.

• • •

"Keste?" Katrina knocked on the door. "Keste Humwolt?"

Silas set the horses grazing and joined her in front of the shack. Something creaked. He touched Katrina's shoulder, nodded towards the window. The shutters were open a crack. An eye blinked in the gap, behind wisps of bone-white hair.

"Have you killed it yet?"

"No," Katrina said. "We-"

"I'm not comin' out till you've killed it. I'm not endin' up like poor Mulberry."

"What happened?" Silas moved forward and the eye squinted at him. "The kid at the inn didn't know-"

"That Hindra boy doesn't know how to find his arse with both hands. So it didn't eat him then?"

"No, he-"

"Good. He's a nice lad, just thick as pigswill. Told him to run for help, soon as I heard him goin' by in the lane."

"Something attacked you?"

"Not me. Mulberry. My cat. Heard him hissin', wailin' in the middle of the night. I went to the window and saw it."

"Out here?" Katrina pointed across the road, where their horses munched the grass.

"Around the back. A horrible thin', standin' over him like a… a demon. Mulberry was… Blood everywhere. Drippin' from its fangs. It looked up at me with these big yellow eyes…"

"Did it try to get inside?"

"I… I don't know. I shut the window and hid in the chest. Stayed there till I heard the birds and knew it was mornin'."

"We'll take a look."

The eye disappeared, the gap disappeared, and a latch clunked into place. Katrina went around the shack. Silas followed, began to draw his sword. She glanced back at him and shook her head.

"Bludgeon?" he said.

"Neither."

On the other side, Keste's eye reappeared between the back window's shutters. Silas nodded to her. Katrina walked over to the red and ginger mess twenty feet from the shack. Mulberry's innards littered the ground. It was hard to believe so much had come from one cat.

Katrina's gaze darted back and forth. She looked up, towards the bushes, then went to them.

"Recognise it?" She pulled aside a clump of vegetation, exposed the shapes printed on the dirt beneath.

"Fox tracks?"

"I told you. This is what it's like most of the time. Animals scare people in the night, and they'll swear they've seen a beast from the bowels of hell. Cats, foxes… Once it was a bear. Couldn't blame them for that one. Ran into it in the forest, and it wasn't much better than facing a monster."

"What happened?"

"Backed away, slowly."

"You or the bear?"

A smile flitted across her lips. They went to the window.

"It was a fox that killed your cat," Katrina said.

"Oh…"

The breeze picked up, and the shack's planks groaned to fill the silence until Katrina spoke.

"We'll be-"

"I can bury him," Silas said. "If you want…"

Katrina looked at him, and he waited for her to chastise him. To say a pair of monster hunters had better things to do than go around digging feline graves.

"Thank you, young man. That'd… Please. If you would. There's a shovel by the outhouse."

Katrina von Talhoffer leaned against the shack, crossed her arms, and nodded towards it. Silas got the spade. He found a spot in the shade of two trees, cleared away russet leaves. The dirt was soft and it didn't take long.

"He was a good cat. Always kept the mice away."

Silas turned, wiped his brow. Keste's hair, eyes, skin, and smock were so close in hue they made her a daylight ghost. A box lay at her feet.

"Let's put him in there," she said. "So the foxes won't get at him."

He nodded. Silas gathered the remains with the shovel and scraped away the crimson soil. Keste averted her eyes till he was done, then helped him seal the box. Soon only a mound of dirt marked Mulberry's demise.

"Someone around here must have a litter," Silas said. "I'm sure you could…"

"No. I won't get another cat." She brushed her cheek. A lock clung beneath her eye. "I'll get a dog. A big, vicious brute. The kind that eats foxes."

They walked Keste back to the shack. She opened the front window's shutters and watched them ride off.

"Where now?" Silas said, after a while.

"We'll try our luck in town."

・・・

Rayya's dreams tumbled away. Her eyelids trembled and the light sealed them again. Why was her bed so strange? Memories washed over her, one by one, and their current swept her towards wakefulness. Her room. Clara's. Ghadi's house. Oh… Lencia.

She sat up on the dead woman's bedclothes.

Clara! Where was-

The door opened. Rayya's lungs froze. She scooted backwards, away from whatever had come for her. Kharjis wielding swords and torches… Purple monsters… Peacekeepers who'd drag her off to the gallows… Lencia, eyes glowering in what was left of her face…

"Morning."

Clara put a tray down on the bed. Savoury smells wafted. Rayya blinked at her. Clara just smiled, and for the barest instant Rayya Shimud wondered if it had all been a dream. Because Clara's smile, that bowl of golden porridge, didn't belong in the same world where her friend bludgeoned a woman to death. But this was a world where her parents lay beside their gateposts, so maybe everything belonged now.

"Your hand…" Rayya said.

Clara lifted her mitt, turned it this way and that. Bandages encased everything down to her wrist. Fingers wriggled inside their wrappings.

"Hurt it," Clara said.

"In the fight?"

"Yeah."

"Let me see…"

Clara's hand drew back.

"It's fine. Really. Eat, before it gets cold."

Rayya opened her mouth to say she wasn't hungry, but her stomach rumbled. She picked up the spoon. Porridge baked her tongue and something crunched between her teeth. She swallowed it down. Her friend had a lot to learn about cracking eggs…

Clara opened a trunk while Rayya ate. She rummaged inside, tossed clothes in all directions. Rayya thought of chiding her. But why did it matter, after what they'd done? Clara Mandrake found a pair of gloves. Big, fat things. She put them on and they fit over her bandages.

"Want anything?"

Clara gestured at mounds of breeches, jerkins, socks, and undergarments. Rayya shook her head. She finished her breakfast, picked up the tray, then put it back down on the bed. Clara went out into the main room. Rayya paused at the threshold. She clenched and unclenched her fists, took a deep breath, and stepped through.

Redness stained the floor, the rug, the chairs. But Lencia was gone and Rayya exhaled.

"Where…?"

She shook her head. It didn't matter. Rayya took her clothes off the rack, pulled them on.

Clara opened the front door and they stepped into the morning.

. . .

"One girl, in all of that…"

Jasmina sighed. Fahmaia nodded, though she only half-heard her. This hilltop wasn't as lofty, the scene before her far less vast. But Lemstras sprawled to the horizon and she shivered. If they failed… No eyes gleamed among the clouds. Yet she imagined Allat's hand all the same, poised to grind the city till all its buildings and denizens were just a smear on the landscape.

"There are believers here," the mawlana said. "Our brothers and sisters. They'll help us do the Goddess' will. And…"

At the edge of the city, the maimed men and woman passed a set of stables. People stared at them. Some spoke, gestured. The trio talked with them and gesticulated with their stumps. Their voices didn't reach the hilltop, but their meaning did. The story of the swamp and their suffering. When it was done, an old man beckoned. He led them along the road. They disappeared under a marble arch which might once have been part of a wall. Fahmaia prayed Allat would them show mercy in whatever lives remained for them.

"Parmeen, Maalam… You're the best riders."

The pair exchanged looks with Jasmina and Azim. After a moment, all four of them nodded.

"Yes, mawlana." Maalam glanced at the stables.

"You'll need us," Parmeen said. "We're few enough…"

"That's why you must ride. And two are safer on their travels."

They went down to the road. People clustered here and there around the stable buildings. Workers tended to the animals, while others loitered. A few conversations died when the Kharjis drew near.

"We want to buy horses," Fahmaia said. "Two of them."

A man and woman whispered nearby. Both wore doublets with elaborate sleeves, and gold glittered on their fingers. The woman's voice rose.

"…their money's just as good… I'll take them if you won't…"

She came over and looked Fahmaia up and down. Her gaze lingered on the mawlana's mask before it met her eyes.

"Ride or pull?"

"Ride."

"This way."

She led the Kharjis to the stalls, pointed out a mare and a stallion. Fahmaia stood back while her warriors inspected the animals — from hoof to tooth.

"How much?"

The merchant named her price. Fahmaia laughed. Numbers went back and forth. It was a long time since she'd haggled. Kharjis almost threw their wares at her, ever since her markings appeared. But her childhood in the bazaars lingered at the back of her mind. Those skills hadn't faded.

Their prices met. Hands shook. Minutes later, Parmeen and Maalam rode away.

"I've heard there's a masjid in the city," Fahmaia said.

"Like a temple for your lot?" the merchant said.

"Yes."

"Yeah, think so. Somewhere in the east quarter. The market-traders and shopkeepers around there can point you towards it."

"Thank you."

The three Kharjis passed through the arch's shadows, into the noise and stink of Lemstras.

"Hey!" A woman in a blue and black tabard jogged over to them at the first crossroads. The butt of her halberd tapped the ground. "No swords."

"Excuse me?" Fahmaia had to stop her hand from going to the hilt of Jamsheed's weapon.

"No one 'cept peacekeepers can wear anything bigger than a knife. Mayor's orders."

"What's the difference between a long knife and a short sword?" Azim said.

"My halberd, up your arse."

He took half a step forward. The peacekeeper's left leg crept back into a combat stance. Fahmaia put her hand on Azim's chest.

"We've only just arrived," she said. "We didn't know."

"Fair enough. Don't blame you for wanting sharp steel on the road. But…"

"We're looking for the masjid."

"That where you'll be staying?"

"We hope so."

"I'll take you. Make sure there's no trouble."

The woman marched them down streets and alleys, through a marketplace where stall-keepers and shoppers stared.

"More bloody Kharjis…"

"Bandits, the lot of 'em…"

"Want to buy some fish? Even your goddess would love these trout!"

The masjid was larger than Fahmaia expected. Atop its steps, marble slabs flanked the entrance. Each supported a pair of feet, sculpted from the same rock.

"Smashed the statues when they bought the place." The peacekeeper shrugged. Her halberd prodded the stone that capped one of the ankles. "Ask me, I thought those gods, or heroes, or whatever they were, brightened the place up."

A seagull squawked overhead.

"Stash your weapons in your lodgings, till you're leaving the city."

"We will. Thank you."

The peacekeeper stood back, and the three Kharjis entered Allat's house.

• • •

The roar came on the wind. Voices melded into a tumult greater than any Clara had heard in her entire life, even at the height of the festival when wine and cider flowed. How many throats did it take to make that much noise? A thousand? A million?

She and Rayya looked at one another.

"Hogmire?" Rayya said.

"Must be."

"Sounds like a battle…"

Shrieks and war cries echoed in Clara's brain. But this wasn't the same. It came at them again, and there was joy amid the ferocity. Their steps quickened. They mounted a rise, and the first buildings lay in front of them. A vista of rooftops rolled away.

People milled around where the road became Hogmire. Two leaned on staves. Another's arm hung inside a sling. One woman held a bloody handkerchief to her nose.

"…should've kicked him right in the…"

"..bowk me dose…"

"…if the bastards win this one, they'll never shut their…"

Clara and Rayya passed between them. A man looked around, then planted himself in front of the girls.

"You two can't play." Gums flapped where his front teeth should've been. "Too small. They'll smash you."

"Oh, bullcrap!" a woman said. She clasped her upper arm, wrenched it, and grimaced when it popped into place. "I wasn't much bigger at my first match. Small and agile. Would've scored too, if some tosser hadn't stamped on my head."

"We just want to get to The Cracked Crown," Clara said.

"Too small." The man crossed his arms, shook his head.

Clara's vision flashed. She'd pull off her glove, tear the bandages away, shove five black blades through his… Those images, impulses, would've frightened her once. It was hard to care about dark thoughts when claws had sprouted from your fingers. She forced them back down. But her eyeballs burned.

"Get out of our way."

She glared up at him.

"Clara…" Rayya touched her arm.

The man blinked, averted his gaze.

"Whatever. You get broken into little pieces, don't come crying to me."

Clara moved around him.

"Wait!" The woman still clutched her injured limb, but pointed with the toe of her boot. "You have to pick a side. Even if you don't play."

"Have to," a man said. Dark red coloured half his grey locks and a quarter of his face. He swayed till his neighbour steadied him. "Folk come to watch, get caught up in the excitement, and jump in. If they're not in colours, causes all sorts of trouble."

Two crates stood side-by-side. Both held piles of sackcloth.

"Purple or green?" the woman said.

A couple of the onlookers wore armless tunics. More of the garments lay in heaps at the others' feet.

"Purple?" Clara said.

A few cheered. One youth booed, till someone clipped him round the ear.

"They're for Hogmire!" The gums shaped a grin. He rapped his fist on the purple saltire which bound his torso. "Still say you're too small, but at least you're with us."

The woman with the relocated arm chanted. A couple more joined in.

"Hogmire, Hogmire, Hogmire! Hog! Hog! Hog!"

"Here." The gum-grinning man held sackcloth in each hand.

Clara took hers, brought it to her face. The purple smelled sweet but sharp. Her nose tapped it and came away damp. Some of the colour stuck to her gloves. She shrugged and put it on. Rayya did the same, then pulled her plait out from under it. The fit wasn't bad.

"The pub's over that way…" The woman pointed with her boot. She bent the leg back as though readying a kick, pivoted on the ball of her foot, and extended it again. "But if you want to join in, Grunshire's goal's there. See the flag?"

A green pennant flapped atop a spire.

"Since you're with us, your goal's…" Another bend, pivot, kick. "…on the other side of town. Can't see any of the flags from here, but you'll know it when you see it. It's the temple. Ball through the doorway to score. Played football before?"

Both girls shook their heads.

"Use your feet on the ball-"

"That's why we call it football." The gum-grinning man tapped the side of his nose. "But you can use your hands on those Grunshire wankers. Knees, elbows, and teeth as well, if you've a mind to."

"Okay…?" Rayya said.

"Good luck!" The woman released her own arm, grimaced, and patted each girl's shoulder.

"Hogmire, Hogmire, Hogmire! Hog! Hog! Hog!"

The battle cry chased them into the streets.

• • •

Rashida looked from the book to her parchment, as though her gaze might carry Allat's scripture across, give it shape in the infidels' script, meaning in their tongue. But the One Goddess didn't oblige with a miracle. And so the imam mulled over sacred verse, weighed up several possible translations, wrote one down, and struck it out.

She rolled the quill between her fingers.

It was impossible. How could she convey the power and beauty of the Goddess' voice, render it in some lesser language? She should just consign the manuscript to the fire… No. Allat smiled when infidels became believers, and divine words would achieve that faster than any preacher's passion or clever arguments. But only if those infidels comprehended them.

Imam Rashida prayed, wrote, rewrote, and gazed at the translation. She allowed herself a smirk. It read even better than she'd hoped.

"Allatu Akbar."

She dipped the quill again, but voices clamoured outside in the prayer room. Rashida frowned. If the youngsters were gossiping again, spreading stories about Barzik Khan and his 'beard of doom'...

The imam went to the mirror. Checked herself for ink marks. Arranged her turban. Assumed a grim expression. When her reflection appeared ready to put the fear of the Goddess into them, she opened the door and strode forth.

"What's all this—"

They stared at her. Fatima and Yasmin were there, with a few more of the congregation, and their mouths gaped. A woman stood in their midst. Dirt and dust clung to her travel garb, yet when she bowed her head there was such grace in the movement that she might've worn the finest silks from Khalib.

"Imam Rashida?"

"Y... Yes."

Rashida's brain tried to return the gesture, but her body didn't respond. The woman's face... Holy words flowed upon her skin. The same verse the imam had just translated passed across the stranger's cheek.

"I'm Fahmaia Hashad. My companions and I request your hospitality, if you'll have us."

The mawlana! A woman with Allat's blessing on her very flesh...

Fahmaia's expression didn't change. A smile hovered on the mawlana's lips, as though it might last forever. But another stranger coughed into her fist.

"Oh... Of... Of course. We'd be honoured. Yasmin, Fatima... Show them to the dormitory. I fear our quarters here are humble. If you'd prefer, I... My home is yours, mawlana."

"Thank you, imam. Truly. But places in the masjid are more than enough. May we speak?"

"Yes. Please... My study."

The mawlana passed her pack to her comrades. They followed Yasmin and Fatima to the stairway. Chatter erupted behind Fahmaia Hashad before she'd gone more than a few feet. Rashida shut the door behind them and hoped it'd muffle the worst of it.

She indicated the armchairs by the fireplace. When Fahmaia sat in the less comfortable of the two, she bit her tongue. If Rashida suggested she take the other instead, would she frown? Denounce the imam for her hedonism? But if she didn't offer... Rashida envisioned hellfire.

The mawlana let out a sigh and settled into the seat.

"Was your journey long?"

"Not so long, but hard and harsh."

"Would you take food and wine?"

"If it's no trouble, imam."

"Rashida, please."

She opened her cupboard. A few moments later, she set a goblet and a saucer of baklava on the table at the mawlana's elbow. Fahmaia sipped the wine. Then she removed her glove, unveiled more of the dancing scripture, and took a piece of pastry between thumb and forefinger.

"This is... wonderful."

"A gift from an elderly sister." Rashida extended her fingers, curled them back, then extended them again. "Forgive me... but may I..."

"Of course."

Fahmaia held out her hand. Rashida's fingers brushed her skin. The script continued to move beneath, and she felt nothing but flesh.

"Allat…"

Fahmaia took another sip. The goblet hid part of her face, and the imam's words came easier.

"Mawlana… The stories they've told, about the village…"

"Traverd?"

"They say the Khan's warriors attacked it."

"It was so."

"Did the villagers… attack one of the faithful? Harm our brothers and sisters?"

Fahmaia sighed. She set aside her cup, leaned in closer to the imam.

"The Goddess sent me a vision while I knelt at prayer. Her judgement looms over the world."

"Allat be praised!"

At last! She'd annihilate the non-believers and… Fahmaia's eyes glinted. The smile seeped from Rashida's lips.

"She intends to destroy the whole world for its sins."

"But… Even the faithful?"

"Everyone will perish. Such is her punishment for what we've allowed to happen."

The imam's brain throbbed with its own heartbeat. She tried to speak but nothing came out. Allat was merciful! She loved the Kharji people! How could this-

"Barzik and I carried out a great sacrifice to earn her forgiveness. Traverd."

"The whole village?"

"Every man, woman, and child. Allat demanded no less."

Rashida's spine crumpled. She slumped back into the armchair. Fahmaia touched the imam's knee and she flinched.

"But we failed. A girl... Clara... escaped into the forest and eluded us. She's come to Lemstras. We must complete the sacrifice."

"You'll... You'll kill her? Here, in the city?"

"We must. For the Goddess. But we'll need your help to find her in this vast place. You and the brothers and sisters of your masjid."

Rashida Al-Taquba stared at the mawlana. Scripture blared in the imam's eyes and mangled her thoughts.

• • •

"Stop!" The woman stood in the middle of the road, and took up a stance that turned her limbs into pink extensions of the green X on her sackcloth tunic. "You can't ride those in there. Not with a match on."

"A match?" Katrina dismounted. "Sounds more like a riot."

"The best footie always does."

Silas jumped down from the saddle. The woman looked from his weapons to Katrina's.

"And you won't be wearing those. Hoggies are a bunch of cheating wankers, but-"

"Piss off!"

"She's right!"

"What about last time-"

"...a cow..."

"...club with nails in..."

"…dressed in full plate…"

"…spikes! Don't forget the spikes…"

"…had a dog fetch the ball and run off with…"

"…nice dog though…"

"Shut up!" The road-blocking woman glared at the others. "Like I was saying… Even Hoggies don't allow weapons in the game."

"We're not here to play football," Katrina said.

"Doesn't matter. Anyone out on the street obeys the rules. No horses, no weapons. If we let you two gallop around, swinging your swords-"

"We wouldn't-"

"…there'd be chaos. Chaos!"

"Fine." Katrina turned to Silas. "Give me your weapons. I'll watch the horses till it's finished. Get us a room and ask around for any news."

"Okay." He undid his belt and passed it over.

"Green or purple?" The woman relinquished her X-shape and went over to the crates.

Silas glanced at his mentor. Katrina shrugged.

"Purple," he said.

"Bastard…" She grinned and handed him the sack. "Hope our lot blackens both your eyes."

Most of the bystanders jeered at him. A few cheered and pumped their fists in the air. Those ones wore more bruises and bandages.

"You played football before?"

"Yeah…"

His ribs twinged where Cryze once stomped him, on her way to scoring yet another goal.

"See those purple flags? That's where you Hoggies're scoring. Our goal's off that way."

Silas donned the tunic.

"If you get involved," Katrina said, "do well. If the locals take a liking to you…"

"Right."

Someone shouted, and everyone else joined in.

"Grunnies're gonna kill ya! Grunnies're gonna kill ya!"

"Hogmire, Hogmire, Hogmire! Hog! Hog! Hog!"

Silas jogged into the town.

• • •

"Watch out!"

Clara pulled Rayya aside. The woman barrelled out of the alleyway, clutching the lower half of her face. Blood poured between her fingers. The corners of her tunic still showed Grunshire's colour, but reds and browns smothered the rest.

"Are you okay?" Rayya said.

The woman didn't look at her. She fell against a wall, staggered off it, and careened down the street. Something glinted on the ground behind her. Clara squatted and examined it.

"Hey! You dropped your… tooth?"

The woman kept going. Clara shrugged, then she and Rayya did the same. They passed homes and shops. Many bore a purple X on their doors, walls, or the shutters that sealed their windows. Various hands had scribbled graffiti in the same hue. Several words and sentences blurred into blotches where stone or wood ended. Exhortations for Hogmire's players, profanities for Grunshire's.

"Local advantage," Clara said.

"But Grunshire won't have to clean their whole town up tomorrow."

"Oh. Yeah…"

Voices raged in the distance and reached them as wordless echoes. The girls worked their way through streets and alleys, till they met another player in the lane between two houses. This one wore a purple cross and a red forehead.

"She had a horseshoe nailed to the bottom of her boot. Cheater!"

They turned side-on and squeezed past.

"Cheater…"

After a few minutes, the shouts came clearer but quieter — as though that mass of noise had shattered and sown Hogmire with its fragments.

"Where is it?" from one direction.

"There!" from another. "No, wait… It's just a rat!"

"I think-" Rayya said.

A woman tore round the corner. Her legs wove this way and that, like the steps of a dance, and muscles thumped along their lengths. A Hogmire tunic flapped around her torso. A brown blob moved at her feet.

She glanced up, grinned, and came towards them. Clara yelled.

"Look out!"

The Grunshire player emerged from an alleyway. He hunched over, panted, but launched himself with a burst of energy. The woman looked at him. Then, an instant before he ploughed into her, she kicked the brown thing. It bounced down the road and bumped against Clara's boot.

"Huh…"

She blinked at it. Trails of stitches laced the object, bound leathery pieces together.

"Clara!"

Her head snapped back up. The woman was on the ground. The man lumbered towards the girls. His eyes narrowed.

"Wait!" Rayya said. "We're just-"

Clara pushed her out of his path. The man snorted, footfalls pounded behind them. His fist swung. And Clara Mandrake's world exploded.

12

Silas ran, but he wasn't fast enough. The Grunshire player punched the girl and the impact spun her around. Silas caught her shoulders. Blood spurted from her mouth, slashed across his tunic. Her feet stumbled, shuffled, and snagged the ball. The girl's eyes fluttered, then hardened like jewels.

"Grunnie bounder!" The woman rose and spat.

"Clara, are you-"

"Give it 'ere!" The man swung again.

Silas shoved the girl into her friend's arms. The Grunnie's fist bounced off him instead, and he'd taken harder punches than that. Silas blasted him in the face with a palm strike. His nose squished and leaked. Silas' other hand slapped his ear and he reeled. The Grunnie threw his arms around Silas, pulled him into a clinch. Silas twisted and threw him down. He hit the ground like a sack of turnips, rolled onto his side, groaned.

Clara let loose a shriek, the cry of a hawk that swooped for murder. She leapt at the man and kicked him between the legs. He curled up, shielded his crotch. She kicked his head.

"Clara!" Her friend touched her shoulder. "Don't!"

"Hey…" The woman grasped her other shoulder, turned her. "No time for that, dear. The rest of the green slime'll be here soon."

"Get off-"

She held up her finger. Clara blinked at it. The digit gestured towards the nearest shouts. They couldn't be more than a street or two away.

"This chap…"

"Silas. But-"

"Jessica." She punched his shoulder. "This chap and I will be the muscle. You and…"

"I'm Rayya. But I don't-"

"…look small and nippy enough. We'll take the hits, you dribble the ball, what?"

"Dribble?"

"Kick along."

"I'm not here to play," Silas said. "I just-"

"We're looking for-" Clara said.

"You're wearing our colour, and Hogmire doesn't tolerate slackers. Hurry up!"

Jessica somehow managed to push all three of them at the same time, and spurred them into motion. They ran down an alley together. The ball bounced at Clara's feet, got loose, and Silas nudged it back to her with his instep. They came out into a marketplace. Figures moved among the empty stalls.

"Grunnies!" Jessica said.

"Hoggies!" a woman said.

Jessica shoulder barged her and she tumbled over a table. Another player went for Clara, for the pig's bladder. Silas hit her with a flying knee. Her jaw crunched. He winced. The four of them ran on, between the stalls. Voices clamoured on all sides.

Grunshire players massed in front of them, across the mouth of a street.

"This way!"

Jessica swerved to the right and swept them along with her, like a sheepdog manoeuvring a flock. The Grunnies advanced. More cries broke out. A band of players in Hogmire purple charged their flank, and a sea of bodies tangled, tumbled, sprawled.

The quartet raced down another road, past shopfronts where scents of bread and roasted meat lingered. A Grunshire player sprang from an alcove. She slammed into Silas and they embraced, banged into Clara and Rayya. Clara yelped and the ball rolled.

"I've got it!" Jessica said.

The woman's forehead bumped Silas' skull, but she didn't get enough weight behind it. He rocked, planted his feet, tossed her away. She rolled, pounced at his legs. Clara kicked her chin and dropped her.

Two Grunnies wrestled with Jessica. She thrashed in their grasp, but her foot captured the ball and rolled it backwards. Rayya intercepted it, lost it, regained it. Silas elbowed the bigger man. The Grunnie punched him back, but Silas took that on his other elbow. The man wailed. His fingers uncurled. Silas hit him three more times and he fell onto his butt.

"Done?"

The man looked up at him, nodded, and held his jaw. His ally had Jessica in a headlock. Silas went for them, but Jessica suplexed the Grunnie. Wood smashed and the Grunshire player disappeared through the window.

Rayya dribbled the ball, kicked it to Silas. He ran it along one wing of their group while Jessica took the other. The girls' legs pumped and they kept pace in the middle.

"There it is!"

Jessica pointed, but they couldn't've missed it. The temple loomed on the opposite side of the square. Purple banners hung across its grey facade, flags fluttered atop its roof. And half a dozen Grunshire players swarmed around its entrance.

"Kill the Hogs!"

"Green rage!"

"Yaaarrrrrrrrrgggggghhhhh!"

• • •

Rashida picked up the wine jug. When had it become so light? The stopper popped and she upended it over her goblet. Liquid poured, trickled, dripped. She shook the jug a few times. Darkness rained and rippled. A half-empty goblet was a forlorn thing.

She sipped, but it cloyed and choked her now. The imam stared at the armchair where the mawlana had sat. Fahmaia Hashad's voice was gone, but its echoes still smothered the study and squashed Rashida against her seat.

It couldn't be right. *Couldn't*. Allat would never...

Again the images came. The mawlana's words wove them till the imam almost believed the vision had been her own. The One Goddess' hand descended to annihilate all the peoples of the world.

Fahmaia was wrong! She'd missed something... She'd...

Rashida drained her goblet. She reached for the jug, picked it up before she remembered, and put it back down.

Allat wouldn't command them to slaughter a village. Not unprovoked! The ancient prophetesses wielded blades and waged wars, brought infidel temples crashing down. But those enemies earned their fate. As did their descendants when they dared fight against believers. Traverd had committed no such crime, no persecution.

And the girl. Clara…

Rashida's fingers tightened around the goblet. A murder here, in her own city, where the unbelievers already despised them. Madness! It'd bring ruin to their masjid, their community.

But the mawlana… Again that face, those markings, hovered before her. The One Goddess had blessed Fahmaia Hashad. Inscribed words on her skin and made the woman her champion. How could she be so wrong, bring about something so monstrous?

The cup dropped from Rashida's hand.

It was a test! The greatest of all tests. It fell to her, a humble imam, to do Allat's will now the mawlana's vision was clouded. Rashida stood. Her foot knocked the goblet aside, sent it spinning. She paced the study.

This was her duty to Allat, to the masjid the Goddess gave her. Rashida Al-Taquba would thwart Fahmaia. She'd prevent this atrocity, and then… The imam's fingers traced invisible lines on her cheek. She smiled. How her congregants would marvel, if Allat rewarded her so. If scripture flowed on their imam's visage…

• • •

Clara's eyes narrowed, her blood pumped. The world compressed into red faces and green crosses. Two of the Grunnies went for Jessica, three for Silas and the ball. The sixth charged at the girls.

Rayya took half a step back. But when Clara didn't budge, she held her ground. Clara had the best friend in the world. And she wasn't going to let anyone hurt her.

Clara strode towards him. The Grunnie's mane flopped around and revealed two widening eyes. He was a stick insect of a man, but still twice as heavy as her. Clara's right hand twitched. Her claws tingled inside the glove and bandages.

He didn't lower his shoulder or pull his arm back to strike. The Grunshire player was just going to mow her down, plough through Rayya, and take them out of the game. But Clara Mandrake had blood on her hands. She didn't mind a little more. When he was almost on her, she fell backwards, braced herself against the ground, and thrust her heel up into his crotch.

The Grunnie doubled over. His eyes bulged, face deepened to a near-purple. He collapsed onto her but Clara's boots held him off. She grabbed his mane, yanked him, and he slumped on his side. The footballer wheezed.

"Hoggie…"

Jessica was down. Both Grunnies booted her. Clara went towards them but the woman called out, pointed even as she shielded herself.

"Ball!"

Silas wove between the three players, dragged the bladder this way and that. One of them slid for it but missed. Another grabbed at him, caught his hand. The third dived and tackled his shins. The ball bounced away. The three Grunnies scrambled for it but Silas' arms and legs ensnared them. All four footballers struggled on the ground, a sixteen-limbed beast.

Clara ran. The two on Jessica peeled away from her. Jessica tripped one, and he landed on his chin. The other raced for the ball. Her eyes met Clara's. Girl and woman pounced. The woman went for the pig's bladder, but Clara Mandrake went for her. She leapt at the Grunnie, kicked and grabbed and gouged. The woman was bigger. Stronger. In a moment she'd batter her off or throw her aside. But Clara only needed one moment.

"Rayya!"

Her friend was already moving. The woman lurched that way with Clara clinging to her, but toppled and had to plant her feet to stay up. Rayya kicked. The ball flew at the temple, struck stone, bounced off.

"Sorry!"

Rayya sprang at the bladder, recaptured it. She kicked again. It arced up high, dropped, and disappeared through the doorway.

"Damn…" The woman set Clara down and sighed. "Good game, anyway."

"Good show, Rayya!" Jessica lifted the girl into a hug.

"Breed them young in Hogmire, they do." The man Clara kicked came up to them, and she prepared for violence. But he laughed and ruffled her hair. "Good pair of legs on this one."

Bells rang out above, echoed through the square. A man in purple robes emerged from the building and held the ball over his head.

"Hogmire wins!" he said.

Cheers, groans, and hundreds of drumming feet mingled with the bells. Players surged towards the temple from all sides.

"Hogmire, Hogmire, Hogmire! Hog! Hog! Hog!"

"Next time, Grunnies."

"Anyone seen my husband? If you stomped him to death, you're doing his chores…"

"Who scored it?"

"We should play with the whole pig next time…"

"…punched him in the face…"

"…threw me through a window…"

Jessica took off her tunic. Everyone else was doing that too. They turned the garments inside out, then put them back on. Clara and Rayya did the same. Soon there was just plain sackcloth on display, albeit with splashes and splodges of crimson.

"Are you okay?" Silas was beside them now.

"Yeah," Clara said. "Thanks for…"

"No problem."

"Oi! Hoggie!" One of the Grunnies he'd wrestled came up behind him and slapped him on the back. "Pub! I'm buying!"

"Well, I-"

"No arguin'!"

Silas shrugged, nodded to the girls, and a pack of players swept him off.

"Are you two coming to The Bleeding Boulder?" Jessica said. "Small beer and pies await."

"We're supposed to see someone at The Cracked Crown," Clara said. "Is that…?"

"Across town. Want me to take you there?"

"If you don't mind…" Rayya said.

"Dear, after that goal, I'd take you all the way to Kessalonia."

Players thronged the streets, leaned on walls, lounged in doorways, sat on windowsills. Blood and bruises, grins and laughter, brightened every face.

"…she kicked me twice!"

"That means she fancies you, mate! Get in there!"

They passed jugs back and forth. A woman offered one to Clara, but even the fumes made her eyes water.

"No, thanks…"

Boys and girls in aprons walked among them. They handed out crimped oblongs from their trays, and gravy mingled with the bloodstains.

"One for you, miss?"

The boy might've been a bit older than Clara, but he gazed at her tunic as though she were a warrior goddess.

"Sure. Thank you."

She took one, passed it to Rayya, and looked at Jessica — but the woman had commandeered a jug from somewhere, and glugged that instead. Clara picked up another pie, bit into it. Pastry crumbled. Gravy spilled onto her tongue, along with chunks of steak and kidney. Her face twinged where she'd taken the punch. The cut stung. But it was worth it, and she munched.

"Hogmire, Hogmire, Hogmire! Hog! Hog! Hog!"

"…that bloke what punched me was well nice…"

"…over there, they play with five balls…"

"…just let us pick it up and carry it."

"Couldn't call it football then, could we?"

A mob cavorted outside the pub. Some kicked a pig's bladder about and gave one another the occasional shoulder barge. Piles of sackcloth marked their goal in lieu of a building. Jessica led them around the game, and deflected the ball when it flew at them.

The inside of The Cracked Crown was just as rowdy. But Jessica muscled her way to the bar, and the girls stuck close behind her.

"Two small beers and an ale, my good woman."

Jessica's coins plinked down on the wood. The barmaid scraped them towards herself, dropped the money into her apron pocket, and slid three drinks in the opposite direction. She was already serving the next customer when Clara spoke.

"Is Jarbul here?"

"In the cellar…" She wielded a collection of tankards and didn't turn around. "…getting another barrel. Shouldn't be long."

"Thanks."

"Good game, you two." Jessica held out her drink.

Their mugs tapped, contents wobbled. Clara drank and oats filled her mouth. It was like drinking a meal.

"Jarb! Kid over there wants you!"

A silver-haired black man lumbered behind the bar, a cask on his shoulder. Sinews strained along his arms. He heaved the barrel onto a stand, grimaced, and rubbed his collarbone.

"Jarbul?"

"Yeah?" He leaned on the bar. "Can I help you?"

"I'm Clara. This is Rayya. We know Ghadi."

"Oh…" His whole face twitched. "Has something…? Is Yallis…?"

"They're… They're okay. She…" Nothing seemed adequate, but she pressed on. "She was really good to us. And she said… She said if we came, you could get us on a wagon to Lemstras."

"Huh. You two on your own? No parents?"

"Not anymore." She touched Rayya's arm.

"I'm sorry."

"Her brother lives in the city. If we could get there…"

"Say no more." Jarbul looked across the taproom, put two fingers to his lips, and whistled. "Simon!"

A man plodded to the bar, all hair and beard and belly. He held a tankard in each hand. A gulp finished one, a second the other. He plonked the vessels down.

"Yep?"

"Got space on your wagon for these kids?"

Simon looked down at them, burped, and wiped his mouth.

"Maybe. How much?"

"We… We don't have any money," Clara said. "But we can work! If there's anything…"

"Name a fair price." Jessica reached into her pouch. "I'll pay it."

"We'll pay you back," Rayya said. "When we're in Lemstras, we'll…"

"Won't hear of it. Least I could do for our champion goal-scorer, what?"

"Got bedrolls and stuff?" Simon said.

"Here." She handed over a fistful of coins. "Be a good chap and find them whatever they need."

"Yeah…" He stared at the mound of money in his palm. "Yeah, okay. I'm heading out soon, mind. Meet you here?"

The girls nodded. He plodded away.

"Thank you so much," Rayya said.

"Don't mention it! How about another round while we're waiting?"

• • •

"Hi!" Silas said.

He lifted his head from the table. Katrina's eye glared down at him, and he grinned at her.

"I've been looking for you," she said.

"Sorry! These blokes, they kept buyin' me drinks, because I beat the crap outta them."

"What?"

"Couldn't refuse. Didn't want to be rude. Like you said, they're our arses and ears!" He covered his mouth and belched into his hand. "'Scuse me. Oh, got us a room though."

"How many have you had?"

"Dunno. I'm a monster hunter, not a counting man… A count?"

"If Gunnar could see you…"

"He'd give me another drink."

"I suppose he would."

"I like your scars. Don't think they're ugly, like all the other trainees said. They're… They're… artistic. Like… Like art."

She blinked at him. Or maybe it was a wink. It was hard to tell with her, so Silas winked back just in case. She sighed.

"Get up."

He stood, fell, and she caught him.

"We goin' monster huntin'? I'll get my sword…"

"No. You're going to get some sleep. Where's our room?"

"Upper… Up the stairs. Third room… Fourth… Fourth room? On the… the…"

She sighed.

"I'll find it."

Katrina draped his arm around her neck and they weaved their way across The Bleeding Boulder's taproom.

• • •

Simon's snore buzzed and grated on the other side of the campfire's embers. He may as well've sawed logs, but there was something restful about it all the same. Clara imagined she was camped outside a bear's cave, while the animal hibernated and dreamt within. Rayya's sleep-breaths rippled closer at hand. She lay and listened to them both for a while.

The night was sharper, crisper than usual. Clouds drifted over the moon and stars, but gloom didn't conquer the field. Clara sat up and stared until she understood that the darkness hadn't changed. Her eyes had. They parted shadows, traced shapes the nocturnal realm should've hidden. Was this how cats saw the world? No wonder they smiled, while humans blundered about and bumped into things…

Bushes rustled across the field. Clara got out of her bedroll, pulled off the gloves, unwrapped her hand. Fingers flexed and claws glimmered. They were blacker than the dark, save for the motes of light they'd captured. The flesh behind them had blackened too, as though their essence seeped into her skin, crept back towards the nearest joint of each digit. Blackened and hardened, like nails or... scales?

It didn't matter. Ducks, not chickens.

She trod the grass and it cooled her feet. That noise came again, a susurration amongst the foliage. Then a thump. Clara slipped through the bushes and the deer looked up at her as it lay on its side. Things sprouted from its flank, plants with feathers instead of leaves. Blood trickled over red-brown patches. Clara's claws yearned for the hunter, but they might've been miles away, deep into their sleep. The deer drew a breath and the arrows heaved.

Clara Mandrake stroked its muzzle and drove her claws into its neck. They went in easier than she expected, parted vessels, spilled crimson. It exploded in her nose. Molten metal. But after a moment it subsided, and her nostrils adjusted as her eyes and ears had done. This was her new existence. Sharp senses and sharper claws. What was there to do but accept it?

A musty, wet-fur scent drifted in with the metallic tang. Four eyes glowed in the undergrowth.

"It's yours," she said. "Eat."

She backed away. The wolves watched, waited. At last they came. Their jaws chomped, tore, tasted her kill. Every so often their eyes, noses, teeth tilted up at her. But she made no move and they bit again.

Clara turned to the heavens, closed her eyes.

The silhouette lurked above her bed. Fingertips on her cheek, a tender shiver. The monster was there. Behind the shadow-man, lithe but powerful. A fresh smell. Fur, though not like the wolves'. Impossible. How could new senses penetrate old dreams? But headless chickens ran, dead ducks flew, and girls grew claws.

Ah!

That odour was out in the world too, well beyond the aromas of earth and leaf and ancient wood. Miles from this place where wolves fed.

"Lemstras."

Her whisper crumbled on the breeze. But if she could smell him, perhaps he'd hear her all the same, somewhere in his monster mind.

"I'm going to Lemstras. Find me there."

• • •

Silas opened his eyes to the morning light, closed them again, and wished he were dead. Maybe he was. That'd explain the wasteland festering inside his mouth…

"Drink this."

His lids half-opened. Katrina held out a cup and Silas' brain shuddered. Memories dislodged, tumbled in front of him. Oh, no… No! No! No!

"Take it."

He sat up, clasped the vessel, and spilled a bit on himself. His mouth gaped but only a rasp came out.

"Drink first. Didn't you have hangovers after your fancy banquets?"

Silas swished the water around his cheeks. It was foul, but he swallowed, then swished another mouthful. By the time the cup was empty, he didn't want to hack his own head off anymore. Not until the next memory-avalanche crashed down on his consciousness.

"I…"

"You were drunk. Now you're sober, and we have work to do. Get changed."

Silas stood up. His vision lurched but he fought the nausea back down. He grappled with his sackcloth tunic, got it off, and tossed it aside.

"Did you learn anything over the ale?"

"Er…"

Katrina sighed and scratched the scars on her cheek.

"Today's a local holiday. Most of the townsfolk are in the same state as you." She lifted her patch, massaged her eye. "Plenty of people loitering around the pubs and streets. We can-"

She stared at the floor, grabbed the tunic.

"Where did you get this?"

"Huh? They gave it to-"

"This blood." She traced a rust-coloured line that bisected the saltire. "Whose is it?"

"Oh. A girl. Clara. Why?"

"There are monster traces. Strong ones."

"That's… She got near a monster?"

"She must've. What do you know about her? Is she a local?"

"I don't think so. She was here with her friend… Rayya."

"Get dressed. Now. Someone has to know where she is."

Silas could only nod. He pulled off his clothes, got changed, and wondered what danger Clara had fallen into.

Part 3

Pink and Black

13

Rashida opened the door to the masjid, blinked, and worried she'd forgotten the date. Rows of young men and women knelt in the middle of the chamber. Their lips intoned prayers. The rug-maker's children were there, alongside the cobbler's. Had a festival ambushed her? Because that was the only time she ever noticed them among her congregants. The imam's eyes widened. Those two brawlers from the marketplace knelt there too. They glanced at their neighbours, imitated every word and movement after a moment's hesitation.

More Kharjis sat or stood in groups at the other end of the room. Dozens of murmurs mingled with the holy words.

"...she said the One Goddess would-"

"Fatima!" Rashida grabbed her arm, pulled her away from Yasmin. "Why are you wearing that?"

She jabbed her finger at the woman's belt. Then Yasmin turned, and polished metal gleamed at her waist too.

"Knives!" The imam glared at each of them. "Wearing knives in the masjid, like a pair of robbers!"

"The mawlana's people wear knives." Fatima pulled free and crossed her arms.

"They're…" Rashida bit back a word, pursed her lips, and found another. "…warriors."

"We'll be warriors too. Jasmina says she'll teach us how to defend our brothers and sisters."

"The prophetesses were warriors," Yasmin said. "And the martyrs who died fighting the non-believers."

"They lived among armies. There's no war here in Lemstras."

The girls' eyes glinted, and all arguments, all admonitions froze on the imam's tongue. Rashida went past them, towards the far corner of the prayer hall. Fahmaia Hashad sat cross-legged in front of a drawing stand. She wielded a quill, and the feather soared and swooped. Inked parchments lay around her. Jasmina and Azim passed other pieces to nearby Kharjis. Most had to tear their gazes from the mawlana to look at them.

Rashida crouched and inspected the ones on the floor. Ink glistened. Drying lines formed faces. Each differed in expression, angle, or the whispers of hair that flittered around it. But all showed the same girl.

"This is…"

"Clara," Fahmaia said.

The child's gaze, the shape of her lips… Clara might've been a lost daughter, as dear to Fahmaia as her own soul. Rashida almost cried. But the imam's eyes hardened.

"What do you expect our people to do if they see her? Stab her in the street?"

"If they learn where we may find her, they can come to me, or Jasmina, or Azim. No one else need bloody their hands. But if they must act, Allat will smile upon them." The mawlana's gaze swept her audience. "Clara isn't our enemy. She's a little girl who's suffered more than any child ever should. When we strike, it will be swift and without cruelty. And we'll pray that the One Goddess embraces her."

Several Kharjis nodded. Rashida looked from face to face, and her heart hammered.

"Excuse me, mawlana… I have… I have matters to attend to."

The imam strode across the prayer hall and left the masjid.

• • •

Vasile Zarabanov unlocked the front door of his shop and tossed a coin into the corner. Metal clinked. A copper avalanche clattered all over the floor. Vasile swore. He gathered the coins one by one, groped beneath a herb-laden bookcase for the last, and returned them to the ledge in front of the idol.

The apothecary went behind the counter. He almost called to Sachin, then sighed and went into the stockroom himself. Mugwort… Damn. The jar held enough for one customer. After that, he'd have to root through the cellar if anyone wanted potent dreams or an empty womb.

"Hello?"

A young woman stood in the middle of the shop. She glanced over her shoulder at the wooden idol, as though the goddess of drugs and healing might be about to pounce.

"Do I have to…?"

"Only if you want to," Vasile said.

She rubbed her cheek, reached into her pouch, and found a coin. The apothecary held his breath, but the girl set it down atop the others and money didn't rain.

"What can I help you with?"

"I'm having nightmares. Bad ones…"

"They always are."

"…with platypuses."

He blinked, coughed.

"Are you with child?"

"Huh? No."

"Do you intend to be, any time soon?"

"No! What's that got to do with it?"

"The same herbs do different things. One moment…"

Vasile returned to the back room and transferred the last of the mugwort to a bag. Maybe this was the goddess' revenge for spilling her offerings. He'd have to make a trip to her temple soon, and drop them in the donation box…

"Here you go. Make it into a tea and drink it before bed. You'll have better dreams."

"No platypuses?"

"If there are, you'll know you're dreaming. And you can just give them a good kick."

"Even the blue one?"

"Kick that one twice."

"Thanks!"

The apothecary sat down after she left, and picked up *Eurydice's Concoctions*. He opened it to his bookmark. Old recipes were hit and miss, but it never hurt to peruse a dusty tome every so often.

"You don't have to…"

A female voice drifted through the window. Vasile stood and put the book away.

"Yeah, I do. Today or tomorrow or sometime…"

The door opened.

"… so it might as well be now."

Grey flesh twitched beneath Sachin's eyelids. He scratched a patch of fuzz on his chin and gazed into the shop.

"Morning…" Vasile said. His apprentice blinked in his general direction. "Are you… I mean, are you sure you should be here?"

Chriki stood behind her boyfriend, met the apothecary's eyes, and gave her head a quick shake.

"Have to." Sachin looked up at last. "Going crazy, just sitting around. Doing nothing. When Chriki's at the theatre, I just… I can work."

Vasile Zarabanov bit his cheek. An apprentice with every reason in the world to have his mind elsewhere… One mistake with a mixture… Dead customer… Angry mob… Flaming torches through the window…

The apothecary sighed. He'd have to keep an eye on Sachin Shimud's work today.

"Yeah, okay."

"Thanks. What needs doing?"

"We're out of mugwort up here. Check the cellar and…"

Sachin's whole face gaped. His eyes goggled, and no longer focused on Vasile. His mouth widened. Lips quivered. More voices came through the window, penetrated the sudden quietness.

"I think it's this one."

"Is that an apothecary's sign? It looks more like…"

"Yeah. That's a bottle, and a pestle and mortar."
"Oh. Like the one I…"
"Yeah."
"Oh."

Sachin Shimud rotated on the spot, like the shadow on a sundial, and his brown face paled. Chriki took a step nearer, put out her hands as if to brace him when he fell. But he stayed up. The door opened and revealed two girls. Sachin's body shook.

"Rayya!"

One of the girls darted at him. They threw their arms around each other, wailed, and babbled. A million words bounced around the store. They dissolved amid sobs and Vasile couldn't make out a single full sentence. He looked at Chriki, mouthed at her.

"Isn't she supposed to be…?"

Chriki looked from him to her boyfriend and the girl, then back again. Her eyes were bigger than Sachin's had been. The actress' shoulders rose and she held her hands to either side, palms upwards.

A man appeared in the doorway. He stepped into the shop, paused, and stared at the scene in front of him. His face reddened. His gaze flicked away, and he pretended to examine a display of colourful bottles. Vasile coughed.

"Sachin. Why… Why don't you, er… go upstairs? Help yourself to… to whatever."

"Y… Yeah. Thanks…"

Tears streamed down his cheeks. The girl's too. He led her to the stairs, went up, and kept looking behind as though she'd disappear the second he took his eyes off her. The other girl moved that way, then stopped.

"I… I should let them…"

She looked around the shop, at Vasile. He could only shrug at Chriki.

"Let's go get you something to eat," the actress said.

"Oh… Okay."

The customer watched until the door closed behind them. He waited a few more moments, came to the counter, glanced behind him.

"Here… I've got… I need a…" He coughed. His face shifted to a deeper red. When he spoke again, he whispered. "I've got… bits… growing on… on me bits."

Vasile sighed. It was going to be one of *those* days…

・・・

The pretty black girl pulled the shop door shut and glanced skyward. A grey mantle hung overhead. But Rayya was under a roof now, warm and safe. Who cared if it rained?

"I'm Chriki," she said.

"Clara."

"Oh… Rayya wrote about you. In her letters."

"You're Sachin's girlfriend?"

"Yeah."

Chriki's mouth shaped the beginning of a word, then another, but neither made it off her tongue. They looked at each other.

"There's a nice tavern nearby. Do you like sweet pastries?"

"Sure."

The actress beamed. She did her best to smile back. Chriki led Clara through the city's streets and scents. Bread, fish, herbs, smoke, human waste. They flowed all around but even the strongest and foulest didn't overwhelm her. Perhaps her nose had claws of its own, and shredded them one by one…

A dog sat outside the tavern. He sniffed at Clara, flinched, and stared.

"Good dog…"

The animal's nose pulled back from her glove, but he didn't try to run when she petted him. Clara rubbed the top of his head, the backs of his ears, and he settled down.

"Do you have a dog at home?" Chriki said. The young woman's face changed. "Oh! I'm sorry… I… I didn't…"

"The pastries smell good."

"Yeah. Let's…" She pushed the door open and they stepped into sticky-sweet aromas. "Grab a table. I'll get them."

"I don't have any-"

"My treat."

"Thanks."

Clara annexed a corner while Chriki stood at the counter. She sat there and her senses reached out. It was like stretching an arm, letting its fingers roam. Details sharpened where they probed. Other sights, sounds, smells faded into the background.

Two old women ate croissants. Cups steamed beside their plates, one mint tea, the other ginger. Fragrant ghosts mingled between them.

"…broke up with his boyfriend…."

"...such a shame. But, you know, my grandson..."
"...get them together..."
"...tomorrow, for dinner?"

They chuckled and flakes stuck to their lips.

A young man dabbed his moustache, which was little more than a line of fluff. He cleared his throat and spoke to the empty seat in front of him.

"I think we should... Well, it's not working out, is it? You like... things... And I like... other... things. Other people!" He groaned and held his head in his hands. "Oh, gods... She's going to stab me, isn't she?"

Over by the door, a-

"Here we go."

Chriki laid the tray down, shared out cups and dishes. The beautiful explosion underneath Clara's nostrils blotted out the rest of the tavern. She picked a diamond-shaped block up by its edges. Chriki glanced at the gloves on Clara's hands, and Clara dredged her brain for excuses. She needed to leave them on because... Open sores? Too gross. Maybe... But the woman just took her own diamond between her fingertips.

Honey, blackberry jam, and crisp, airy layers stuffed Clara's senses. She munched and crunched her way through, and wished Rayya were there to taste it.

When the last bit of pastry vanished into Clara's mouth, Chriki stopped nibbling and put the rest of hers down.

"Sachin thought you were..." She dropped Clara's gaze, fiddled with the teapot.

"Yeah..."

Blood-coloured tea poured into Clara's cup. Sour, fruity. Shadows wobbled in its depths. Ella Mandrake had always loved rosehip and hibiscus. Clara drank, washed it around her mouth, and let it fill her from head to toe.

"They said it was…" Chriki glanced over her shoulder. "Kharjis?"

"Yeah."

Chriki averted her eyes again, shaped the beginnings of questions but didn't utter them. Clara sighed and just told the story. The night raid. Kharjis and swords and screams and fire. But not the monster. Never the monster. Then the escape, through the forest, to Ghadi's house. The kind woman, the road to Hogmire. The Darthuns' farm. She bludgeoned Lencia to death a second time in her memories, but trapped her there and skipped to the town and its silly, brutal, glorious game. To the wagon that brought them to Lemstras, where Rayya cried but would be okay.

The tale hung above the tea and crumbs. For a while they both just drank, while wisps played on their faces.

"Do you have any family?" Chriki said.

"Only mum."

"I'm so sorry…"

The woman's shoulders twitched, as though she'd lunge at Clara, pull her into a hug, squeeze her. Chriki's eyes glistened. Words half-formed and died on dark lips.

"Would you…? Would you like another pastry?"

Clara wasn't hungry, but nodded anyway and smiled when Chriki did. The woman bounded back to the counter. She returned with a pastry twice as large as the last one. Clara bit off a piece. Chriki still smiled, but wiped the corner of her eye.

"What will…?" She swallowed. "Will you…?"

The woman sipped tea. Clara filled the silence before she could try again.

"Rayya said you're an actress."

"Oh! Yes. I… I act. On stage. In plays and…"

"What kind?"

"I'm in a comedy at the moment."

"Is it good?"

"The playwright thinks it is." She rolled her eyes. "But her idea of humour…"

Clara gnawed the pastry, coaxed her with a question or two when the stories sagged, and let the actress share all the trials and tribulations of her craft.

• • •

A fresh round of sobs broke out above Vasile's head. He sighed at the ceiling, and wished he could go for a walk instead of eavesdropping on their grief. But he could hardly ask his apprentice to mind the shop…

The apothecary whistled, and drowned out the worst of it. He kept the tune up until his cheeks hurt and the door opened.

A Kharji woman came inside, adjusted her turban, and frowned at the idol. Would she storm back out? That'd happened once before, though it may've been because he'd dropped a bottle of stinkweed essence. The woman shook her head and came to the counter.

Someone wailed upstairs. The customer looked from the ceiling to the apothecary.

"Sorry. There's... My apprentice had some deaths in the family."

"My condolences."

"How can I help you?"

The woman's eyes darkened.

"There are rats in my cellar..."

• • •

"Lunch?" the barkeep said.

"Please." Silas leaned against the bar. One of his bruises groaned, and he shifted his weight. "What's good?"

"Pork and beetroot stew."

"Sure. Two bowls, when my... friend..." The word slotted into place easier than he'd expected. "...gets here."

He handed over the money and crossed The Bleeding Boulder's taproom. A few drinkers and diners nodded at him from their seats, or raised a hand. All bore cuts and bruises. They might as well've been guild insignias. He returned each gesture and claimed a couple of spots at the end of a table.

Katrina came through the door a few minutes later. The barkeep brought bowls and bread over before she'd even sat down.

"Anything?" She prodded the stew with a chunk of crust.

"No." Silas touched the skin beneath his eye. "How about..."

"Too many people cavorted through those streets. Can't pick up any trails."

Pork slid apart between Silas' teeth.

"Do we ride on, or keep asking around?"

"We'll spend one more night here. If we don't find anything by the end of the day, we'll leave at first light."

"Hope she's okay…"

They split up outside the pub. Silas wandered in a different direction from the morning, glanced at every girl's face. Maybe Clara and Rayya had eaten at that-

"Oh! Sorry!"

The woman's voice hit him at the same time as the rest of her. Something banged Silas' temple. He staggered, but his leg swung, the ball of his foot stamped on the ground, and he stayed up. The young woman sat down and books fell around her. One bounced off her head. She rubbed the spot and jumbled her hair into a haystack.

"Sorry," he said.

"At least there're no puddles…" She picked up a tome, laid another on top of it. "Mad Jess'd kill me if I ruined one of these."

Silas gathered a few of the heftier volumes, then frowned.

"Mad Jess?"

"Oh… That's what we call the professor. Her name's Jessica, and…"

"Long legs, with more muscle than most people's whole bodies? Talks like-"

"Like this, what? That's the one."

"She's a professor?"

"Ancient history and languages. Speaks things most people don't know exist. Amy."

"Amy?" Silas tried to recall if his tutors had mentioned such a tongue. "Oh… Right. Silas."

He hefted his stack. Amy's inched upwards.

"Just put them on top." Her knees and shoulders shook.

"Why don't I carry them?"

"You sure?"

"Yeah. I'd like to see your professor."

Her face sank.

"Look... I know I gave you a hard knock, but there's no need to complain. I wouldn't mind with any of the others, but Mad Jess makes us do sprints. Sprints! And sometimes-"

"I just want to talk to her about someone."

"Oh. Okay. That'd be great then…"

Silas bent his legs and let her slide her books atop his. He wedged the portable library under his chin.

"It's not far," she said. "Just up this way…"

Amy led him down an alley. At the other end, mansions surrounded a courtyard. She unlatched a gate and held it open for him.

"That's a noble crest." He tilted his upper body at the gatepost. "The Viovania family."

"This used to be theirs, before they donated it."

"A whole house?"

"One of the Viovanias really liked ancient languages. Or the professor. Probably the professor. Unless she just beat it out of him."

They went through a side entrance, into a corridor. Amy knocked on the second door along.

"Come in!"

The voice and volume were familiar. She might've been barking a command mid-game. Amy turned the handle, shoved it open, then stepped back. Silas carried the tomes inside.

"Put them anywhere." Jessica leaned over the codices and papyri on her desk. She glanced up. "And… Silas? What the devil are you doing here, old chap?"

"The books were heavy," Amy said. "So…"

"Students…" The professor shook her head. "Weak as kittens, half of them. You can go."

Amy shut the door behind her. Silas set the books down against the wall, beside a similar pile, and made a few adjustments when it swayed.

"Fancy enrolling? Might be able to get a good school football team going."

"No. Thanks."

A red and black gown hung on the back of a chair. The hat that rested on the seat resembled a gateau. The rest of her attire was more practical, but just as fine. Silas tried to place her alongside the woman with a sackcloth tunic and blood dripping off her knuckles.

"You're a… teacher?"

She grinned.

"Surprised, what? Can't make a living kicking the old bladder around and knocking people's teeth out. Look, I'd love to chat about the game… Talk both your ears off… But I have to be getting back to this. Texts don't translate themselves, worse luck."

"Sure. I'll just… Listen, do you know what happened to Clara and Rayya? Are they still in Hogmire?"

"No, they'll be off in Lemstras by now."

"Lemstras? You're sure?"

"That's where they wanted to go. Saw them onto the cart myself, not long after the game. Merchant took them. Chap named Simon."

"Oh… Thanks."

Jessica nodded. Silas went out into the corridor, left the school, and jogged back to the pub.

• • •

Rayya, Sachin, and his master stood around the counter when Chriki brought her back. Redness threaded her friend's eyes. But Rayya held Sachin's hand, rested her head on his arm, and a smile played on her lips. Clara tried to match it.

"If you're thirsty…" The apothecary fiddled with a sprig, plucked pale green buds one by one. "…there's still some tea upstairs."

"I'm okay, Mr.…."

"Zarabanov. Don't try to say it. No one else does. Vasile." He finished stripping the sprig, put it aside, and picked up another. "So… You two'll need somewhere to lay your heads."

Rayya looked up at her brother.

"We thought… maybe we could stay with you?"

Sachin and Chriki exchanged glances.

"We…" he said.

"It's just…" she said.

Vasile snorted.

"I've seen their place. Barely room for one person to lie down straight, let alone four. His old room upstairs is better, but youngsters will put up with anything so they can have a bit of-"

Sachin coughed.

"...*privacy* in the morning. And they weren't going to have that with my thin walls."

Gazes drifted to jars, bottles, and floorboards.

"Anyway... I haven't had any luck getting a lodger to fill it yet. You're welcome to it tonight..."

"Thank you," Rayya said.

"Yeah, thanks," Clara said.

"But if you want it long-term, I can't afford to let it go for nothing. Room and board cost money."

"We'll work," Rayya said. "If there's anything..."

"Rayya's clever." Sachin squeezed his sister's hand. "Just like me. And you said you might need a shop kid, now I'm messing with mixtures all the time."

"And turning things purple..." Vasile scratched his jaw. "The stuff in the cellar needs putting in order, for a start. I could maybe find enough chores for *one*."

Clara's stomach murmured. This was it. Rayya had family, a place in the world. *She* didn't. But she kept her face steady. Maybe she'd prowl the alleys like a stray cat. Or run away into the forest and live with the wolves. Kill deer, squat by their carcasses, chew bloody chunks with the rest of the pack. Whatever happened, she wouldn't be a chicken. She wouldn't stumble around till she-

"There might be something at the theatre." Chriki touched Clara's shoulder. "Odd jobs. Lugging things around, helping with the stage and props. I'll ask."

"Thanks."

Clara's fingers curled inside her gloves. Her claws tingled. She tore her thoughts away from murky futures, but her smile quivered.

• • •

Rashida took a deep breath. It didn't help, but she took another, whispered a prayer.

"Allat guide me."

She composed her face, checked it in the mirror. Her smile wobbled. Her hands did too, and purple-blackness sloshed inside the goblets. The imam prayed until they stopped. Her smile returned, but it was a gash on the mirror-woman's face. She discarded it and waited till something better found its place there.

"Allatu Akbar."

Rashida went to the study door. She put the goblets down on her desk, turned the handle, eased it open a crack. Shadows covered the hall. Fahmaia Hashad knelt at their centre, hands cupped in her lap, gathering her prayers.

The imam reached for the goblets and her heart thumped. Which way round? Had she put them down this way, or that way? If she got it wrong… No. She knew which was which. Djinn wouldn't vanquish her by whispering doubts in her ear, thwart her from doing Allat's will. Rashida Al-Taquba picked up both vessels and nudged the door further open with the toe of her shoe.

Fahmaia murmured the last words of her prayer. The mawlana's hands rose. Palms, fingers, and pieties washed over her cheeks. She smiled at the imam. Her markings swam in shadow.

"Did the One Goddess reveal anything new?"

Rashida sat and offered the cup in her right hand. Fahmaia accepted it, mouthed a word of thanks, and gazed at the blackness within. The imam's heartbeat pounded through her body, echoed in every muscle.

"No visions. Allat waits for us to fulfil our promise."

Scripture snaked across her brow. Words flashed in Rashida's skull. That verse warned against false prophets and the evil they wrought in the name of piety. A sign? It must be! Allatu Akbar!

"I know our presence troubles you."

"No, mawlana! I…"

"I understand, truly. Those of us who serve the One Goddess with steel as well as prayer must seem savage to you who dwell in the cities, and do other portions of her work instead."

"Forgive me. I… We…"

Her hand shook. She brought the goblet to her lips. A sip became a glug, then a quaff. Sweetness and fire filled her head and hit her brain faster than they should've. The world shone at its edges. Fahmaia drank too, just a taste. Rashida wanted to scream.

"Allat asks hard things of us all. The sacrifice, the burden, has fallen on you as well as Barzik's warriors."

The mawlana drank again. Rashida's throat tightened. She couldn't breathe! She'd picked the wrong cup! She was going to… to…

"Are you all right?"

"I…" The imam's mouth widened and hung from her face.

"Let us pray. Together."

Fahmaia drained her goblet. Rashida's features froze. Her body shook.

"Imam? You look… look…"

The mawlana's brow creased. Her eyelids quivered. Fingers twitched and the goblet rolled on the carpet. Fahmaia thudded on her side. Spasms wrenched her body. Her spine bent backwards, forwards, stretched her out and crunched her up into a ball. Limbs flailed, drummed. They flopped like trout on the planks of a fisherman's boat.

Rashida exhaled.

The stairs creaked. Jasmina's voice floated down.

"Mawlana? Are you…?"

The imam snatched up her goblet, grabbed at the other, fumbled. She swore under her breath and grasped it. Rashida ran for the doorway. The balls of her feet launched her, almost didn't touch the floor. She tossed the cups into an armchair. Closed the door. Leaned against it. Sucked the whole universe into her lungs.

Wood pressed on the back of her head, and the cry from the other side shuddered through her skull.

"Mawlana!"

Rashida Al-Taquba shut her eyes and prayed.

14

"That's a large camp." Katrina patted her horse's neck. "I didn't think any of the gypsy caravans were nearby this season."

Campfires dotted the horizon. Flame and moonlight daubed wagons, far across the plain. Silas moved to tie the animals but she waved him back.

"Let's pay them a visit. They might have decent rations to swap. Maybe a story or two."

"If they wanted company, they'd've camped closer to the road."

"Gypsies always have time for trade and tales."

Silas shrugged and they tramped over the grass with their steeds. The nearest fire was some distance from the rest, away from where the wagons rested and horses grazed. Groups of men and women crouched around the others, but only two gypsies sat here. The pair stopped eating. They watched the monster hunters approach.

"Sastipe." Katrina bowed her head.

"Hello," the woman said.

The man nodded to them and Silas did the same.

"I'm Katrina, of the von Talhoffers. This is Silas, of the Renshaws. Which clan do we have the honour of meeting?"

The two gypsies glanced at one another.

"We're clanless," the woman said. "Just fellow travellers who've come together for protection."

Wood crackled. A twig snapped and sparks rose between them.

"I'm Parmeen. Pleased to meet you."

"Maalam," the man said. "Likewise."

"May we?" Katrina gestured.

After a moment, Parmeen nodded. Katrina pulled a pack off her horse and squatted by the fire. Silas crouched beside her.

"We've just come from Hogmire. Got some of their salted meats, if you want to trade. We'd love something sweet... Maybe a honey cake?"

"Dried dates?"

"Sure."

Katrina took a package from her bag and passed it over the fire. Parmeen reached out.

"It's blessed too, if you want a bit of divine favour."

"Oh?"

Her fingers hovered, then withdrew.

"The local priest cures his own. Every piece goes on his altar and gets offered to his god."

"Actually... We've got enough meat in the wagons."

"Ah... How about-"

"You can just have these."

"You're sure?"

"Please."

"Thank you."

Parmeen opened a bag, turned it, and shook several black shapes into Katrina's hands. She looked at Silas.

"Uh... Maybe just one?"

She held the bag towards him. He plucked out a sticky, fleshy blob, popped it in his mouth, and chewed at its sweetness. Katrina masticated one of her own while she spoke.

"Have you or your people seen anything strange on the road?"

"Strange?" Parmeen glanced at Maalam.

"Carcasses maybe, that don't look like the work of a wolf. Tracks halfway between feet and paws."

"No, nothing like that."

The two women talked a little longer. Silas and Maalam's eyes met, but the gypsy said nothing.

"Thank you again for the dates."

"Think nothing of it."

"Good travels."

"And you."

Silas murmured a farewell and Maalam did the same. He and Katrina led their horses halfway back to the road before she spoke.

"Had many dealings with gypsies?"

"Not really. They sometimes camp on a corner of our estate, but…"

"How'd their clothes look to you?"

"Same as usual." He shrugged. "Baggy breeches, flowing shirts…"

"Easy enough for one to pass for the other, among outsiders who don't know how the scarves should be knotted, or which order they're supposed to wear those leather bracelets in. But gypsies never turn their noses up at a blessing. They'll take their luck from any god who'll give it. Kharjis won't."

Silas let out a low whistle.

"Do you think…?"

"It could be innocent enough. After what happened in Traverd, Kharji merchants might dress themselves up as gypsies so people won't shun their goods or drive them off."

Grass whispered underfoot. The back of Silas' neck prickled.

"Shall we ride on a bit?" he said.

"Let's."

• • •

Clara slid out of bed. A floorboard groaned and she winced, but Rayya didn't stir on the mattress. A wave of hair covered most of her friend's face. Yet the edge of a smile peeked out between the streams, and a shaft of moonlight framed it. Clara's own mouth curved too.

She sat there for a while, and clouds hid the heavens. The darkness didn't deepen much. Didn't mask the glove on her hand.

"It's the hand I killed her with…"

Clara sighed. Rayya's eyes, her hug, had made the lie a blade. It carved Clara Mandrake's tongue right down the middle, sliced its way along her throat, split her heart. But what else could she have said? That she wore it because…?

She took the glove off and laid it on the bedside table, undid the knot at her wrist. The bandages came away but didn't lose their shape. A phantom hand. That'd taken some practice, and Clara wished she could show her mother. Ella Mandrake would smile at her daughter's artfulness. But then she'd see what lay underneath, and she'd scream or cry…

Scales covered the ends of her fingers, almost to the middle joints. Black bumps grew further along. Soon they'd sprout and devour the rest, all the way to the knuckles. The skin on the back of her hand had already darkened a shade. Her palm too. When those night-scales took them, what then? Would she have to bandage her whole arm? Her entire body? Wear a mask?

And why didn't any of this frighten her?

Clara's fingers and claws fluttered. No tightness squeezed her flesh or constricted her joints. The scales were as natural, as comfortable as her skin. She might've been born with them.

She went to the window. Hid her hand behind the sill, though there was no one to see. Shutters blinded the other buildings. Nobody sauntered below. People slept, and only Clara Mandrake wanted to lope through the night.

His scent was stronger now. She sniffed it on the breeze, drew it deep inside. The monster was coming. And then? Maybe he'd tear her apart and scatter her black-scale-blood all over Lemstras. Or…

The moon broke free and bathed her. She lifted her hand, held it to the sky. Silver flowed between her claws.

• • •

Fahmaia opened her eyes and the camp was aflame. Purple, turquoise, emerald fire blazed above the tents, lapped at yellow skies. Scents of cinnamon, offal, lime, and her mother's perfume slapped her in the face, echoed in her ears. The children ran around the conflagration. They whooped and waved wooden swords and sang while everything burned.

"One Goddess, One Goddess, glaring in the sky…"

"Stop that!" The mawlana grabbed Aisha's arm. "Allat will punish you for such blasphemy."

Aisha giggled and broke free.

"Mawlana, mawlana, glaring on the ground…"

Where was Barzik Khan? Why did he allow this madness? Fahmaia ran through the rainbow inferno.

"Her brow's hot as a forge. Where's that doctor?"

Barzik's pleasure palace shone with the jewels of a thousand reflected flames. She pushed its golden doors. They swung away, struck the walls, and thunder boomed through a hall that stretched forever. Serpent-limbed men and women slithered and entwined on cushions and couches. Their scales glistened in all the hues of the cosmos.

"Mawlana!" The walrus sprawled upon his throne. When he opened his mouth, tusks grated on the black metal of his beard and the sound scraped Fahmaia's bones. "What's wrong?"

"Empty the masjid, before this illness spreads. Azim and I will stay with her."

"The camp's on fire, Barzik."

"Then we must offer a sacrifice to appease Allat!" The walrus warlord flumped onto his feet, tottered, and waved his sword over his head. "Sacrifice! Sacrifice!"

A hundred coils grasped daggers. The snake-people took up the cry and steel glittered on all sides.

"Sacrifice!" The word hissed off razor edges. "Sacrifice! Sacrifice!"

They writhed towards her and Fahmaia ran.

"Sacrifice! Sacrifice!"

She flew through the doorway and plummeted, into an ocean of stars that shattered into wine and voices and honey.

"Yasmin, are they all gone?"

"The imam's in her study, praying. I sent the others away and barred the door."

"Good. You go too."

"I want to stay. Please!"

"You mustn't-"

"Someone has to wait downstairs, and let Fatima in when she's back with the doctor."

"Okay. But…"

Fahmaia crested a wave and then the ocean was the sky and she was far below, atop the hill. Cities sprawled and millions screamed. She screamed with them. The idol from Traverd towered above streets and temples, but now she was flesh. So were the five totem djinn, with maws that could eat mountains. Others loomed beside and beyond them. Every false god and goddess of the non-believers. They rampaged through civilisations, shouldered one another aside, snatched at settlements, seized men, women, and children, tossed them into their mouths. Tongues thrashed. Thousands of mortals churned and wailed.

Fahmaia clawed her cheeks, moaned prayers at the heavens. Allat would save them! The One Goddess' eyes would open and she'd-

But the One Goddess was down there with the rest. She squatted over the minarets and masjids, drove her hands into their midst, and a million Kharjis shrieked in her fists. Her eyes shone. Her mouth gaped. Cheeks tore, saliva poured out, and villages drowned. The One Goddess crammed Fahmaia's people into her maw. Bones and souls crunched between Allat's teeth.

The mawlana's markings flashed across the backs of her hands and lashed blasphemies into her brain.

• • •

"Sorry." Chriki held the shop door open. "We start early at the theatre."

Clara stepped outside and tasted the morning gloom. The sky had brightened a little, but shadows still bathed the street. They embraced her and rippled over her skin.

"I want Beth to meet you before rehearsals start, while she's in a better mood."

A gust blew between the shops. Motes of debris tumbled around their boots. Chriki pulled up her hood and bit her lip.

"I have a shawl in here…" The actress unbuckled her bag.

"Thanks, but it's okay."

"But…"

"Really. It's fine. I don't get cold."

Chriki glanced at Clara's gloves.

"Apart from my hands…"

"Okay. But if you change your mind…"

The roads and alleys were still quiet. But if she focused, stretched her senses, noises buzzed all around. Lemstras woke and ate breakfast and argued with slugabed children. A mother laughed at her daughter's joke. Clara sighed, smiled, and brushed the wall of their house with her fingertips.

"Did Vasile feed you?"

"Yeah. He made us stuffed eggs."

"His favourite. He must like you."

A clamour rose in the distance and intensified with every stride. Dozens of voices and as many odours. They swept her up into a maelstrom of flesh, fish, and shouts.

"…better than a smack in the mouth…"

"Trout! If you don't eat enough fish, the sea god'll drown you next time you're on the water! Trout!"

"…not beef, is it?"

"…no, but squirrel's cheaper…"

Chriki took Clara's arm. They squeezed among stalls, shoppers, and youths lugging crates or barrels.

"Here's good for most things…" Chriki slid between two bruisers, and Clara popped through the gap like a stopper from a bottle. "If you want a bracelet or something, you're better off going to…"

A trout-wielding woman moved, and a pair of eyes widened in that sliver of space. The boy held a piece of parchment with both hands, as though reading a missive. But he gazed over its edge instead. Clara's right hand tensed and her vision narrowed. He wore a Kharji shirt…

The boy got up from the box he sat on, took a step towards her. A man banged into him and knocked him back down.

"Watch where you're going! Bloody Kharjis…"

Chriki pulled her onward, the crowd shifted behind them. Clara looked over her shoulder before they turned down a side street, but he'd disappeared amid the throng.

"There are Kharjis here."

"Oh…" Chriki squeezed Clara's left hand. "Yeah. But these ones… They aren't raiders. They're just…"

Clara's fingers tightened. Chriki yelped.

"Sorry…"

"It's okay. You don't… You don't have to be scared."

Scared? Clara's claws strained inside their bonds. She'd rip his face off and blow her nose on it…

The theatre was just another building. Rain had worn away at the stone, and the wood smelled damp. She'd never been to one before, but she'd expected something… grander? Chriki smiled at her and Clara hoped it didn't show on her face.

"Just wait…"

The actress opened the door and gestured for Clara to lead the way.

"Oh!"

Chriki giggled.

"Yeah."

Painted scenes covered all four walls of the vestibule. On the left, actors performed. Three different plays took place side-by-side. It should've been cramped, cluttered, but Clara grinned and wished she could hear them all at once. On the other walls, audiences cheered and laughed and wept.

"Look up." Chriki pointed.

Broken edges framed it, as though a storm had torn the roof off and opened the building to the heavens. Stars twinkled. A dozen faces peered down at the stages.

"That's Thespia. Goddess of drama."

"All of them?"

"She wears different faces. Different aspects. That's how she looks when she watches a farce… That's for tragedy…"

One face roared with laughter. Another blushed. A third scowled, but not at the stage.

"What about that one?"

"That's Thespia the Avenger. She punishes audience members who talk during the play."

"How?"

"She beats them up," a woman said from the doorway opposite.

"Really?"

"Well, ushers wearing her mask. But they do it in her name."

The woman's smirk was missing at least three teeth, and her nose turned one way, then the other. But the body beneath that fighter's face was soft and plump.

"Beth, this is Clara. Clara, Beth."

"Hmm…"

Beth took Clara's chin. Clara resisted for an instant, but it felt like her jaw would break off, so she let the woman tilt her head upwards.

"Not the prettiest I've seen, but if we slap enough war paint on her…"

Clara glared. She'd plunge her fingers through the woman's flab, grab her intestines, yank them-

"She's not an actress. You said we needed more stagehands…"

"Right, right." Beth released her. "What can you do?"

"What do you need me to do?"

"Any good at slashing things?"

Clara bit her lip.

"We've got some old costumes. We need them mangled a bit, like they've been through the wars. Rips, tears. That sort of thing. Last girl was useless. Stabbed herself in the leg. You safe with sharp things?"

"Yeah." Otherwise you'd be picking up your guts, she thought.

"Good. I'll give you a try. Lots to get done. If you do cut yourself, you can bleed on them as much as you want. A bit of blood'll work well on these…"

"Great…"

Beth turned on her heel, strode away, and called back over her shoulder.

"Show the kid where to go, then get yourself ready. That crazy cow of a playwright's made *another* change…"

• • •

Fatima hissed between her teeth.

"Are you strong enough to carry me?" the doctor said.

"No, but-"

"Then stop complaining."

Doctor Zubeida's cane tapped the ground. One shoe stepped, the other dragged. Fatima's fingers whitened around the medic's bag. Goddess… She wanted to take her by the shoulder and propel her down the street like a battering ram.

Two infidel women laughed and staggered towards them. Wine jugs dangled from their hands.

"So I grabbed him by the bits and gave them a good hard squeeze!"

"You didn't!"

"I did! He squeaked like a-"

She stumbled, bumped into the doctor. Fatima growled and shoved her. The woman's arms windmilled. Her heels kicked at the ground then flew out from under her. She sat down, the jug shattered, and she roared.

"Oi! I'll have you for that! I'll-"

Fatima grasped the handle of her knife.

"Stop!" Doctor Zubeida moved between them. "This foolishness won't help your friend, will it?"

The upright drunkard helped the other woman to her feet. Neither met Fatima's eyes, and they hurried off. The two Kharjis continued to the masjid.

"Take my arm, child."

Fatima bristled, but helped the doctor up the stairs to the entrance. She pushed the door but it didn't budge.

"Hey!" She hammered on it. "Let us in!"

Wood and iron grated. There was a thunk. The door opened, and the doctor shuffled inside.

"Why was that locked?" Fatima stormed past Yasmin. "Where is everyone?"

"I sent them home. Jasmina said to."

"Very wise." Doctor Zubeida followed them across the prayer hall. "We don't want everyone getting sick, if it's contagious."

She gripped the banister, hobbled up the staircase, then tapped and shuffled her way to the sickroom door.

Jasmina and Azim sprang up when it opened, a pair of tigers. Swords hung from their belts.

"Those won't help a sick woman." The doctor moved around Jasmina, to the bed. "Not unless she needs amputation."

Azim's eyes glinted.

"If anyone comes for the mawlana, even death itself, they'll have to fight us first."

Doctor Zubeida snorted and muttered something under her breath, then spoke out loud.

"Bring me my bag."

Jasmina stood aside and Fatima crossed the room. The mawlana's body shuddered on the blanket. Her face glistened. Droplets trickled over script that stalled, sped, and juddered.

"So the tales are true." The doctor touched Fahmaia's cheek, then her brow. "Open the bag."

"Are you a believer?" Jasmina said.

"She comes to the masjid." Fatima unbuckled the satchel, pulled its sides apart, and held it out. "Her mother did too."

"For the Eids. The One Goddess doesn't need me every day, but my patients do."

Zubeida leaned over the mawlana, as though she intended to kiss her. She sniffed her lips instead. Then she whirled round, and Fatima flinched. The doctor reached into her bag.

"Did anyone share her last meal?"

"We all ate with her," Jasmina said.

"And no one else got sick?"

"No. You-"

The doctor shushed her, took a green leaf from a pouch, and pressed it against the inside of the mawlana's mouth. Fahmaia twitched, shook. Azim moved towards them but Jasmina waved him back. After a few seconds, Zubeida removed the leaf and turned it between her fingers.

"Has she thrown up?"

"No." Jasmina nudged a bucket with her boot. "Only drool."

"Ink. Quill. Parchment." She knelt before the bedside table. "Hurry up, girl."

Fatima pulled them out of the satchel. Doctor Zubeida licked the tip of the quill, dipped it, and scribbled. She looked over at Jasmina but didn't stop writing.

"Do you know where Zarabanov's is?"

"This is our first time in Lemstras."

"I know it," Yasmin said.

"Give Vasile these notes." She held the parchment by its edges. "He'll know what to do."

"An infidel?" Jasmina said.

"An apothecary."

Yasmin took it from her and left. Footsteps pounded down the stairs.

• • •

Clara laid the wedding dress on the table. She probed ruffles and other flourishes that belonged on a cake, brushed patches where threads frayed or hints of yellow stained the whiteness. Had a real bride worn it? It must've looked gorgeous among summer blossoms or winter snow…

She picked up the knife and slashed it. Fabric tore like flesh.

Clara wounded it a few more times. The bride's blood spattered purple blooms, reddened the snow. She tossed the dress onto one pile and took a tunic from the other. No, not a tunic… Embroidery unfurled across the table. Emerald dye had faded to grass, but the robe belonged on an emperor, or maybe a hero. Clara stabbed it, twisted the blade. Assassinated the emperor. Murdered the hero. They fell on the palace floor, raised their hands, and made long, silly speeches.

Her fingertips tingled.

Why was she using this stupid, clumsy knife? Her claws were keener, quicker, deadlier. They'd eviscerate the whole heap, slaughter all the princesses, witches, warriors, and kings. Strew the room with their guts and gore. Clara tugged the glove off her right hand, pinched the knot-

The door opened. She jumped back.

"Sorry." The man's head bobbed like a bird's. "Didn't mean to scare you."

"I was… I was just…"

"Hurt yourself?"

Clara's hand dropped to her side. The claws burned.

"Want me to take a look?"

"No! I… I'm fine. It's not… It isn't…"

"Ah. Disfigured?"

"Y… Yeah."

"Nothing to worry about. We get all sorts through here. When a performance is on, can't tell which bits are real and which are fake anyway. I'm Cyril, by the way. Those are my clothes you're ruining."

"I was just… Beth said…"

He grinned.

"I mean, I'm in charge of costumes."

He walked over to the piles, picked out the wedding dress, and held it up. The bride's corpse dangled in front of him.

"Very nice work."

"Thanks. I'm Clara."

"Right. Chriki's friend. She sent me. Would you like to see her rehearse? Seems a shame to slave away in this little cubbyhole while there's magic going on."

"Sure, but…" She glanced at the ones she hadn't butchered. "I've still got those to do."

"We can bring them with us."

He stooped and lifted the entire mound. Clara put her glove back on and followed him to the door.

"Knife. Can't slice these up without that, can you?"

Clara didn't know if the smile was forced or not, but it warmed her face. She got the blade and they went along a series of passages that wound through the building's innards. The last one brought them into a corridor with more of those wall paintings. Forests and throne rooms and the decks of ships. Then a blank, cream-coloured stretch. Cyril looked round.

"We ran out of paint."

"Really?"

"Nah. Every time a play does well, it goes up there."

"Will this one be next?"

"Heh. We'll see…"

Double doors opened into a cavern. Rows of seats cascaded away from them, down into darkness, then emerged in the aura of lantern-light before the stage.

"Sit where you want. Beth'll want me down with her, so she can complain about the outfits."

Clara found a seat in the shadows. Cyril dumped the clothes next to her and half-walked, half-skipped down a stairway. She took the topmost garment and draped it over the back of the chair in front. A shirt. A long, billowing shirt... Clara pulled it off the chair and stabbed the Kharji woman through her heart.

"Let's get this started then." Beth stood in front of the stage. She gestured to one of the wings, then took her seat. "Before Miss Playwright decides to write the scene out from under us again."

"Now look here!" Another woman sprang to her feet. The sleeves of a patchwork dress flapped. It might've been made from bits of Clara's victims. "Those changes were-"

Several people shushed her. She huffed and fell back into her seat. A harp played somewhere, and a woman strutted onto the stage. A purple gown swept behind her like a mystical river. The actress strode back and forth, crossed its full width three times before Clara recognised her. Even then, it was unreal. The face was almost Chriki's. But way she held her jaw, moved her limbs... An empress walked the stage.

"Where are my warriors?" The voice wasn't hers either. Not the girl from the pastry shop. "There's supposed to be a parade to celebrate my splendid victory!"

A man rolled in from the opposite wing. His belly bulged against his tunic.

"All dead, Majesty. They died in your splendid victory."

The playwright barked laughter. A couple of the others coughed.

"What? All of them?"

"Their spouses and children mourn as we speak."

"Then dress *them* in the warriors' armour. I want a parade, and I'm going to have one!"

Clara grinned and the drama bounced onward. Chriki's voice, her mannerisms, piped humour into the words like custard into a bun. Soon everyone laughed at the jokes. The playwright looked from side to side and Clara caught the edge of her smirk.

The knife continued its work. She murdered victim after victim, but didn't watch them die. The theatre really was magic. A place for strange and silly things. Even a girl with claws and scales. Maybe she'd live here, lurk beneath the stage. Pop out and scare little children until a heroine slew her. Then do the same night after night, play after play…

Clara sighed and shredded another dress.

• • •

Fatima paced the prayer hall. The carpet ate the sound of her steps, but each one still thudded in her head. What if the doctor's pokes, prods, and strange tests did nothing? If that apothecary's drug couldn't save her? The mawlana, Allat's chosen… If the One Goddess didn't spare her from this illness, wouldn't that be a sign? They might all perish soon after, when Allat's wrath crashed down upon them.

She knelt. Her thoughts spun, but her lips and limbs fell into the rhythm of prayer, and after a few minutes her brain and being submerged in those words, those motions. Fatima prayed for the Goddess' mercy, her blessing. She prostrated herself, touched her forehead to the floor, lifted it, and froze there on her hands and knees.

The carpet's pattern… Had it always been flawed? Fatima frowned. She'd prayed in this spot before, gazed upon those colours and geometric designs dozens of times. Maybe hundreds. How had she never noticed?

Fatima's index finger touched the splodge, then rubbed across the neighbouring fibres. She lowered her face, shifted around on all fours, and found more spots amid the dye. Fatima glared. Which idiot spilled wine in the prayer hall? She'd have to tell the imam and-

Wine.

There was…

But…

Fatima knelt there and a thousand things banged against the inside of her skull. When the study door opened, her muscles tensed. She almost spoke but bit down on her tongue let the burst of pain spread through her face. Fatima prostrated herself. Her lips fluttered but uttered no prayer. Imam Rashida passed through the chamber and headed to the washroom.

Everything in her head crunched into a single thought. If the imam performed the ritual wash before her prayers, she'd be gone for many minutes. Fatima's eyes narrowed. She sprang up, went into the study.

Several of the imam's books lay open on her desk, alongside an inked parchment, a quill, and her goblet. A single purple-black drop rested at the bottom of the cup. Fatima opened the cupboard, ran her fingers across jugs and bottles. Wine. Water. Ink. She plucked a smaller vessel from behind two others. Fatima pulled out the stopper, sniffed it, and swore. She blinked a few times. Sealed the bottle. Put it back where she'd found it. Closed the cupboard.

She knelt in the prayer hall when the imam returned from the washroom. Fatima's mouth shaped empty syllables. She gazed down at the carpet as though she contemplated the greatness and mercy of Allat.

Her eyes and mind burned.

15

Rayya's hand trembled. She should call for Sachin. Have him come down, and… And laugh at her, like he did when she was small. Her eyes narrowed. After everything she'd been through, this wasn't going to beat her. Rayya Shimud gripped the top of the jar with her fingertips and lifted it. The spiders burst into motion. Finger-legs kicked and scuttled. One of the beasts fell off and disappeared among the bottles below. Another scurried to the bottom of the jar. A third came up towards her fingers.

"Argh!"

She shook the jar like a madwoman. Dust and spiders dropped into the junk. Rayya turned, then danced a jig when one of them appeared near her boots. She shuddered. Imagined the crunch, the goo… But she managed to get past without stepping on it.

Rayya put the jar into the box with the other things, took a deep breath. Spices, herbs, and something like melted wax, fought inside her nose. Apothecary perfume. She smiled, picked up her spoils, and went up the cellar steps.

"Spiders?" Sachin looked round from the table.

"No…"

She sighed. He grinned and her mouth widened with it.

"Vasile likes them." He got up. "They don't mess with the stock, and they eat the things that might."

He held out his arms.

"It's okay." Rayya went past him and set the box down. "Not that heavy."

She took out the jar she'd liberated from the arachnids, wiped it with a forearm. Greyness smeared her sleeve. Her grip slipped off the lid when she tried to open it.

"Let me…"

"I can do it." Rayya shifted her body and held it away from him. "Vasile will think I'm useless if I need you to do everything."

"He isn't even here."

"That's not the point."

She braced it on the table, rubbed both hands on her breeches, and got a better grasp. Her fingers hurt, but the lid popped. She put it aside and sniffed. Mushrooms and mould. Rayya shook a piece out into her palm.

"Mum used to make these into tea, when we were sick."

"Old wives' tale," Sachin said. "They don't do much in a tea."

"I loved drinking it."

"Yeah. Me too…"

She put it back in, closed the lid, and wrote the mushroom's name on a sliver of parchment. Rayya bound the label to the jar and put it on a shelf. Sachin peered over her head.

"He'll like that. Vasile says he can never read my writing. Yours always was neater."

She sorted through the rest, while Sachin chopped, soaked, and mangled herbs. Dried leaves. Desiccated berries. Something that floated in brine. Rayya lifted it, turned it around, and frowned. She'd mistaken it for a pickled pig's foot in the gloom below, but it looked more like-

"I'll…" Sachin coughed and snatched it away from her. "I'll take that."

"What is it?"

"It's from a hanged man. Used in love tonics."

They worked in silence for a while, until the shop door opened. Rayya went out behind the counter.

"Hi! How can-"

Her throat tightened.

"Is Vasile here?"

The Kharji's eyes bored into her. Rayya took a step backwards and bumped into a shelf. A sprig of rosemary tickled her cheek. She had a knife! The Kharji had a knife on her belt! Steel. Fire. Screams. Her parents, lying in the-

"Sorry." Sachin moved in front of her. "He's out gathering herbs. Won't be back till late."

The Kharji swore. Her gaze flicked from Sachin to Rayya, and Rayya looked away.

"The mawlana's ill. We need something to cure her."

"I'm Vasile's apprentice. Maybe I can help?"

The woman swore again, but she handed him a rolled-up piece of parchment. Sachin unfurled it and read.

"This is Doctor Zubeida's hand."

"You know her?"

"I've prepared things for her before."

The Kharji's shoulders unstiffened. Sachin pursed his lips, carried on reading, then looked up at her.

"I can mix an elixir. It should do what she wants."

"Should?"

"I can't promise-"

"If she dies..." Her eyes flashed.

"Wait here."

He went through to the other room. Rayya darted after him, leaned in close, hissed in his ear.

"She's a Kharji!"

"I know." Sachin pinned the parchment's corners to a board on the wall and read it once more. "So's the doctor."

"They killed mum and dad!" Rayya winced, glanced at the doorway. The woman was out of sight and she exhaled. "You can't..."

"Doctor Zubeida's a good woman. She helps people, even the ones who can't pay. She's never killed anyone."

"They burned our village. Our house."

"Other Kharjis did. Not the ones in Lemstras. Does that girl out there look like she goes around with a bunch of raiders in the wilderness?"

"No..."

She tried to grunt but it became a sniff and her eyes watered. Sachin hugged her.

"Sit down. It's okay."

Sachin whooshed around the room. His hands, his steps, didn't falter or fumble. She'd never seen him move like this in the Shimud house. He grabbed ingredients, measured, cut.

"Mind putting some water on the fire?"

Rayya nodded and filled a pot from the jug. Sachin ground pebble-like things under a pestle. Rayya shivered. When the water boiled, Sachin threw a handful of herbs into it. He brewed and poured, mixed and sprinkled. It might've been a game from their childhood. But his eyes and lips were firm. His fingers nipped and pinched motes of dried leaves or powders, and didn't drop a single grain.

He filled a bottle, smothered a wisp of steam with the stopper, and went to the counter. Rayya held back for a second or two, then followed.

"Here you go."

Sachin put the vessel down, held onto it as he named his price. The Kharji's hand went for her belt. Rayya's mouth opened. But the woman's fingers darted to the opposite side from her weapon and Rayya swallowed the scream. The Kharji's eyes widened. She groaned.

"I forgot to bring the money."

"Oh…"

She and Sachin stared at one another. Rayya's heart quivered.

"I'll come back with it later. I swear, by the Goddess."

"I…"

"The mawlana needs this!" Her eyes hardened. Her fingers scratched at the pouch, inched towards the sheath. "I-"

"Fine." Sachin released the bottle. "Just bring the money when you can."

"Thank you."

She snatched the elixir, strode to the door, and ran off. Sachin closed it behind her. He came back and Rayya threw her arms around him.

• • •

Apostates moaned. Their heads lolled, torsos slumped. Spikes transfixed their wrists and ankles. Eyes looked down as Fahmaia wove between the poles, but their gazes drifted like the wind.

"Help…" The woman's tresses hid her face.

"You renounced the Goddess." Fahmaia pressed onward. "I can't save you."

The mawlana ran. The shriek chased her.

"And *you* renounced all the others!"

"There's only one," she whispered. "Only one."

"One Goddess, One Goddess, glaring in the sky…" The children's song drew her though she didn't want to go. "Wherever she looks, little children die."

Leaves crunched underfoot. She walked among dead trees and their music echoed above.

"Mawlana, mawlana, glaring on the ground…" Their heads giggled and rocked the branches that impaled them. "Whenever she walks, horrors will abound."

Another crunch, then a crack. Bones broke beneath her boots. Fahmaia ran and they cracked, crunched, cracked forever. Someone else ran too. A girl.

"Clara!"

The girl looked over her shoulder and laughed.

"Mawlana, mawlana, couldn't save the world! Angering the Goddess, into fire hurled!"

Fahmaia leapt, tackled her. They crashed to the ground, smashed through ribcages and femurs and skulls. She went for Clara's throat but the skeletal tide swept them apart and Fahmaia screamed.

Bone dust filled her mouth. Herbs and honey and-

The mawlana thrashed. Faces hovered around her.

"Get the bucket! She's-"

"Mawlana, can you-"

Foulness surged up her throat, gushed from her nose and mouth. Voices blared but no words found her brain. Her head slumped back down into softness. The bottom half of her face stung. It didn't matter. The darkness took it all away.

• • •

"She was amazing." Clara pulled herself up onto the counter. "Like a real queen."

"Sachin said she was good."

Rayya bent over the collection of green things, picked one up, and held it closer to the candle. She mumbled an incomprehensible word, then put it into a jar. Clara's heels drummed on the wood.

"In this one bit-"

"Clara! Could you-"

"Oh. Sorry." Her legs went still. "Want a hand?"

"Sure."

She jumped down and surveyed Vasile's bounty. Clara didn't recognise everything, but she knew enough. Together they sorted them, piece by piece.

"They turn these things into cures and salves." Rayya plucked berries off a twig. "It's like magic."

"Which one turns cats purple?"

"I don't know. But I'll make Sachin teach me."

Rayya's smile shone. Clara sucked in the smell of herbs and her muscles softened. Her friend had landed. And Rayya's head was already growing back…

Clara grinned as she sorted.

Duck. Duck. Duck. Duck. Duck.

The stairs creaked. Vasile came down into the shop, rubbed his neck, and grimaced.

"When I said you had to work, I didn't mean all night. The rest'll keep till morning."

"Thanks…" Rayya glanced up long enough to smile at him. "But I want to get them done."

Vasile looked to Clara, but she just shrugged. Rayya Shimud didn't leave things half-done. The apothecary locked the front door and took the key.

"If you need to go outside…"

"Yeah, we know," Clara said.

"Goodnight."

"Goodnight," they chorused.

He went back up the stairs and the girls carried on.

"I'll be the best apothecary." Rayya scraped a mushroom. Flecks peeled away and fell onto the counter.

"Better than Sachin?"

Rayya smirked.

"Always. And if you like the theatre, you'll be an actress."

"I can't act."

"Just pretend. Everyone in Lemstras will go see your plays, cry their eyes out-"

"Or laugh their guts out…"

"Gross. Then they'll come here and buy something to make them feel better. We'll make a fortune."

"I'll break them, you'll fix them."

"Exactly." Her smile wavered. She looked at Clara's gloved hand. "Oh… I didn't…"

"It's okay."

The candle flickered. They worked in silence for a minute or two.

"Is this one mugwort?" Clara said.

"Yeah. Just…" Rayya turned her head and yawned.

"Go to bed. I can do the rest."

"It isn't your job."

"You'll be an apothecary. I'll be a Rayya-looker-afterer, so you don't forget to eat and sleep. It's fine. I'm not tired. It'll give me something to do."

"Thanks."

Rayya touched her left hand. Coolness tingled through Clara's flesh. Would it still feel good when Rayya held scales instead of skin? She forced a smile and wished her friend goodnight.

Wax dribbled down the candle.

Clara closed the last jar, swept the debris away. Her eyes weren't heavy. Even inside the shop, the night air soothed them. She left the light and meandered through the shadows. Stroked herbs on the shelves. Picked up bottles, set them back down. She wandered into the other room. Smiled at Rayya's writing on the labels. Rolled her eyes at the mess on Sachin's table.

She went down into the cellar, wrapped herself in odours and gloom. Spiders scuttled. Miniscule eyes watched her.

"Will I be scarier than you?"

Spider-steps answered her, but she didn't understand them anyway. Clara thought about rummaging through the stock. Maybe something interesting or sinister lurked amid all that junk... But she could already see Rayya's scowl. She climbed back up the stairs.

A knock echoed through the shop. Then another, and a woman's voice.

"Hello?"

Clara went to the front door, turned the handle. It didn't budge. She brought her face closer to the wood.

"Sorry. We're closed. If it's an emergency, I can wake up Mr. Zarabanov. But..."

"I need to pay him. Or the boy."

"Sachin?"

"He made something for me. I said I'd come back with the money. Could you...?"

"The door's locked, and I don't have the key. Hang on..." She unlatched the shutters and opened the window. "Over here. Just pass it through."

"Thanks. I..."

The Kharji appeared at the window. A pouch dangled from her fingers. She stared at Clara. Clara took a breath. This girl didn't kill Ella Mandrake, didn't burn Traverd to the ground. She was just a customer, and-

"Clara?"

"Huh?"

Clara blinked.

"Is your name Clara?"

"Yeah... How...? Hey!"

The pouch clinked on the floor. The Kharji grasped the edges of the window and pulled herself up onto the sill.

• • •

Ink shone. The words dried and dulled under Rashida's nose. She tried to conjure up fresh ones, but they lodged in her mind and the quill remained in the inkwell like a sword in a soldier's corpse. The imam rubbed her eyes. Everything blurred, then settled, though a haze still hung around the edges.

She opened the cupboard and her hand stopped an inch away from the wine jug. Rashida closed it again. She went back to her desk, sat down, and pondered Allat's lore. The same scripture that covered the mawlana's skin…

The imam closed her eyes and cupped her hands.

"Goddess, please end Fahmaia Hashad's suffering. She has strayed, and threatens the peace and prosperity of our brothers and sisters. But you once smiled upon her. May you show her mercy in the next life, and let her atone for her sins. But please, let this be over. Insha'Allat."

She brushed her hands over her face, picked up the quill, and translated another line. The imam dipped the nib again. Eyes and mind flicked across the next verse, envisioned the shape it would bear in the infidels' tongue.

The door creaked.

Rashida's breath hardened. Ink dripped, but she yanked the quill aside and it bloomed on a piece of scrap parchment.

"Imam?" Jasmina said.

"Come in!"

Rashida readied her face. Dreamt up words. She'd have to console the whole community… The door opened. Jasmina came into the study, and Rashida's intestines turned to stone.

"Is she…?"

But the woman's eyes told the tale.

"The doctor says she'll recover."

"Has… Has the mawlana spoken?"

The imam's hand quivered. More ink drops blossomed. But she steadied it, formed a phantom smile. Jasmina hadn't come with a sword in her grasp, so…

"Not yet. She's sleeping."

"Allat be praised. Thank you for letting me know."

Jasmina nodded and left. Rashida put the quill down, got up, and shoved her fingers into her mouth to stifle a scream. Fahmaia would wake, speak. Denounce the imam. Send Jasmina and Azim to hack her to pieces. Or else come herself, eyes blazing, scripture flashing…

Rashida would die for Allat. She'd become a martyr, and feast at the One Goddess' banquets. But… The imam's jaws clamped together. Teeth grated. Her congregation would know nothing of that. To them, she'd be a traitor. Perhaps even an apostate! Generations would grow up cursing her name. She tottered, put a hand on her desk.

Words hovered beneath her. The translation… Her gift to Allat and all the souls it might save… It couldn't perish! Her work and reputation were too important. Rashida took her satchel, laid the parchments inside. She closed each book and added them too. The bag hung like a sack of bricks. Its strap dug into her shoulder.

Rashida Al-Taquba stood in the prayer hall. Her gaze swept its walls, followed the patterns on the carpet. She wiped her cheek. The imam left her masjid and strode through the night.

One day she'd return. After Fahmaia's folly destroyed the mawlana. Her congregation would weep and embrace her. They'd speak of her books and letters, the salvation she'd brought to the Kharji people. Her eyes stung, but she thanked Allat for the vision, prayed it would come to pass.

Rashida's shoulder ached. She switched the satchel to the other side. Not far now. She'd take her mother's prayer beads, money, and some clothes. Hire a horse? It'd been a long time since she'd ridden. Maybe a wagon…

"Imam?"

Footsteps echoed in the alley. Rashida turned.

"Fatima? Is… Is something wrong?"

"I know."

"W… What do you mean?"

Rashida took a step backwards. Shadows covered the girl's face, but the knife glinted.

"You tried to kill the mawlana."

"Wait!" The imam took off the strap. Her fists clenched around it. "You don't understand…"

"Allatu Akbar!"

She lunged. Rashida swung the satchel at her head. Fatima's left arm rose, blocked it. The young woman staggered a step. Rashida pulled it back, flailed again, and crumpled. Agony twisted through her guts.

"Fatima…"

The bag thudded by her feet. She grasped at the girl's shirt, but her fingers wouldn't close.

"Death to apostates."

Fatima's cheek glistened. Rashida's legs fell away, and the night closed around her.

• • •

Clara backpedalled.

"What're you-"

The Kharji's eyes shone. It didn't make sense. This was stupid, crazy. But Clara knew that look. She tore off her glove, cast it aside. The woman struggled in the window, shifted her shoulders inside its frame. Clara undid the knot, gripped the sheath of bandages, and froze.

Rayya…

Not here. Not here. Not here.

Clara ran. The woman swore. Clara dashed across the back room, to the rear door. Something thudded on the shop floor. Clara tore at the bolts. Iron grated, clunked. She yanked it open, ran through the yard. She attacked another bolt. It caught her skin, pinched and pierced. Footsteps pounded. Wood bashed the wall. Clara sprinted into the alley, through shadows and starlight.

She turned down another passage. A gash between two houses. Her boots ate the ground and her heartbeat pumped fire through her muscles. Was the noise closer behind now? Didn't matter. Just needed to take her as far away as possible, through the tangle of backstreets…

Clara turned again, hurtled onward. Bricks loomed ahead of her.

"Stupid place for a wall…"

But as good a place to fight and die as any. Clara took off her bandage-glove, shoved it into her belt. Footfalls echoed away as the Kharji appeared.

Clara Mandrake angled her body, hid her right hand. She took a step towards the woman and the Kharji faltered.

"I'm sorry." The Kharji's knife hand trembled. She planted one foot in front of the other, and her knee shook too. "I…"

Clara smiled. Her own limbs didn't twitch, save for the curl and uncurl of her fingers.

"How do you know my name?"

The Kharji's feet shifted.

"If you're going to kill me, I want to know why."

"The mawlana…" Her knuckles whitened on the handle. "I have to…"

Clara sniffed. How had she never smelled fear before, when it stank like that? A lake of sweat and piss. And beyond it, something else…

"Did you follow me from my village?"

"No… Not me. The mawlana, and… I'll make this quick. I promise. She doesn't want you to suffer…"

"You mean the snake-woman?"

The Kharji blinked at her.

"The one with things that move on her face. I saw her… She told you to kill me?"

"You're the last one. We have to save the world!"

"What-"

The Kharji lurched forward. Her blade shivered. Clara slipped aside and clawed at her. The woman flinched, cried out. Coppery perfume tingled in the air.

Clara darted, thrust her fingers at the woman's face. The Kharji caught hold of her, behind the thumb. Twisted. A digit dug into the back of Clara's hand and pain shot through her joints. The Kharji wrenched the wristlock, drove Clara down onto one knee.

"Djinn!"

Clara growled, thrashed. But her elbow bent and she landed on her back. The Kharji's knee crushed her ribcage, pinned her down. The blade glimmered. And Clara grinned.

The woman's head snapped round, followed the girl's gaze to the rooftop. She made a sound. It died when the purple shape landed on her, knocked her off Clara, ground her into the dirt. Pink talons slashed and she died too. Clara sat up, held her wrist. The monster's eyes gleamed over the Kharji's corpse.

"Hello, Clara Mandrake." His accent made each word magic. "My name is Xerachus."

Flesh ripped under his claws.

"She's already dead."

"And now her death will look like the work of weapons."

"Oh."

"We must speak, but away from here. Come."

The monster sprang onto the wall that severed the alley.

"I can't…"

But Clara got up, coiled her legs, and jumped. Her hands latched onto the top, feet scrabbled till she clambered up next to him. Xerachus nodded and jumped down on the other side. He loped away, looked over his shoulder, and carried on going.

Clara followed, through the city's bowels. Amid the rats and refuse. He vanished but the purple-pink scent lingered. She chased it to the gates of the park, over the grass. Into the copse where he waited.

"I've dreamed about you." Clara sat in front of him. Close enough for claws, whether pink or black. "In my room. Inside the wardrobe."

"Just dreams?"

"I don't..."

"Do you remember your father?"

"No. He died when I was... Oh."

Her eyes closed. The shadow-man leaned over her bed. Warm fingers stroked her and she shivered...

"He... He..."

"Touched you. Hurt you. I stopped him."

"Mum said..."

"My claws were thinner then." They fluttered in front of his face, carved the air. "I slid one into his brain. She thought he had a fit, like a deranged prophet, and bled within his skull."

Clara waited for the inner girl to shriek, for the distant child to weep over her father. But that Clara was gone. Perhaps she'd never been there at all.

"I stopped him, but I was too late. The damage was done. When I returned to Traverd, weeks ago... when I smelled your scent... I knew. So I waited."

"In my wardrobe."

"I can... melt... into dark places. To hide and heal."

"Why didn't you show yourself? Talk to me?"

"What would you have done, Clara Mandrake? What would you have done if I had revealed myself?"

"Screamed and run for help."

"I had to wait for the change. But you surprised me. Sensed my presence before that."

"You saved me and Rayya. From the Kharjis."

"You were my responsibility."

"Have you come to cure me?"

"There is no cure. You will continue to change."

"To kill me then?"

"Do you want me to slay you, Clara Mandrake?"

"No."

"Then I will not."

She held out her hand, spread her fingers. Placed her claws against his.

"Is this where all monsters come from?"

"Some."

"Like you?"

"Yes."

"So what happens now?"

"You cannot hide your claws and your scales forever. You must abandon this place."

"Like a duck…"

"I do not understand."

"Nothing. I'll live in the forests. With the wolves."

"No. We will wander together, until you are strong enough for this world."

"Oh…"

"We can leave tonight, if you wish."

"No. I… I can't. Rayya…" She sighed. "Not tonight."

"You are in danger. If one Kharji found you…"

"I know."

"Very well. I will wait for you here. Finish your human life as you see fit. When you are ready, come to me."

"What if someone sees you?"

"They will not."

Xerachus stood and went to an oak, touched the crack that marred its trunk. The monster poured himself into the blackness. In moments he was gone.

16

"That's from the Caracallan Empire." Silas pointed.

Cracks and pockmarks scarred the arch, but its marble still gleamed in the morning light.

"I suppose there's a Caracallan amphitheatre on your family's estate? Perhaps a set of baths, or a villa?"

"No! Just a…. Well, a temple." He could've sworn she smirked, but when he looked round there was no trace of it. "More of a small shrine, really."

They led their horses towards the stables. Grooms and porters were at work, brushing manes, re-shoeing a stallion, lugging baggage. Others sat around on crates, chewed and chatted. Silas went up to the nearest loiterers.

"Excuse me. We're looking for a couple of girls. They're about ten or-"

"Bit young for you, aren't they?"

The man's nose split his grin. A few people chuckled, until Katrina glared at them.

"They're called Clara and Rayya," he said. "Would've got here a couple of days ago, on a merchant's cart from Hogmire. One's got dark skin, wears her hair in a long braid. The other's olive-skinned. She had a cut on her mouth, where she got punched."

"Oh!" A woman came over, clutching a horseshoe. "The little footballers."

"Yeah. You talked to them?"

"Had to, when I saw that one's face. Thought the bloke they rode with might've done it to her. Was all set to give him the stable special…" Her doublet flexed. The horseshoe-fist snapped a right cross. "But she said it was from the game and looked to be telling the truth."

"She was. Do you know where they went?"

"Asked the way to Zarabanov's. The apothecary shop."

"Whereabouts?"

"You head straight down the road, then…"

Silas nodded along to each instruction and lodged them in his brain.

"Got somewhere to stay in the city?"

"Not yet," Katrina said. "Know somewhere decent?"

"Marlow's place is just up the road. Your stuff'll be safe there, and you won't wake up with things scuttling around your privates."

Silas coughed.

"If you stable your horses with me, my lads and lasses won't walk off with anything either. You can come back for it later, or send one of Marlow's kids. They'll fetch and carry for a couple of coins."

Katrina paid her price. The woman shook her hand, then Silas'.

"Might want to leave those swords here. Or stow them in your rooms. New law. Knives and daggers are fine, but you can't wear swords on the street anymore."

"Has there been trouble?" Katrina said.

"Ever since Traverd. You two heard about that?"

"We were there. When the militia burned the bodies."

"Was it as bad as they say?"

"Worse."

The stable-mistress muttered something that might've been a prayer or profanity.

"We have Kharjis in the city. People've been picking fights with them, and they're giving as good as they get. Harsh words and punches in the street mostly. But last night two of them bit it. Mayor's scared and the peacekeepers are too. If they catch you carrying swords, they'll come down hard."

"Thank you for the warning."

"Want me to hang on to them?"

Silas touched his pommel, but Katrina shook her head and he took his hand off it.

"We'll keep them in our room," she said.

Katrina took a couple of bags off her horse. Silas did the same. The monster hunters went into Lemstras, skirted a cart heading in the opposite direction, and wandered along the road. Two women in blue and black tabards accosted them before they'd gone a dozen yards.

"Halt!" The younger woman lowered her halberd and aimed its point at Silas' chest. "By order of the-"

The other peacekeeper sighed, grabbed her companion's weapon, and pointed it skyward.

"Sorry. This one's new. Blasted commanders made us rush all the recruits into uniform."

The girl reddened.

"But she's right. No-"

"No swords on the street." Katrina nodded. "We're on our way to Marlow's."

"We'll walk with. Not that we don't trust you, but…"

"You have a job to do."

The inn wasn't much further. All four of them went inside, and the elder peacekeeper went to the bar.

"Two strong wines, Marlow. Need to settle the girl's nerves before she skewers some poor traveller."

The youngster leaned in to Silas.

"I wasn't going to skewer you."

He didn't know what to say to that, so he just nodded.

"And these two want a room."

The man named a price, took Katrina's money, and handed over a key. They went upstairs and dumped their bags. Katrina unbuckled her belt, detached her scabbard. She brought a dagger out of her pack and wore that across from her bludgeon instead. Silas did the same.

Their escorts were still drinking at the bar when they went back down. They exchanged nods, then the monster hunters headed into the street.

"Untrained youths with uniforms and polearms." Katrina's eye narrowed. "They're as likely to start trouble as quell it."

Silas wanted to go back into the inn. Take the girl aside. Tell her what it felt like when you saw blood on your blade and life sloughing from someone's eyes. He walked on instead.

They rounded a corner, passed a few shops. Kids lurked in the shadows under the awnings, cast glances as they set up displays or served customers. The shoppers hurried away with their purchases. A Kharji came down the street and people whispered. She stopped, glared at a shopkeeper.

"What're you looking at?"

"Nothing, love."

The merchant dropped her gaze and fumbled with her wares. The Kharji walked off. Silas turned side-on to avoid her shoulder. She snorted and said something in another language.

There were more of them just before the crossroads. Four youths stood close together but spoke as if bellowing across a town square.

"...the imam. Allat watch over her."

"...stabbed..."

"I heard a peacekeeper say they cut her throat."

"Beheaded."

"No. Stabbed. My sister helped wash the body. The peacekeepers are full of crap."

"Bloody infidels..."

"A bunch of them kicked her turban up the street. Pissed on it!"

Across the road, two girls whispered. One of them giggled. A Kharji boy stormed towards them.

"You think it's funny?"

"What?"

"Think you can laugh at our imam?"

"I wasn't! We were just-"

He seized a handful of ginger hair and she wailed. The other girl grabbed his forearm.

"Get off her!"

A Kharji woman ran at her, shoved her chest. The girl fell backwards and smacked the wall. The other two Kharjis advanced.

"Want me to cut your nose off?" He shook the ginger girl.

"No! Please!"

"Then the imam can laugh, when she looks down and sees you in the hellfire."

"Oi!" Silas strode at them. The other three Kharjis closed ranks. "Let her go. Now."

The boy wrenched her head and she screamed. He tossed her aside. She rolled on the ground, came up on her knees. Dust and dirt clung to her hair. The Kharji pulled out his knife. Two of the others did the same. The fourth gawped at them.

"Wait!" She turned her body, as though to run. But her eyes didn't leave them. "We-"

Silas took the bludgeon off his belt. The one who'd manhandled the girl lunged. Silas tapped the Kharji's wrist. The Kharji yelped, dropped his blade.

"Stop!"

The unarmed girl leapt at Silas. He threw a push-kick at her abdomen and she landed on her back. Silas whirled round, but the other two were already running. One held his forearm. The woman clutched her shoulder. Katrina lowered her bludgeon and let it dangle from her hand.

"Kuffar bastard!"

The Kharji boy spat at Silas, but it splatted on the ground between them. He glared, stepped towards the monster hunter. Silas drew back his bludgeon, took aim at the lad's collarbone. But the woman who hadn't drawn her weapon was back up. She grasped the boy's shoulder.

"Don't! The peacekeepers…"

He grunted but followed her. The two of them ran after their companions. Their victims gawked at Silas and Katrina, then disappeared down an alley.

"That's right!" A woman outside the tailor's shop pumped her fist in the air. "Bash the stinkin' Kharjis!"

Katrina pursed her lips.

"Come on…"

Silas nodded. They turned down another street and continued towards the apothecary shop.

• • •

Sergeant Gunther kicked the pickpocket a few more times. The kid groaned, rolled on the ground, and clutched his crotch.

"Now…" He added one more, but lighter this time. "Are you going to do any more robbing?"

"No! No!"

"You sure?" The next kick was just a tap.

"No! I mean… Yes! Yes!"

"Glad to hear it." Gunther turned to his partner. "You can take it from here, can't you?"

"Sure, sarge!" The young woman drew back her boot.

The pickpocket yelped. Gunther sighed and blocked the kick with his sole.

"I meant take him away."

"To jail?"

"To his parents. I know them. They'll give him a good hiding."

"Oh…"

She dragged the boy to his feet and led him off. He hobbled, but he'd get over that. The best justice lingered on the body for a while and stuck in the mind forever. Gunther made a mental note to tell the girl that.

The sergeant sauntered down the street and whistled his favourite tune. As he passed the last house, he let out a sigh. Lemstras was a fine place. But his own mentor had taught him that a peacekeeper needed somewhere away from the crap, literal or otherwise. So he trod over the grass. Ran his hand along marble, which dozens of peacekeeper buttocks had worn smooth over the years. Pulled himself up onto the fallen column. His muscles relaxed and he sighed again.

Gunther took a pinch of chew-weed from his pouch, popped it in his mouth. He masticated the clump till its staleness dissolved into a sharp-sweet mass. Chew-weed and a decent view. What more did a man need? He leaned back. Trees swayed on the horizon.

He frowned.

A cart trundled out from the wood. Men and woman flanked it, traipsed over the grass. Gunther murmured. Maybe they'd do the sensible thing and leave it on the plain… But they continued towards the city. Gypsies…

"Oi!"

Gunther beckoned the driver when the cart drew near the column. The other gypsies stared at him. But the man with the black mane jumped down from the vehicle and came over. His beard clinked. How many necklaces and amulets hid under that thing? Seemed pointless to wear them like that, but the peacekeeper didn't pretend to understand gypsy ways.

"Good morning." The man bowed his head.

"You've picked the wrong road."

"Oh? It's brought us to Lemstras, has it not?"

"Yeah. But it's narrow. Some of the turns'll be a tight squeeze for that cart of yours. Most wagons take one of the others, so they don't block up the street."

"A thousand apologies."

"What're you selling, anyway?"

"Fruit, clothes, trinkets…"

"Brought a fair few people for merchant work, haven't you?"

Another gypsy shifted her weight from foot to foot.

"My clan's heard so much about your city. No one wanted to miss its sights."

Gunther snorted.

"Don't know about sights, but the ale's good and the food won't kill you. If you…"

He glanced round. A woman in Kharji clothes came along the road. She stopped in front of the bearded man then looked at Gunther.

"Jasmina." The gypsy nodded. His hidden jewellery rattled.

"Kh… Barzik." She nodded back.

Kh'Barzik… He'd never get used to those gypsy names.

"If you'll excuse us, peacekeeper, our customers are waiting."

Another gypsy climbed into the driver's seat. The bearded man walked alongside it with the Kharji. Similar, weren't they, Kharji and gypsy clothes?

"Hey, wait…"

The man and woman looked over.

"Got any apples?"

The man reached into the cart. His beard clanked, but nothing gleamed beneath it.

"You're in luck, my friend."

He tossed a green ball to Gunther, who caught it one-handed.

"Thanks."

The gypsy bowed. Gunther took a bite. The crunch brought a flood of juice that mingled with the chew-weed. He sighed, munched away, and watched the gypsies pass.

• • •

"Like this…"

Rayya cracked the egg. Gloop dripped into the pan. The yolk flopped after it, but not a single shell-flake.

"Oh…" Clara picked one up in her glove. "Hmm…"

"Maybe you should…" Rayya sighed and covered it with a smile. "Let me."

She took it, tapped it, opened it. Lard sizzled and spat. Sulphurous smells turned Vasile's kitchen into an appetising underworld. Clara hugged her.

"Hey! Careful!"

Rayya jerked and droplets flew at them. Clara shielded her friend with her arm. They fizzed on her skin but she didn't care. Rayya laughed and Clara beamed.

"What was that for?"

"Because you're the best egg-cracker in the world."

"Um... Thanks?" She added rashers of bacon, and porcine hell was even more wondrous.

Rayya cooked, and the smile hollowed out behind Clara's lips. She couldn't tell her friend. Not now. It'd have to be later, in the evening. Right before she...

"Morning!" Vasile came into the kitchen, yawned, and sniffed. "Better than your brother cooked."

"Really?"

Rayya grinned and filled their plates. They sat around the table, gobbled away, and Clara dreamt. She'd hack her hand off. Stop the scales before they spread. Live here forever, and... Bacon tore in her mouth. Flesh and blood and death. Her claws twitched.

"Hey, could I borrow a hood? It's cold outside."

"If you want." Vasile chewed a chunk of bread. "Might be a bit big for you."

"That's okay."

They ate, cleaned up. Vasile gave her the garment and it fit on her shoulders well enough. She pulled the cowl over her head. It was almost a blanket, but it'd do. Downstairs, the apothecary picked up a box and went off to make his deliveries. Rayya stationed herself behind the counter. Clara wanted to hug her again, but held back. No crazy Clara routine. Not yet. Save that for tonight...

She went to the door. It opened and she jumped back.

"Sorry." Sachin turned side-on and slid past her.

"You're late!" Rayya said. "I was here early. Slacker..."

"You live upstairs."

"Details."

"And there was a fight…"

"Huh?" The grin vanished. "Are you-"

"I'm fine. But a boy had his nose broken, and I stopped to help him." He touched Clara's arm. "Be careful out there. I hear it wasn't the only one. The Kharjis are scrapping with everyone today."

Clara's fists clenched.

"Why?" Her voice throbbed. She swallowed, tried again. "What happened?"

"Two of their lot got killed last night."

"Two?" She blinked.

"One of them was Rashida Al-Taquba. Their leader."

"The snake-woman?"

Her face lit up before she could stop it. Sachin and Rayya stared.

"Huh?" His brow creased.

"I… I saw one with stuff on her skin. Markings?"

"No, I've seen Rashida. Their imam, or whatever. She didn't wear anything like that."

"Oh. Well, I should…"

She waved to Rayya and left the shop. A dead woman's voice echoed in her ears.

"The mawlana…"

That was it. Not imam. Mawlana.

"You're the last one."

That meant Rayya was safe, didn't it? But… She chewed the side of her tongue. Should she have told Rayya? Destroyed her smile and made her cringe every time the door opened? Clara's eyes narrowed. Her friend shouldn't have to live in the same city as their parents' murderers.

Ah! Before she left, she'd write a message, wrap it around a rock, throw it through their window. They had a temple or something. A... masjid? She'd tell them Clara Mandrake was leaving Lemstras, and they could come after her if they wanted.

She spread her fingers.

Blood. Blood. Blood.

Clara grinned under her hood.

• • •

They'd almost unloaded the first cart when the second rolled into the yard behind the masjid.

"Mawlana."

"Barzik."

Fahmaia embraced the warlord, but kept her face away from his beard. She let go and stepped back.

"Your sword... I..."

"So be it. The Goddess' blessings are hers to give or take. Perhaps she'll favour us with another, once we've earned it."

Warriors clambered over the vehicle, handed down barrels and boxes. Foodstuffs and other goods flowed into the masjid. She grimaced. None of these gifts would go to waste today, with a whole congregation to feed afterwards.

"Are we in time to pay our respects? Jasmina told us... An imam!" The warlord's eyes flashed. "An imam, struck down like a dog!"

The back of Fahmaia's throat twinged, but she nodded. Let the dead have their secrets...

"Allat foresees everything," she said. "I thought our warriors would help search for the girl, not protect our brothers and sisters."

"Our eyes and blades are ready."

He tilted his head at the cart. Azim passed a bundle of weapons down to Jasmina, who carried them inside. Barzik and the mawlana followed her. Fahmaia gave instructions, had things laid in the storeroom, then led the newcomers into the prayer hall.

Congregants knelt around the space in the middle of the chamber. White shirts and trousers shone like candles. Redness stained their eyes. Most were dry now, but Fatima wailed and sprawled over Yasmin. Tears darkened the cloth that swaddled the corpse. Had the two been more than friends and sisters in faith? Fahmaia wished she'd known the girl better, and Lemstras' other believers. This was an imam's role she had to play. But Rashida lay there too, so what else could she do?

"Brothers, sisters. This is Barzik Khan."

Their gazes fastened on the warlord. He bowed his head.

"Forgive me for intruding here, today of all days."

"The infidels killed Yasmin!" Fatima glared at him. "They murdered her!"

"There will be justice for her, and the imam."

Fatima looked away and wiped her eyes. The Khan clasped her shoulder, then kissed Yasmin on the forehead. He went to Rashida's corpse and did the same. In spite of everything, Fahmaia's eyes stung.

"My warriors will defend every believer as if you were our own flesh and blood. I swear this by Allat and our sword arms."

The mourners shuffled to make space, and Barzik knelt among them. His warriors found places of their own. Fahmaia cupped her hands and intoned scripture. When the last word left her lips, the congregants' own prayers whispered through the hall. The mawlana murmured laments for the young woman, then mustered up what she could for the imam.

"Allat, forgive Rashida Al-Taquba. She erred, but she loved her masjid and her community of believers. Let your mercy guide her in the next life."

Fahmaia gave them a few moments before she prayed aloud once more. Then everyone anointed their faces.

"Allatu Akbar!" Fatima's fist thrust upward and others followed.

The cry echoed around them.

"Allatu Akbar! Allatu Akbar! Allatu Akbar!"

The worshippers rose. They bore the corpses into the air, ferried them from hand to hand as they marched out of the masjid. Their chant flowed into Lemstras.

"Allatu Akbar! Allatu Akbar!"

Fahmaia Hashad wrapped her face, donned her gloves, and followed them.

• • •

Silas stopped at the door of the apothecary shop and looked at Katrina.

"Let me go first. They know me."

"You think my face might scare them?"

"Well…"

"Go on then."

He opened it and entered an ocean of aromas. A blend of gardens, banquets, and childhood medicines.

"Silas?" Rayya stood behind the counter, alongside a youth with an almost identical nose and smile. "What're you doing here?

"I…"

Rayya and the boy looked past him.

"Oh. This is Katrina. Katrina, Rayya and…"

"My brother. Sachin."

"We're looking for Clara. Is she here?"

"She's gone to the theatre. She works there now." Rayya looked from him to Katrina, then back again. Her smile faltered. "Is something wrong?"

"No-"

"Yes," Katrina said.

"Maybe? Look, we just have to-"

Katrina reached for her eyepatch. Silas opened his mouth, but she lifted it before he could speak. He winced and waited for the kids to scream. They wore matching frowns instead.

"That looks infected," Rayya said.

"I could mix up a-"

"Monster signs."

"Huh?" both siblings said.

"The traces are strong too." Katrina's gaze swept the shelves. "Do you have monster parts here? Hair? Ground scales?"

"No, nothing like that," Sachin said.

Rayya looked away.

"Rayya…" Silas waited till her eyes met his. "Have you and Clara been near a monster?"

"Yeah."

"What?" Sachin took her by the shoulders. "Where? How…?"

"In our village. It… It lived in Clara's wardrobe, and scared her. For days. Then-"

"That's ridiculous." Katrina crossed her arms. "Monsters don't lurk around to frighten little girls. They eat them and go on their way."

"I know it sounds crazy! That's why we… we didn't tell anyone."

"Your village… You lived in Traverd?"

She nodded.

"The monster came out when the Kharjis were in Clara's bedroom. It attacked them, and we ran. That's how we got away."

"Did the monster touch you? Bleed on you?"

"No."

Katrina scratched her scars.

"Even then, the traces wouldn't be this fresh. This strong. Not days later. You haven't seen it again?"

"Only that one night. After that… It didn't matter."

Katrina scowled, but Silas nodded. Traverd… The stench came back to him, assaulted his throat.

"Where's the theatre?" he said. "We'll have to talk to Clara."

Rayya looked to Sachin. The boy gawped for a second or two, till Katrina coughed. Then he blurted out some directions. Katrina turned and left. Silas thanked him and followed, but Rayya's voice stopped him in the doorway.

"Is Clara in danger?"

"I… I'll make sure she's okay. Promise."

He forced a smile. Rayya returned it, but her lips quivered.

...

"Damn Kharjis! Stop hogging the street!"

"Two down! Good start, that!"

"Where's your im-am, where's your im-am, where's your im-am over there?"

"Kharji scum, going down! Kharjis, Kharjis, going down!"

"Ha ha ha ha ha!"

Shouts, songs, and cheers drew Clara. She jogged towards the din, away from the theatre. People ran with her and past her. Some laughed, hollered. Others growled like beasts. A few wore no expression, made no sound, but meandered along with the rest.

A Kharji procession filled the street ahead. Men and women in white clothes marched past and bore two bundles.

"Oi!" A cart driver slammed her palm against her seat. "Hurry up! Some of us've got places to be!"

Several Kharjis glared at her. One spat in her direction. It fell short, but another cry went up.

"Kharji scum!"

A turnip flew from the crowd. It hit a Kharji's shoulder and the young woman whirled round, clenched her fists. A couple of bystanders backed away. But others jeered.

"Come on then!"

"Can't chop us up like you lot did in Traverd!"

More vegetables flew. The Kharjis babbled in both languages. Some waded into the crowd, went for the missile-throwers. Dozens of hands pushed them away. One Kharji pulled his fist back to smash a man's face, but a masked woman yelled at him and he withdrew.

That woman…

Her! It had to be!

Nearby, a boy held a box of onions. Wares or weapons? Clara didn't know and didn't care. She grabbed one. He might've shouted at her, but the chaos drowned him out. Clara hurled it.

The onion spun towards the woman. She slapped it aside without looking, and Clara Mandrake glared. The Kharjis went past. Some of the bystanders got on with their business, drove their carts or carried their goods. But others surged after the funeral procession. Clara hesitated. A press of bodies swept her along and she surrendered to it.

No wall or fence encircled the cemetery. The Kharjis filtered between the tombstones, towards their portion — where a hole gaped, and shovels protruded from a mound of earth like a hedgehog's spikes. The crowd spread among the graves but kept their distance.

"Kharjis, in the ground! Kharjis, Kharjis, in the ground!"

"Traverd!" Clara's voice broke through the others. Her eyes blazed. "Traverd! Traverd!"

"Traverd! Traverd! Traverd!"

"They killed my mum!"

Clara took her glove off, held it in her mouth. She undid the knot, tugged at the bandage-mitt, dropped it at her feet. A little kid peered over her mother's shoulder. The infant's eyes widened. Clara put the glove back on and touched a finger to her lips. The mother carried her kid away. The child's face stared till it disappeared. Clara's claws twitched. If she got close to the masked woman, it'd only take a second…

"Kharji scum, out of here! Kharji scum, out of here!"

"Traverd! Traverd! Traverd!"

A band of youths carried the taunts into the Kharji area. Several Kharjis moved towards them, but the masked woman called out and they picked up shovels instead.

"Traverd! Traverd! Traverd!"

"Murderers! You're all murderers!"

"You killed my cousin!"

The mourners worked together. Those with tools passed them on, but many used their hands instead of waiting. Shovelfuls and fistfuls of dirt fell together. Soon it was done.

"Screw you and screw your goddess!"

One boy darted closer than the rest. He lobbed a clod of earth and it exploded across a young woman's back. Grime clung to white cloth.

"Ha ha ha ha ha!"

The Kharji ran at him. He backed away, but she lunged, hit him in the face. His limbs flopped like a ragdoll's. The boy's head cracked against a gravestone. He lay there, didn't move, and crimson trickled on granite. People screamed. Half a dozen charged at the Kharji. She held her ground until other mourners pulled her back.

"He's dead! They killed him!"

A woman knelt by the boy. More clustered around her and the cry spread.

"Get them! Get the Kharjis!"

The crowd rushed over the graves. Someone knocked Clara and she bumped between several elbows. Taunts and war cries and shrieks for calm mixed together and it was all just noise. Fists flew. Shovels swung. Blood splattered on white and brown and everything else.

Clara slid through them. Barged where she had to. Where was the masked woman? Where–

A man smashed into her and she sprawled on the grass. She tried to get up, but a girl fell on her, pinned her down. Clara howled. She wrestled, and the girl groped at her face.

"Sorry!" Blood smeared the girl's eyes. She stank of urine. "I'm sorry! Please!"

Clara grunted and helped her up.

"Traverd! Traverd! Traverd!"

"Allatu Akbar!"

The Kharjis were running. But it wasn't a rout. They moved together, one beast with a hundred legs, guarded their flanks and rear. Most of the crowd fled from them. The rest caught fists or forearms and tumbled.

For several seconds there were only groans, sobs, and wails. Then the shouting started again. A new mob formed, left the injured and the cowards in their wake. Clara ran with them.

"Kill the Kharjis! Kill the Kharjis! They murdered my mum! They murdered the Shimuds! They murdered everyone! Kill the Kharjis!"

Another crowd had already gathered at the foot of the masjid's steps.

"They're inside!" a woman said.

"Tear it down!" A man threw a turnip and it bounced off the wall.

"Burn them out! Burn them out!"

"You lot, get back!" A peacekeeper ran in front of the mob, held her halberd across her chest. "Now!"

Other men and women in black and blue tabards formed up beside her.

"Those Kharjis killed my boy!"

"Where the hell were you?"

"Peacekeepers my arse!"

"Wankers!"

The middle of the crowd surged. Youths tussled, some in tabards, some in jerkins or bare-chested. Polearms shoved. A man took a shaft in the face, toppled backwards, but there wasn't room to fall.

"Traverd! Traverd! Traverd!"

"Disperse, all of you!"

"They're murderers! Let us at them!"

"Get back! We'll deal with them, but get back!"

Heat washed over Clara's hood.

"Watch it with that torch!" someone said.

More flames lapped above people's heads. The peacekeepers yelled. Some tried to penetrate the crowd, but bounced off as though they'd run into a wall.

"Look!"

"They're coming out!"

"Get them!"

"Oh, hell…"

Kharjis poured from the masjid, fanned out at the top of the stairs. Swords shone in the sunlight.

"Go back inside!" A silver-haired peacekeeper banged the butt of her halberd on the ground. "No weapons out here. We'll-"

"Keep them away from Allat's house." The masked woman turned her blade and its edge glimmered. "We'll defend it with our blood if we have to."

"Damn Kharjis!"

"Traverd! Traverd! Traverd!"

More voices cried out, but fewer bodies pressed against the line of tabards.

"We'll handle this," the peacekeeper said. "No more bloodshed."

"They killed my son!"

"Whoever did that will answer for it, but you'll disperse…" She turned back to the masjid. "And you Kharjis will take your swords inside."

The Kharjis and the mob glared at each other. Clara's fingers itched. She wanted to plough through the peacekeepers, charge up the stairs. Rip the masked woman's heart out. But a forest of swords and halberds stood between them, and the Kharji would live. Burn more villages. Murder more people like Ella Mandrake and the Shimuds.

Unless…

Clara squeezed and shoved and elbowed her way through the crowd. People yelped and yelled but she kept going, pushing, hitting, till the mob spat her out at its edge. She threw back her hood.

"Mawlana! I'm Clara Mandrake. Come and kill me."

17

Fatima's grip tightened around the sword. Her fingers sunk into grooves where another warrior's grasp had worn away the leather. She prayed she'd do that brother or sister proud.

"For Yasmin," she whispered.

Her gaze flayed the crowd. She pictured their vital points, the places her blade would spill blood and life. A woman's eyes met hers. Fatima glowered and she looked away. The Kharji grinned. Non-believers were cowards.

"Mawlana! I'm Clara Mandrake. Come and kill me."

The girl yelled at the edge of the crowd, and heads turned.

"Barzik!" Fahmaia went down onto the next step. Peacekeepers flinched in the street. "That's her! The girl from Traverd!"

Clara walked backwards a few paces, held her arms out to the sides as though she challenged the entire universe.

"Kill me, mawlana. Kill me, like you killed my mum."

"Get back!" The silver-haired peacekeeper levelled her halberd at Fahmaia. The others did the same. "Get back, or-"

"Kill me now, or I'll leave Lemstras and you'll never find me."

The girl backed away, and... Goddess! She actually smiled. Fatima prayed for such courage.

"Go, mawlana!" Azim raised his weapon. "Allatu Akbar!"

He leapt from the top of the stairs. Soared above the peacekeepers. Landed in their midst, roaring, cleaving. Everyone shouted. One man went down. Halberd points skewered the Kharji, but his sword still swung.

"Allatu Akbar!"

Other warriors sprang or charged down the steps. They crashed into the peacekeepers, into the crowd. Clara ran. Barzik Khan, the mawlana, and Jasmina skirted the melee and raced after her. A peacekeeper tried to intercept them, but another Kharji tackled her to the ground and they rolled amid the chaos.

"Allatu Akbar!"

A rock clipped Fatima's shoulder. Pain burst and turned to fire. She stormed down the stairs. An infidel hurled a torch, flames flashed over her head. Another threw a vegetable but it went wide. Then she was on them.

"Allatu Akbar!"

The man screamed and Fatima hacked his face. Her sword thudded instead of slicing, jarred her arm. But blood splashed and the man went down and Fatima cleaved, left and right.

"Allatu Akbar!"

A woman fled but there was nowhere to go. Bodies held her in place and Fatima slashed her across the back. The Kharji cut and cut and everything stank of bladders and bowels and smoke.

Hands grabbed her. She twisted, kicked, bit. A boy yelped and she tried to chop his neck, but her sword caught on something. Pain lanced her side. Her legs crumpled.

Fatima fell and her blood gushed and boots stamped on her hands, her shins. Tendrils snaked over the masjid. Yellow tongues lapped within its windows. She tried to shout, tried to warn the others. But an ocean flooded her mouth and black waves washed over her.

...

"Either Lemstras has taken up football," Katrina said, "or there's a riot happening over there."

A wisp of smoke rose above the rooftops. The wind carried it their way, along with the clamour. Silas frowned.

"Should we go help?" he said.

"We aren't peacekeepers. If we waded into a street battle, we'd likely as not catch one of their halberds in the gut."

"Clara might've got caught up in it. Could be why she didn't make it to the theatre."

"She'll go back home eventually. Better to wait for her there than fight our way through half the citizenry."

"Yeah, I suppose…"

They walked on. At the end of the street, a park sprawled in the sunlight. The monster hunters turned at its railings, but something darted at the edge of Silas' vision and he glanced, stopped, grabbed the bars. A girl sprinted over the grass. Two Kharji women came through the gates, chased after her. Swords flashed in their hands. A bearded man followed, but he stopped at the entrance and faced a pair of peacekeepers.

Katrina was already vaulting over the railings. Silas went after her, shouted as they ran.

"That's her! That's Clara!"

Katrina swore. Then a second time, louder than before, and Silas joined her. Another figure hurtled across the grass, from the opposite direction. This one was purple.

"Clara!" Silas waved his arms. "Watch out!"

She glanced at him, but didn't change direction. Clara went straight for the monster and it went for her. Katrina and Silas sped up. The masked Kharji called out, pointed at them.

"Jasmina!"

The other woman peeled away from the chase.

"Take her." Katrina gripped her bludgeon. "I've got the monster."

Silas' right hand closed around his club. His left drew the dagger. Jasmina slowed at the same time as him. Their chests rose and fell as they took up their stances.

"Stay back." The woman advanced, both hands on her weapon. "We have to do this. We won't harm you if-"

The bludgeon lashed out. She tapped it aside with the flat of her blade, made a cut of her own. He caught it on the dagger. Metal clinked, clanged. War music. Jasmina thrust and he dodged, struck to break her blade. But she was better than that and steel slid away before he struck. She sliced at his face. Both his weapons rose and it rang out across the park. Sword, dagger, and bludgeon locked. Muscles strained. Their eyes met.

Silas kneed her between the legs. Twice.

She buckled. He stabbed her in the side of the neck, twisted the dagger. Blood spurted. Jasmina fell. Silas dropped his bludgeon and snatched the sword from her fingers.

"Allatu Akbar!"

The bearded man charged at him. Behind, two bodies lay by the gates. Silas grimaced and adopted a long blade, short blade stance. This Kharji didn't slow down as Jasmina had. He chopped mid-run, and Silas leapt aside. The man pivoted, lunged. Silas parried with the dagger, thrust with the sword, and steel sang. Silas drove his dagger into the opening. Its point stabbed at the Kharji's breast, hit his beard, and clinked. Silas' arm shuddered. The Kharji threw his weight forward, sword on sword. Silas tried to shuffle. A leg hooked his and he staggered, flailed.

The Kharji slashed. Silas put up his sword. Metal grated. The Kharji's blade snaked around his, darted, and Silas cried out. Agony sliced the back of his forearm. His sword fell from his hand. The Kharji kicked his legs out from under him. Silas landed on his back, tried to roll. But the Kharji's boot stamped on his wrist, pinned the dagger.

That mass of beard loomed above as the Kharji's sword came down.

• • •

Katrina swung her bludgeon. The monster leapt back, hissed. She swept through the strike and brought the weapon round from another angle. Its claws raked at her face. She slipped aside but pain cut across her cheek, ripped through good skin and scars.

They circled one another. The monster lunged and she snapped a hit at its forearm. It growled, snatched the limb back. If she had her sword…

Katrina took aim. Perhaps a-

Silas cried out. The girl howled.

Katrina's gaze met the monster's. They both ran.

Silas was on the ground, the Kharji above him. And that was Barzik Khan. She'd seen sketches of the warlord's damn face, and now it would haunt her dreams with all the others, because they were too far and she was too slow, just like last time…

Katrina sprang. The sword came down. Steel struck iron and the note they made fluttered through her muscles. She shoved him back, away from Silas. Khan adjusted his footing. His eyes flicked, took her measure. He lunged and their weapons clinked again and again. The warlord's blade danced, too swift and sure to take the bludgeon's force straight-on. Katrina swung at his hands and wrists. His collarbone. Temple. Barzik Khan slipped or turned each strike.

If she had her sword…

Anguish pierced her abdomen, burst through her torso. The warlord twisted his blade and it gushed along her limbs. The bludgeon thumped on the ground. Barzik Khan's eyes flashed, because she was done. He'd killed dozens… hundreds? And he knew what his blade was doing to her innards, churning organs, spewing life from her body. Death was a formality.

But she was Katrina von Talhoffer.

She drew her dagger and it plunged through his left eyeball. He fell first, and she smiled at that. Then she was down too. Her torso raged at her, but pain didn't matter now.

"Katrina!"

Silas knelt, tried to staunch the flow.

"Won't work," she said.

The world fluttered, dark and light.

"Keep your eyes open! Focus on me, okay? Just… Listen! That day, in the dormitory… I knew you were there. I let them talk, because… So you'd…"

Her laugh rattled inside her skull.

"I know. Made me think you might be cunning enough for this life…"

This time the darkness clung.

• • •

Clara ran towards Xerachus, but he was too far, the thump of boots on grass too close behind. She stopped, threw her glove aside. Turned and shrieked and clawed.

The mawlana slowed down, pulled away. Talons ripped her mask and tugged the fabric. It shifted, blinded her. The Kharji leapt backwards. Clara darted in but the sword flashed between them, spun a web of steel while the woman snatched at the garment. She threw the cloth aside. Black script whooshed across her face.

"Please. I'll make this quick. I promise you won't suffer…"

"You killed my mum."

Clara lunged. The mawlana cut. Her right hand caught the blade. Bones shuddered, scales scraped. But no redness trickled from Clara Mandrake's palm. All was black, from claws to wrist.

"The djinn have tainted you. Let me-"

Clara pulled, tried to wrench the weapon away. The mawlana kicked her ribs. Bone cracked, her lungs convulsed. Clara howled. She clutched the sword, twisted away from the next kick, shielded her flank. It bashed the side of her skull instead. She rolled on the grass. The world wobbled. Stars exploded. Clara got up, fell down again. Her head banged the ground and another galaxy erupted.

She lay on her side. White and purple whirled before her. So beautiful… Pink too. And red. Smells spun around with everything else. Fur and fury and her mother's egg porridge…

Xerachus hissed.

The mawlana and the monster sharpened, and Clara groaned, forced herself up onto her knees. Crimson dyed the Kharji's garb. Blood on snow. But more flowed from Xerachus' hide.

"Run, Clara Mandrake. Run…"

She stood, tottered. Everything shook. The mawlana's sword gleamed, silver and scarlet. Xerachus threw himself at the Kharji but the blade moved too. His belly opened. Guts stank, dangled. He crumpled.

The mawlana's chest heaved. Flecks of blood and spittle clung to her lips. The markings quickened, slowed, quickened. Her eyes fastened on Clara Mandrake.

"Allatu Akbar!"

The Kharji took a step, then staggered as though an invisible fist punched her. Something slapped down on the grass behind. The mawlana turned. Silas crouched a dozen yards away and clutched his forearm. She made a sound, twisted back to face Clara.

Clara tore her throat out. The Kharji fell, and the writing stopped at the same time as her eyes.

Xerachus' throat rumbled. She didn't know if it was a laugh or a groan.

"Go, Clara Mandrake."

She knelt. Blood oozed between fur and scales.

"Can you heal? You said…"

"Darkness…" He gazed at the sun. "Nowhere to go."

"There's one place…"

Their eyes met, and then he was gone. Clara sighed. She picked up the dagger, grabbed the mawlana's mask, and went to Silas. He flinched.

"What…? What are you?"

"I'm a monster."

"But-"

"Here." She set his knife down, held out the fabric. "Bandage that."

He stared at her, but took it and wrapped it around his arm.

"Go to Vasile Zarabanov's apothecary shop. They'll help you. It's over-"

"I've been there."

She yanked off the hood and dropped it beside him.

"That's Vasile's. And tell Rayya… Tell her I'm sorry, and I love her, and she's the best friend in the world. And tell her I'm safe. Okay?"

"Yeah."

Clara waited till he'd finished, made sure the bandage was good, then stood up.

"Wait… We could… Maybe we can…"

"Help me?" Clara turned her hand. Scales drank the sunlight.

"Yeah…"

"It's okay. I know what to do." She smiled at him. "I have to be a duck."

"Huh?"

Clara walked a few steps. Then she flew.

• • •

The boy twitched beneath his blankets. He murmured in his sleep, but the words meant nothing. A floorboard creaked beyond the door. Wood groaned, and footsteps padded away till the other sounds of the house swallowed them.

Perhaps she'd been wrong. But she'd linger till she knew for certain. If the boy was safe, she'd move on. If not…

Her claws tingled.

Clara Mandrake melted into the wardrobe's shadows. She drifted towards slumber, and the place Xerachus dreamt his endless dream, in the darkness of her heart.

Acknowledgements

I wrote the latter half of this novel as a Camp NaNoWriMo project during the April 2017 session. My cabin mates' dedication and productivity were a constant source of inspiration, and their banter (whether about tea, *Doctor Who*, the German judicial system, singing contests, or literary tattoos) made the month fly by. So, thank you to every member of The Novelland Adventurers.

If a proverbial tree falling in the woods doesn't make a sound unless there's someone around to hear it, a novel doesn't exist until another person's read it. Fortunately, I have great people in my life whom I can conscript as beta readers. Thank you to Lena Gkika, Aaron Doyle, Niki Pladson, Khadijah Amin, Laurence Viollet, and Kathleen Trembath, for reading *Clara Mandrake's Monster* and making it real.

Aaron Doyle illustrated many of my stories and lore blurbs during our time at 5th Planet Games, and since then he's always been someone I can go to whenever I want a great piece of art. If you bought this novel because of its cover, that's Aaron's magic at work.

And, of course, thank you to everyone who's reading this. If you've got this far without throwing the book or your electronic device across the room, we can hopefully both walk away satisfied. Feel free to ask any questions on my Goodreads author page. You can also find me on Twitter (@Ibrahim_S_Amin), though I mostly just rant about things there.

About the Author

Ibrahim S. Amin was educated at the Manchester Grammar School, the University of Newcastle, and the University of Manchester. He wallowed in education for as long as he could, earning his PhD in Classics & Ancient History. At that point he ran out of excuses and joined the real world — where he now writes to support his unhealthy takeaway addiction.

His previous books are *The Monster Hunter's Handbook: The Ultimate Guide to Saving Mankind from Vampires, Zombies, Hellhounds, and Other Mythical Beasts* (published in Italian as *I Fratelli del Vampiro*), and the graphic novel *Jihad Squad*.

Printed in Great Britain
by Amazon